FROSTBITE

FROSTBITE

RICHELLE MEAD

razOr
bill

Frostbite

RAZORBILL

Published by the Penguin Group ·
Penguin Young Readers Group
345 Hudson Street, New York, New York 10014, U.S.A.
Penguin Group (USA) Inc., 375 Hudson Street, New York, New York 10014, U.S.A.
Penguin Group (Canada), 90 Eglinton Avenue East, Suite 700, Toronto, Ontario, Canada M4P
2Y3 (a division of Pearson Penguin Canada Inc.)
Penguin Books Ltd, 80 Strand, London WC2R 0RL, England
Penguin Ireland, 25 St Stephen's Green, Dublin 2, Ireland
(a division of Penguin Books Ltd)
Penguin Group (Australia), 250 Camberwell Road, Camberwell,
Victoria 3124, Australia (a division of Pearson Australia Group Pty Ltd)
Penguin Books India Pvt Ltd, 11 Community Centre, Panchsheel Park,
New Delhi – 110 017, India
Penguin Group (NZ), 67 Apollo Drive, Rosedale, North Shore 0632, New Zealand
(a division of Pearson New Zealand Ltd.)
Penguin Books (South Africa) (Pty) Ltd, 24 Sturdee Avenue,
Rosebank, Johannesburg 2196, South Africa

Penguin Books Ltd, Registered Offices: 80 Strand, London WC2R 0RL, England

30

Library of Congress Cataloging-in-Publication Data is available

Printed in the United States of America

For Kat Richardson, who is very wise.

PROLOGUE

THINGS DIE. BUT THEY DON'T always stay dead. Believe me, I know.

There's a race of vampires on this earth who are literally the walking dead. They're called Strigoi, and if you're not already having nightmares about them, you should be. They're strong, they're fast, and they kill without mercy or hesitation. They're immortal, too—which kind of makes them a bitch to destroy. There are only three ways to do it: a silver stake through the heart, decapitation, and setting them on fire. None of those is easy to pull off, but it's better than having no options at all.

There are also good vampires walking the world. They're called Moroi. They're alive, and they possess the incredibly cool power to wield magic in each of the four elements— earth, air, water, and fire. (Well, *most* Moroi can do this—but I'll explain more about the exceptions later). They don't really use the magic for much anymore, which is kind of sad. It'd be a great weapon, but the Moroi strongly believe magic should only be used peacefully. It's one of the biggest rules in their society. Moroi are also usually tall and slim, and they can't handle a lot of sunlight. But they do have superhuman senses that make up for it: sight, smell, and hearing.

Both kinds of vampires need blood. That's what makes

them vampires, I guess. Moroi don't kill to take it, however. Instead, they keep humans around who willingly donate small amounts. They volunteer because vampire bites contain endorphins that feel really, really good and can become addictive. I know this from personal experience. These humans are called feeders and are essentially vampire-bite junkies.

Still, keeping feeders around is better than the way the Strigoi do things, because, as you might expect, they kill for their blood. I think they like it. If a Moroi kills a victim while drinking, he or she will turn into a Strigoi. Some Moroi do this by choice, giving up their magic and their morals for immortality. Strigoi can also be created by force. If a Strigoi drinks blood from a victim and then makes that person drink Strigoi blood in return, well . . . you get a new Strigoi. This can happen to anyone: Moroi, human, or . . . dhampir.

Dhampir.

That's what I am. Dhampirs are half-human, half-Moroi. I like to think we got the best traits of both races. I'm strong and sturdy, like humans are. I can also go out in the sun as much as I want. But, like the Moroi, I have really good senses and fast reflexes. The result is that dhampirs make the ultimate bodyguards—which is what most of us are. We're called guardians.

I've spent my entire life training to protect Moroi from Strigoi. I have a whole set of special classes and practices I take at St. Vladimir's Academy, a private school for Moroi and dhampirs. I know how to use all sorts of weapons and can land some pretty mean kicks. I've beaten up guys twice my size—both in and out of class. And really, *guys* are pretty much the only ones I beat up, since there are very few girls in any of my classes.

Because while dhampirs inherit all sorts of great traits, there's one thing we didn't get. Dhampirs can't have children with other dhampirs. Don't ask me why. It's not like I'm a geneticist or anything. Humans and Moroi getting together will always make more dhampirs; that's where we came from in the first place. But that doesn't happen so much anymore; Moroi tend to stay away from humans. Through another weird genetic fluke, however, Moroi and dhampirs mixing will create dhampir children. I know, I know: it's crazy. You'd think you'd get a baby that's three-quarters vampire, right? Nope. Half human, half Moroi.

Most of these dhampirs are born from Moroi men and dhampir women getting together. Moroi women stick to having Moroi babies. What this usually means is that Moroi men have flings with dhampir women and then take off. This leaves a lot of single dhampir mothers, and that's why not as many of them become guardians. They'd rather focus on raising their children.

As a result, only the guys and a handful of girls are left to become guardians. But those who choose to protect Moroi are serious about their jobs. Dhampirs need Moroi to keep having kids. We *have* to protect them. Plus, it's just . . . well, it's the honorable thing to do. Strigoi are evil and unnatural. It isn't right for them to prey on the innocent. Dhampirs who train to be guardians have this drilled into them from the time they can walk. Strigoi are evil. Moroi must be protected. Guardians believe this. I believe this.

And there's one Moroi I want to protect more than anyone in the world: my best friend, Lissa. She's a Moroi princess. The Moroi have twelve royal families, and she's the only one left in hers—the Dragomirs. But there's something else that makes Lissa special, aside from her being my best friend.

Remember when I said every Moroi wields one of the four elements? Well, it turns out Lissa wields one no one even knew existed until recently: spirit. For years, we thought she just wasn't going to develop her magical abilities. Then strange things started happening around her. For example, all vampires have an ability called compulsion that lets them force their will on others. Strigoi have it really strongly. It's weaker in Moroi, and it's also forbidden. Lissa, however, has it almost as much as a Strigoi. She can bat her eyelashes, and people will do what she wants.

But that's not even the coolest thing she can do.

I said earlier that dead things don't always stay dead. Well, I'm one of them. Don't worry—I'm not like the Strigoi. But I did die once. (I don't recommend it.) It happened when the car I was riding in slid off the road. The accident killed me, Lissa's parents, and her brother. Yet, somewhere in the chaos—without even realizing it—Lissa used spirit to bring me back. We didn't know about this for a long time. In fact, we didn't even know spirit existed at all.

Unfortunately, it turned out that *one* person did know about spirit before we did. Victor Dashkov, a dying Moroi prince, found out about Lissa's powers and decided he wanted to lock her up and make her his own personal healer—for the rest of her life. When I realized someone was stalking her, I decided to take matters into my own hands. I broke us out of school to run off and live among humans. It was fun—but also kind of nerve-wracking—to always be on the run. We got away with this for two years until the authorities at St. Vladimir's hunted us down and dragged us back a few months ago.

That was when Victor made his real move, kidnapping her and torturing her until she gave into his demands. In the process, he took some pretty extreme measures—like zapping me and Dimitri, my mentor, with a lust spell. (I'll get to *him* later). Victor also exploited the way spirit was starting to make Lissa mentally unstable. But even that wasn't as bad as what he did to his own daughter Natalie. He went so far as to encourage her to turn into a Strigoi to help cover his escape. She ended up getting staked. Even when captured after the fact, Victor didn't seem to display too much guilt over what he'd asked her to do. Makes me think I wasn't missing out on growing up without a father.

Still, I now have to protect Lissa from Strigoi *and* Moroi. Only a few officials know about what she can do, but I'm sure there are other Victors out there who would want to use her. Fortunately, I have an extra weapon to help me guard her. Somewhere during my healing in the car accident, spirit forged a psychic bond between her and me. I can see and feel what she experiences. (It only works one way, though. She can't "feel" me.) The bond helps me keep an eye on her and know when she's in trouble, although sometimes, it's weird having another person inside your head. We're pretty sure there are lots of other things spirit can do, but we don't know what they are yet.

In the meantime, I'm trying to be the best guardian I can be. Running away put me behind in my training, so I have to take extra classes to make up for lost time. There's nothing in the world I want more than to keep Lissa safe. Unfortunately, I've got two things that complicate my training now and then. One is that I sometimes act before I think. I'm getting better at avoiding this, but when something sets me off, I tend to punch first and then find out who I actually hit later. When it comes to those I care about being in danger . . . well, rules seem optional.

The other problem in my life is Dimitri. He's the one who killed Natalie, and he's a total badass. He's also pretty good-looking. Okay—more than good-looking. He's hot—like, the kind of hot that makes you stop walking on the street and get hit by traffic. But, like I said, he's my instructor. *And* he's twenty-four. Both of those are reasons why I shouldn't have fallen for him. But, honestly, the most important reason is that he and I will be Lissa's guardians when she graduates. If he and I are checking each other out, then that means we aren't looking out for her.

I haven't had much luck in getting over him, and I'm pretty sure he still feels the same about me. Part of what makes it so difficult is that he and I got pretty hot and heavy when we got hit with the lust spell. Victor had wanted to distract us while he kidnapped Lissa, and it had worked. I'd been ready to give up my virginity, and Dimitri had been ready to take it. At the last minute, we broke the spell, but those memories are always with me and make it kind of hard to focus on combat moves sometimes.

By the way, my name's Rose Hathaway. I'm seventeen years old, training to protect *and* kill vampires, in love with a completely unsuitable guy, and have a best friend whose weird magic could drive her crazy.

Hey, no one said high school was easy.

ONE

I DIDN'T THINK MY DAY could get any worse until my best friend told me she might be going crazy. Again.

"I . . . what did you say?"

I stood in the lobby of her dorm, leaning over one of my boots and adjusting it. Jerking my head up, I peered at her through the tangle of dark hair covering half my face. I'd fallen asleep after school and had skipped using a hairbrush in order to make it out the door on time. Lissa's platinum blond hair was smooth and perfect, of course, hanging over her shoulders like a bridal veil as she watched me with amusement.

"I said that I think my pills might not be working as well anymore."

I straightened up and shook the hair out of my face. "What does that mean?" I asked. Around us, Moroi hurried past, on their way to meet friends or go to dinner.

"Have you started . . ." I lowered my voice. "Have you started getting your powers back?"

She shook her head, and I saw a small flash of regret in her eyes. "No . . . I feel *closer* to the magic, but I still can't use it. Mostly what I'm noticing lately is a little of the other stuff, you know. . . . I'm getting more depressed now and then. Nothing even *close* to what it used to be," she added hastily, seeing my face. Before she'd gone on her pills, Lissa's moods could get so low that she cut herself. "It's just there a little more than it was."

"What about the other things you used to get? Anxiety? Delusional thinking?"

Lissa laughed, not taking any of this as seriously as I was. "You sound like you've been reading psychiatry textbooks."

I actually *had* been reading them. "I'm just worried about you. If you think the pills aren't working anymore, we need to tell someone."

"No, no," she said hastily. "I'm fine, really. They're still working . . . just not quite as much. I don't think we should panic yet. Especially you—not today, at least."

Her change in subject worked. I'd found out an hour ago that I would be taking my Qualifier today. It was an exam—or rather, an interview—all novice guardians were required to pass during junior year at St. Vladimir's Academy. Since I'd been off hiding Lissa last year, I'd missed mine. Today I was being taken to a guardian somewhere off-campus who would administer the test to me. Thanks for the notice, guys.

"Don't worry about me," Lissa repeated, smiling. "I'll let you know if it gets worse."

"Okay," I said reluctantly.

Just to be safe, though, I opened my senses and allowed myself to truly feel her through our psychic bond. She had been telling the truth. She was calm and happy this morning, nothing to worry about. But, far back in her mind, I sensed a

knot of dark, uneasy feelings. It wasn't consuming her or anything, but it had the same feel as the bouts of depression and
anger she used to get. It was only a trickle, but I didn't like it. I
didn't want it there at all. I tried pushing farther inside her to
get a better feel for the emotions and suddenly had the weird
experience of touching. A sickening sort of feeling seized me,
and I jerked out of her head. A small shudder ran through my
body.

"You okay?" Lissa asked, frowning. "You look nauseous
all of a sudden."

"Just . . . nervous for the test," I lied. Hesitantly, I reached
out through the bond again. The darkness had completely disappeared. No trace. Maybe there was nothing wrong with her
pills after all. "I'm fine."

She pointed at a clock. "You won't be if you don't get moving soon."

"Damn it," I swore. She was right. I gave her a quick hug.
"See you later!"

"Good luck!" she called.

I hurried off across campus and found my mentor, Dimitri Belikov, waiting beside a Honda Pilot. How boring. I
supposed I couldn't have expected us to navigate Montana
mountain roads in a Porsche, but it would have been nice to
have something cooler.

"I know, I know," I said, seeing his face. "Sorry I'm late."

I remembered then that I had one of the most important
tests of my life coming up, and suddenly, I forgot all about

Lissa and her pills possibly not working. I wanted to protect her, but that wouldn't mean much if I couldn't pass high school and actually become her guardian.

Dimitri stood there, looking as gorgeous as ever. The massive, brick building cast long shadows over us, looming like some great beast in the dusky predawn light. Around us, snow was just beginning to fall. I watched the light, crystalline flakes drift gently down. Several landed and promptly melted in his dark hair.

"Who else is going?" I asked.

He shrugged. "Just you and me."

My mood promptly shot up past "cheerful" and went straight to "ecstatic." Me and Dimitri. Alone. In a car. This might very well be worth a surprise test.

"How far away is it?" Silently, I begged for it to be a really long drive. Like, one that would take a week. And would involve us staying overnight in luxury hotels. Maybe we'd get stranded in a snowbank, and only body heat would keep us alive.

"Five hours."

"Oh."

A bit less than I'd hoped for. Still, five hours was better than nothing. It didn't rule out the snowbank possibility, either.

The dim, snowy roads would have been difficult for humans to navigate, but they proved no problem for our dhampir eyes. I stared ahead, trying not to think about how Dimitri's aftershave filled the car with a clean, sharp scent that made me want to melt. Instead, I tried to focus on the Qualifier again.

It wasn't the kind of thing you could study for. You either passed it or you didn't. High-up guardians visited novices during their junior year and met individually to discuss students' commitment to being guardians. I didn't know exactly what was asked, but rumors had trickled down over the years. The older guardians assessed character and dedication, and some novices had been deemed unfit to continue down the guardian path.

"Don't they usually come to the Academy?" I asked Dimitri. "I mean, I'm all for the field trip, but why are we going to them?"

"Actually, you're just going to a *him*, not a *them*." A light Russian accent laced Dimitri's words, the only indication of where he'd grown up. Otherwise, I was pretty sure he spoke English better than I did. "Since this is a special case and he's doing us the favor, we're the ones making the trip."

"Who is he?"

"Arthur Schoenberg."

I jerked my gaze from the road to Dimitri.

"What?" I squeaked.

Arthur Schoenberg was a legend. He was one of the greatest Strigoi slayers in living guardian history and used to be the head of the Guardians Council—the group of people who assigned guardians to Moroi and made decisions for all of us. He'd eventually retired and gone back to protecting one of the royal families, the Badicas. Even retired, I knew he was still lethal. His exploits were part of my curriculum.

"Wasn't . . . wasn't there anyone else available?" I asked in a small voice.

I could see Dimitri hiding a smile. "You'll be fine. Besides, if Art approves of you, that's a great recommendation to have on your record."

Art. Dimitri was on a first-name basis with one of the most badass guardians around. Of course, Dimitri was pretty badass himself, so I shouldn't have been surprised.

Silence fell in the car. I bit my lip, suddenly wondering if I'd be able to meet Arthur Schoenberg's standards. My grades were good, but things like running away and getting into fights at school might cast a shadow on how serious I was about my future career.

"You'll be fine," Dimitri repeated. "The good in your record outweighs the bad."

It was like he could read my mind sometimes. I smiled a little and dared to peek at him. It was a mistake. A long, lean body, obvious even while sitting. Bottomless dark eyes. Shoulder-length brown hair tied back at his neck. That hair felt like silk. I knew because I'd run my fingers through it when Victor Dashkov had ensnared us with the lust charm. With great restraint, I forced myself to start breathing again and look away.

"Thanks, Coach," I teased, snuggling back into the seat.

"I'm here to help," he replied. His voice was light and

relaxed—rare for him. He was usually wound up tightly, ready for any attack. Probably he figured he was safe inside a Honda—or at least as safe as he could be around me. I wasn't the only one who had trouble ignoring the romantic tension between us.

"You know what would really help?" I asked, not meeting his eyes.

"Hmm?"

"If you turned off this crap music and put on something that came out after the Berlin Wall went down."

Dimitri laughed. "Your worst class is history, yet somehow, you know everything about Eastern Europe."

"Hey, gotta have material for my jokes, Comrade."

Still smiling, he turned the radio dial. To a country station.

"Hey! This isn't what I had in mind," I exclaimed.

I could tell he was on the verge of laughing again. "Pick. It's one or the other."

I sighed. "Go back to the 1980s stuff."

He flipped the dial, and I crossed my arms over my chest as some vaguely European-sounding band sang about how video had killed the radio star. I wished someone would kill this radio.

Suddenly, five hours didn't seem as short as I'd thought.

Arthur and the family he protected lived in a small town along I-90, not far from Billings. The general Moroi opinion was split on places to live. Some argued that big cities were the best since they allowed vampires to be lost in the crowds; nocturnal activities didn't raise so much attention. Other Moroi, like this family, apparently, opted for less populated towns, believing that if there were fewer people to notice you, then you were less likely to be noticed.

I'd convinced Dimitri to stop for food at a twenty-four-hour diner along the way, and between that and stopping to buy gas, it was around noon when we arrived. The house was built in a rambler style, all one level with gray-stained wood siding and big bay windows—tinted to block sunlight, of course. It looked new and expensive, and even out in the middle of nowhere, it was about what I'd expected for members of a royal family.

I jumped down from the Pilot, my boots sinking through an inch of smooth snow and crunching on the gravel of the driveway. The day was still and silent, save for the occasional breath of wind. Dimitri and I walked up to the house, following a river rock sidewalk that cut through the front yard. I could see him sliding into his business mode, but his overall attitude was as cheery as mine. We'd both taken a kind of guilty satisfaction in the pleasant car ride.

My foot slipped on the ice-covered sidewalk, and Dimitri instantly reached out to steady me. I had a weird moment of déjà vu, flashing back to the first night we'd met, back when he'd also saved me from a similar fall. Freezing temperatures or not, his hand felt warm on my arm, even through the layers of down in my parka coat.

"You okay?" He released his hold, to my dismay.

"Yeah," I said, casting accusing eyes at the icy sidewalk. "Haven't these people ever heard of salt?"

I meant it jokingly, but Dimitri suddenly stopped walking. I instantly came to a halt too. His expression became tense and alert. He turned his head, eyes searching the broad, white plains surrounding us before settling back on the house. I wanted to ask questions, but something in his posture told me to stay silent. He studied the building for almost a full minute, looked down at the icy sidewalk, then glanced back at the driveway, covered in a sheet of snow broken only by our footprints.

Cautiously, he approached the front door, and I followed. He stopped again, this time to study the door. It wasn't open, but it wasn't entirely shut either. It looked like it had been closed in haste, not sealing. Further examination showed scuffs along the door's edge, as though it had been forced at some point. The slightest nudge would open it. Dimitri lightly ran his fingers along where the door met its frame, his breath making small clouds in the air. When he touched the door's handle it jiggled a little, like it had been broken.

Finally, he said quietly, "Rose, go wait in the car."

"But wh—"

"Go."

One word—but one filled with power. In that single syllable I was reminded of the man I'd seen throw people around and stake a Strigoi. I backed up, walking on the snow-covered lawn rather than risk the sidewalk. Dimitri stood where he was, not moving until I'd slipped back into the car, closing the door as softly as possible. Then, with the gentlest of movements, he pushed on the barely held door and disappeared inside.

Burning with curiosity, I counted to ten and then climbed out of the car.

I knew better than to go in after him, but I had to know what was going on with this house. The neglected sidewalk and driveway indicated that no one had been home for a couple days, although it could also mean the Badicas simply never left the house. It was possible, I supposed, that they'd been the victims of an ordinary break-in by humans. It was also possible that something had scared them off—say, like Strigoi. I knew that possibility was what had made Dimitri's face turn so grim, but it seemed an unlikely scenario with Arthur Schoenberg on duty.

Standing on the driveway, I glanced up at the sky. The light was bleak and watery, but it was there. Noon. The sun's highest point today. Strigoi couldn't be out in sunlight. I didn't need to fear them, only Dimitri's anger.

I circled around the right side of the house, walking in much deeper snow—almost a foot of it. Nothing else weird about the house struck me. Icicles hung from the eaves, and the tinted windows revealed no secrets. My foot suddenly hit something, and I looked down. There, half-buried in the snow, was a silver stake. It had been driven into the ground. I picked it up and brushed off the snow, frowning. What was a stake doing out here? Silver stakes were valuable. They were a guardian's most deadly weapon, capable of killing a Strigoi with a single strike through the heart. When they were forged, four Moroi charmed them with magic from each of the four elements. I hadn't learned to use one yet, but gripping it in my hand, I suddenly felt safer as I continued my survey.

A large patio door led from the back of the house to a wooden deck that probably would have been a lot of fun to hang out on in the summer. But the patio's glass had been broken, so much so that a person could easily get through the jagged hole. I crept up the deck steps, careful of the ice, knowing I was going to get in major trouble when Dimitri found out what I was doing. In spite of the cold, sweat poured down my neck.

Daylight, daylight, I reminded myself. Nothing to worry about.

I reached the patio and studied the dark glass. I couldn't tell what had broken it. Just inside, snow had blown in and made a small drift on pale blue carpet. I tugged on the door's handle, but it was locked. Not that that mattered with a hole that big. Careful of the sharp edges, I reached through the opening and unlocked the handle's latch from the inside. I removed my hand just as carefully and pulled open the sliding door. It hissed slightly along its tracks, a quiet sound that nonetheless seemed too loud in the eerie silence.

I stepped through the doorway, standing in the patch of

sunlight that had been cast inside by opening the door. My eyes adjusted from the sun to the dimness within. Wind swirled through the open patio, dancing with the curtains around me. I was in a living room. It had all the ordinary items one might expect. Couches. TV. A rocking chair.

And a body.

It was a woman. She lay on her back in front of the TV, her dark hair spilling on the floor around her. Her wide eyes stared upward blankly, her face pale—too pale even for a Moroi. For a moment I thought her long hair was covering her neck, too, until I realized that the darkness across her skin was blood—dried blood. Her throat had been ripped out.

The horrible scene was so surreal that I didn't even realize what I was seeing at first. With her posture, the woman might very well have been sleeping. Then I took in the other body: a man on his side only a couple feet away, dark blood staining the carpet around him. Another body was slumped beside the couch: small, child-size. Across the room was another. And another. There were bodies everywhere, bodies and blood.

The scale of the death around me suddenly registered, and my heart began pounding. No, no. It wasn't possible. It was day. Bad things couldn't happen in daylight. A scream started to rise in my throat, suddenly halted when a gloved hand came from behind me and closed over my mouth. I started to struggle; then I smelled Dimitri's aftershave.

"Why," he asked, "don't you ever listen? You'd be dead if *they* were still here."

I couldn't answer, both because of the hand and my own shock. I'd seen someone die once, but I'd never seen death of this magnitude. After almost a minute, Dimitri finally removed his hand, but he stayed close behind me. I didn't want to look anymore, but I seemed unable to drag my eyes away from the scene before me. Bodies everywhere. Bodies and blood.

Finally, I turned toward him. "It's daytime," I whispered. "Bad things don't happen in the day." I heard the desperation in my voice, a little girl's plea that someone would say this was all a bad dream.

"Bad things can happen anytime," he told me. "And this didn't happen during the day. This probably happened a couple of nights ago."

I dared a peek back at the bodies and felt my stomach twist. Two days. Two days to be dead, to have your existence snuffed out—without anyone in the world even knowing you were gone. My eyes fell on a man's body near the room's entrance to a hallway. He was tall, too well-built to be a Moroi. Dimitri must have noticed where I looked.

"Arthur Schoenberg," he said.

I stared at Arthur's bloody throat. "He's dead," I said, as though it wasn't perfectly obvious. "How can he be dead? How could a Strigoi kill Arthur Schoenberg?" It didn't seem possible. You couldn't kill a legend.

Dimitri didn't answer. Instead his hand moved down and closed around where my own hand held the stake. I flinched.

"Where did you get this?" he asked. I loosened my grip and let him take the stake.

"Outside. In the ground."

He held up the stake, studying its surface as it shone in the sunlight. "It broke the ward."

My mind, still stunned, took a moment to process what he'd said. Then I got it. Wards were magic rings cast by Moroi. Like the stakes, they were made using magic from all four of the elements. They required strong Moroi magic-users, often a couple for each element. The wards could block Strigoi because magic was charged with life, and the Strigoi had none. But wards faded quickly and took a lot of maintenance. Most Moroi didn't use them, but certain places kept them up. St. Vladimir's Academy was ringed with several.

There had been a ward here, but it had been shattered when someone drove the stake through it. Their magic conflicted with each other; the stake had won.

"Strigoi can't touch stakes," I told him. I realized I was using a lot of *can't* and *don't* statements. It wasn't easy having your core beliefs challenged. "And no Moroi or dhampir would do it."

"A human might."

I met his eyes. "Humans don't help Strigoi—" I stopped. There it was again. *Don't*. But I couldn't help it. The one thing we could count on in the fight against Strigoi was their limitations—sunlight, ward, stake magic, etc. We used their weaknesses against them. If they had others—humans—who would help them and weren't affected by those limitations . . .

Dimitri's face was stern, still ready for anything, but the tiniest spark of sympathy flashed in his dark eyes as he watched me wage my mental battle.

"This changes everything, doesn't it?" I asked.

"Yeah," he said. "It does."

Two

DIMITRI MADE ONE PHONE CALL, and a veritable SWAT team showed up.

It took a couple of hours, though, and every minute spent waiting felt like a year. I finally couldn't take it anymore and returned to the car. Dimitri examined the house further and then came to sit with me. Neither of us said a word while we waited. A slide show of the grisly sights inside the house kept playing in my mind. I felt scared and alone and wished he would hold me or comfort me in some way.

Immediately, I scolded myself for wanting that. I reminded myself for the thousandth time that he was my instructor and had no business holding me, no matter what the situation was. Besides, I wanted to be strong. I didn't need to go running to some guy every time things got tough.

When the first group of guardians showed up, Dimitri opened the car door and glanced over at me. "You should see how this is done."

I didn't want to see any more of that house, honestly, but I followed anyway. These guardians were strangers to me, but Dimitri knew them. He always seemed to know everybody. This group was surprised to find a novice on the scene, but none of them protested my presence.

I walked behind them as they examined the house. None of them touched anything, but they knelt by the bodies and studied the bloodstains and broken windows. Apparently, the Strigoi had entered the house through more than just the front door and back patio.

The guardians spoke in brusque tones, displaying none of the disgust and fear I felt. They were like machines. One of them, the only woman in the group, crouched beside Arthur Schoenberg. I was intrigued since female guardians were so rare. I'd heard Dimitri call her Tamara, and she looked about twenty-five. Her black hair just barely touched her shoulders, which was common for guardian women.

Sadness flickered in her gray eyes as she studied the dead guardian's face. "Oh, Arthur," she sighed. Like Dimitri, she managed to convey a hundred things in just a couple words. "Never thought I'd see this day. He was my mentor." With another sigh, Tamara rose.

Her face had become all businesslike once more, as though the guy who'd trained her wasn't lying there in front of her. I couldn't believe it. He was her *mentor*. How could she keep that kind of control? For half a heartbeat, I imagined seeing Dimitri dead on the floor instead. No. No way could I have stayed calm in her place. I would have gone on a rampage. I would have screamed and kicked things. I would have hit anyone who tried to tell me things would be okay.

Fortunately, I didn't believe anyone could actually take

down Dimitri. I'd seen him kill a Strigoi without breaking a sweat. He was invincible. A badass. A god.

Of course, Arthur Schoenberg had been too.

"How could they do that?" I blurted out. Six sets of eyes turned to me. I expected a chastising look from Dimitri for my outburst, but he merely appeared curious. "How could they kill *him*?"

Tamara gave a small shrug, her face still composed. "The same way they kill everyone else. He's mortal, just like the rest of us."

"Yeah, but he's . . . you know, Arthur Schoenberg."

"You tell us, Rose," said Dimitri. "You've seen the house. Tell us how they did it."

As they all watched me, I suddenly realized I might be undergoing a test after all today. I thought about what I'd observed and heard. I swallowed, trying to figure out how the impossible could be possible.

"There were four points of entry, which means at least four Strigoi. There were seven Moroi . . ." The family who lived here had been entertaining some other people, making the massacre that much larger. Three of the victims had been children. ". . . and three guardians. Too many kills. Four Strigoi couldn't have taken down that many. Six probably could if they went for the guardians first and caught them by surprise. The family would have been too panicked to fight back."

"And how did they catch the guardians by surprise?" Dimitri prompted.

I hesitated. Guardians, as a general rule, didn't get caught by surprise. "Because the wards were broken. In a household without wards, there'd probably be a guardian walking the yard at night. But they wouldn't have done that here."

I waited for the next obvious question about how the wards had been broken. But Dimitri didn't ask it. There was no need. We all knew. We'd all seen the stake. Again, a chill ran down my spine. Humans working with Strigoi—a large group of Strigoi.

Dimitri simply nodded as a sign of approval, and the group continued their survey. When we reached a bathroom, I started to avert my gaze. I'd already seen this room with Dimitri earlier and had no wish to repeat the experience. There was a dead man in there, and his dried blood stood out in stark contrast against the white tile. Also, since this room was more interior, it wasn't as cold as the area by the open patio. No preservation. The body didn't smell bad yet, exactly, but it didn't smell right, either.

But as I started to turn away, I caught a glimpse of something dark red—more brown, really—on the mirror. I hadn't noticed it before because the rest of the scene had held all of my attention. There was writing on the mirror, done in blood.

Poor, poor Badicas. So few left. One royal family nearly gone. Others to follow.

Tamara snorted in disgust and turned away from the mirror, studying other details of the bathroom. As we walked out, though, those words repeated in my head. *One royal family nearly gone. Others to follow.*

The Badicas were one of the smaller royal clans, it was true. But it was hardly like those who had been killed here were the last of them. There were probably almost two hundred Badicas left. That wasn't as many as a family like, say, the Ivashkovs. That particular royal family was huge and widespread. There were, however, a lot more Badicas than there were some other royals.

Like the Dragomirs.

Lissa was the only one left.

If the Strigoi wanted to snuff out royal lines, there was no better chance than to go after her. Moroi blood empowered Strigoi, so I understood their desire for that. I supposed specifically targeting royals was simply part of their cruel and sadistic nature. It was ironic that Strigoi would want to tear apart Moroi society, since many of them had once been a part of it.

The mirror and its warning consumed me for the rest of our stay at the house, and I found my fear and shock transforming into anger. How could they do this? How could any creature be so twisted and evil that they'd do this to a family—that they'd want to wipe out an entire bloodline? How could any creature do this when they'd once been like me and Lissa?

And thinking of Lissa—thinking of Strigoi wanting to wipe out her family too—stirred up a dark rage within me.

The intensity of that emotion nearly knocked me over. It was something black and miasmic, swelling and roiling. A storm cloud ready to burst. I suddenly wanted to tear up every Strigoi I could get my hands on.

When I finally got into the car to ride back to St. Vladimir's with Dimitri, I slammed the door so hard that it was a wonder it didn't fall off.

He glanced at me in surprise. "What's wrong?"

"Are you serious?" I exclaimed, incredulous. "How can you ask that? You were there. You saw that."

"I did," he agreed. "But I'm not taking it out on the car."

I fastened my seat belt and glowered. "I hate them. I hate them all! I wish *I'd* been there. I would have ripped *their* throats out!"

I was nearly shouting. Dimitri stared at me, face calm, but he was clearly astonished at my outburst.

"You really think that's true?" he asked me. "You think you could have done better than Art Schoenberg after seeing what the Strigoi did in there? After seeing what Natalie did to you?"

I faltered. I'd tangled briefly with Lissa's cousin, Natalie, when she became a Strigoi, just before Dimitri had shown up to save the day. Even as a new Strigoi—weak and uncoordinated—she'd literally thrown me around the room.

I closed my eyes and took a deep breath. Suddenly, I felt stupid. I'd seen what Strigoi could do. Me running in impetuously and trying to save the day would have only resulted in a quick death. I was developing into a tough guardian, but I still had a lot to learn—and one seventeen-year-old girl couldn't have stood against six Strigoi.

I opened my eyes. "I'm sorry," I said, gaining control of myself. The rage that had exploded inside me diffused. I didn't know where it had come from. I had a short temper and often acted impulsively, but this had been intense and ugly even for me. Weird.

"It's okay," said Dimitri. He reached over and placed his hand on mine for a few moments. Then he removed it and started the car. "It's been a long day. For all of us."

When we got back to St. Vladimir's Academy around midnight, everyone knew about the massacre. The vampiric school day had just ended, and I hadn't slept in more than twenty-four hours. I was bleary-eyed and sluggish, and Dimitri ordered me to immediately go back to my dorm room and get some sleep. He, of course, looked alert and ready to take on anything. Sometimes I really wasn't sure if he slept at all. He headed off to consult with other guardians about the attack, and I promised him I'd go straight to bed. Instead, I turned toward the library once he was out of sight. I needed to see Lissa, and the bond told me that was where she was.

It was pitch-black as I walked along the stone walkway that crossed the quad from my dorm to the secondary school's main building. Snow completely covered the grass, but the sidewalk had been meticulously cleared of all ice and snow.

It reminded me of the poor Badicas' neglected home.

The commons building was large and gothic-looking, more suited to a medieval movie set than a school. Inside, that air of mystery and ancient history continued to permeate the building: elaborate stone walls and antique paintings warring with computers and fluorescent lights. Modern technology had a foothold here, but it would never dominate.

Slipping through the library's electronic gate, I immediately headed for one of the back corners where geography and travel books were kept. Sure enough, I found Lissa sitting there on the floor, leaning against a bookcase.

"Hey," she said, looking up from an open book propped up on one knee. She brushed a few strands of pale hair out of her face. Her boyfriend, Christian, lay on the floor near her, his head propped up on her other knee. He greeted me by way of a nod. Considering the antagonism that sometimes flared up between us, that was almost on par with him giving me a bear hug. Despite her small smile, I could feel the tension and fear in her; it sang through the bond.

"You heard," I said, sitting down cross-legged.

Her smile slipped, and the feelings of fear and unease within her intensified. I liked that our psychic connection let me protect her better, but I didn't really need my own troubled feelings amplified.

"It's awful," she said with a shudder. Christian shifted and linked his fingers through hers. He squeezed her hand. She squeezed back. Those two were so in love and sugary sweet with each other that I felt like brushing my teeth after being around them. They were subdued just now, however, no doubt thanks to the massacre news. "They're saying . . . they're saying there were six or seven Strigoi. And that humans helped them break the wards."

I leaned my head back against a shelf. News really did travel fast. Suddenly, I felt dizzy. "It's true."

"Really?" asked Christian. "I figured that was just a bunch of hyped-up paranoia."

"No . . ." I realized then that nobody knew where I'd been today. "I . . . I was there."

Lissa's eyes widened, shock coursing into me from her. Even Christian—the poster child for "smartass"—looked grim. If not for the horribleness of it all, I would have taken satisfaction in catching him off guard.

"You're joking," he said, voice uncertain.

"I thought you were taking your Qualifier . . ." Lissa's words trailed off.

"I was supposed to," I said. "It was just a wrong-place-and-wrong-time kind of thing. The guardian who was going to give me the test lived there. Dimitri and I walked in, and . . ."

I couldn't finish. Images of the blood and death that had filled the Badica house flashed through my mind again. Concern crossed both Lissa's face and the bond.

"Rose, are you okay?" she asked softly.

Lissa was my best friend, but I didn't want her to know

how scared and upset the whole thing had made me. I wanted
to be fierce.

"Fine," I said, teeth clenched.

"What was it like?" asked Christian. Curiosity filled his
voice, but there was guilt there too—like he knew it was wrong
to want to know about such a horrible thing. He couldn't stop
himself from asking, though. Lack of impulse control was one
thing we had in common.

"It was . . ." I shook my head. "I don't want to talk about it."

Christian started to protest, and then Lissa ran a hand
through his sleek black hair. The gentle admonishment
silenced him. A moment of awkwardness hung between us
all. Reading Lissa's mind, I felt her desperately grope for a
new topic.

"They say this is going to mess up all of the holiday visits,"
she told me after several more moments. "Christian's aunt is
going to visit, but most people don't want to travel, and they
want their kids to stay here where it's safe. They're terrified
this group of Strigoi is on the move."

I hadn't thought about the ramifications of an attack like
this. We were only a week or so away from Christmas. Usually, there was a huge wave of travel in the Moroi world this
time of year. Students went home to visit their parents; parents came to stay on campus and visit their children.

"This is going to keep a lot of families separated," I murmured.

"And mess up a lot of royal get-togethers," said Christian.

His brief seriousness had vanished; his snide air was back. "You know how they are this time of year—always competing with each other to throw the biggest parties. They won't know what to do with themselves."

I could believe it. My life was about fighting, but the Moroi certainly had their share of internal strife—particularly with nobles and royals. They waged their own battles with words and political alliances, and honestly, I preferred the more direct method of hitting and kicking. Lissa and Christian in particular had to navigate some troubled waters. They were both from royal families, which meant they got a lot of attention both inside and outside of the Academy.

Things were worse for them than for most Moroi royals. Christian's family lived under the shadow cast by his parents. They had purposely become Strigoi, trading their magic and morality to become immortal and subsist on killing others. His parents were dead now, but that didn't stop people from not trusting him. They seemed to think he'd go Strigoi at any moment and take everyone else with him. His abrasiveness and dark sense of humor didn't really help things, either.

Lissa's attention came from being the last one left in her family. No other Moroi had enough Dragomir blood in them to earn the name. Her future husband would probably have enough somewhere in his family tree to make sure her children were Dragomirs, but for now, being the only one made her kind of a celebrity.

Thinking about this suddenly reminded me of the warning

scrawled on the mirror. Nausea welled up in me. That dark anger and despair stirred, but I pushed it aside with a joke.

"You guys should try solving your problems like we do. A fistfight here and there might do you royals some good."

Both Lissa and Christian laughed at this. He glanced up at her with a sly smile, showing his fangs as he did. "What do you think? I bet I could take you if we went one on one."

"You wish," she teased. Her troubled feelings lightened.

"I do, actually," he said, holding her gaze.

There was an intensely sensual note to his voice that made her heart race. Jealousy shot through me. She and I had been best friends our entire life. I could read her mind. But the fact remained: Christian was a huge part of her world now, and he played a role I never could—just as he could never have a part of the connection that existed between me and her. We both sort of accepted but didn't like the fact that we had to split her attention, and at times, it seemed the truce we held for her sake was paper thin.

Lissa brushed her hand against his cheek. "Behave."

"I am," he told her, his voice still a little husky. "Sometimes. But sometimes you don't want me to. . . ."

Groaning, I stood up. "God. I'm going to leave you guys alone now."

Lissa blinked and dragged her eyes away from Christian, suddenly looking embarrassed.

"Sorry," she murmured. A delicate pink flush spread over her cheeks. Since she was pale like all Moroi, it actually sort of made her look prettier. Not that she needed much help in that department. "You don't have to go. . . ."

"No, it's fine. I'm exhausted," I assured her. Christian didn't look too broken up about seeing me leave. "I'll catch you tomorrow."

I started to turn away, but Lissa called to me. "Rose? Are you . . . are you sure you're okay? After everything that happened?"

I met her jade green eyes. Her concern was so strong and deep that it made my chest ache. I might be closer to her than anyone else in the world, but I didn't want her worrying about *me*. It was my job to keep her safe. She shouldn't be troubled about protecting me—particularly if Strigoi had suddenly decided to make a hit list of royals.

I flashed her a saucy grin. "I'm fine. Nothing to worry about except you guys tearing each other's clothes before I get a chance to leave."

"Then you better go now," said Christian dryly.

She elbowed him, and I rolled my eyes. "Good night," I told them.

As soon as my back was to them, my smile vanished. I walked back to my dorm with a heavy heart, hoping I wouldn't dream about the Badicas tonight.

THREE

THE LOBBY OF MY DORM was abuzz when I sprinted downstairs to my before-school practice. The commotion didn't surprise me. A good night's sleep had gone far to chase away the images from last night, but I knew neither I nor my classmates would easily forget what had taken place outside Billings.

And yet, as I studied the faces and clusters of other novices, I noticed something weird. The fear and tension from yesterday were still around, certainly, but something new was there too: excitement. A couple of freshmen novices were practically squealing with joy as they spoke in hushed whispers. Nearby, a group of guys my own age were gesturing wildly, enthusiastic grins on their faces.

I had to be missing something here—unless all of yesterday had been a dream. It took every ounce of self-control I had not to go over and ask somebody what was happening. If I delayed, I'd be late for practice. The curiosity was killing me, though. Had the Strigoi and their humans been found and killed? That would certainly be good news, but something told me that wasn't the case. Pushing open the front doors, I lamented that I'd just have to wait until breakfast to find out.

"Hath-away, don't run-away," a singsong voice called.

I glanced behind me and grinned. Mason Ashford, another novice and a good friend of mine, jogged up and fell in step with me.

"What are you, twelve?" I asked, continuing on toward the gym.

"Nearly," he said. "I missed your smiling face yesterday. Where were you?"

Apparently my presence at the Badica house still wasn't widely known. It wasn't a secret or anything, but I didn't want to discuss any gory details. "Had a training thing with Dimitri."

"God," muttered Mason. "That guy is always working you. Doesn't he realize he's depriving us of your beauty and charm?"

"Smiling face? Beauty and charm? You're laying it on a little thick this morning, aren't you?" I laughed.

"Hey, I'm just telling it like it is. Really, you're lucky to have someone as suave and brilliant as me paying this much attention to you."

I kept grinning. Mason was a huge flirt, and he liked to flirt with me in particular. Part of it was just because I was good at it and liked to flirt back. But I knew his feelings toward me were more than just friendly, and I was still deciding how I felt about that. He and I had the same goofy sense of humor and frequently drew attention to ourselves in class and among friends. He had gorgeous blue eyes and messy red hair that never seemed to lie flat. It was cute.

But dating someone new was going to be kind of difficult when I still kept thinking about the time I was half-naked in bed with Dimitri.

"Suave and brilliant, huh?" I shook my head. "I don't think you pay nearly as much attention to me as you do your ego. Someone needs to knock it down a little."

"Oh yeah?" he asked. "Well, you can try your best on the slopes."

I stopped walking. "The what?"

"The slopes." He tilted his head. "You know, the ski trip."

"What ski trip?" I was apparently missing something serious here.

"Where have you been this morning?" he asked, looking at me like I was a crazy woman.

"In bed! I only got up, like, five minutes ago. Now, start from the beginning and tell me what you're talking about." I shivered from the lack of movement. "And let's keep walking." We did.

"So, you know how everyone's afraid to have their kids come home for Christmas? Well, there's this *huge* ski lodge in Idaho that's exclusively used by royals and rich Moroi. The people who own it are opening it up for Academy students and their families—and actually any other Moroi who want to go. With everyone in one spot, they're going to have a ton of guardians to protect the place, so it'll be totally safe."

"You can't be serious," I said. We reached the gym and stepped inside out of the cold.

Mason nodded eagerly. "It's true. The place is supposed to be amazing." He gave me the grin that always made me smile in return. "We're going to live like royalty, Rose. At least for a week or so. We take off the day after Christmas."

I stood there, both excited and stunned. I hadn't seen this coming. It really was a brilliant idea, one that let families reunite safely. And what a reunion spot! A royal ski lodge. I'd expected to spend most of my holiday break hanging out here and watching TV with Lissa and Christian. Now I'd be living it up in five-star accommodations. Lobster dinners. Massages. Cute ski instructors . . .

Mason's enthusiasm was contagious. I could feel it welling up in me, and then, suddenly, it slammed to a halt.

Studying my face, he saw the change right away. "What's wrong? This is cool."

"It is," I admitted. "And I get why everyone's excited, but the reason we're getting to go to this fancy place is because, well, because people are dead. I mean, doesn't this all seem weird?"

Mason's cheery expression sobered a little. "Yeah, but we're alive, Rose. We can't stop living because other people are dead. And we have to make sure *more* people don't die. That's why this place is such a great idea. It's safe." His eyes turned stormy. "God, I can't wait until we're out of here in the field. After hearing about what happened, I just want to go tear apart some Strigoi. I wish we could go now, you know? There's no reason. They could use the extra help, and we pretty much know everything we need to."

The fierceness in his voice reminded me of my outburst yesterday, though he wasn't quite as worked up as I'd been. His eagerness to act was impetuous and naive, whereas mine had been born out of some weird, dark irrationality I still didn't entirely understand.

When I didn't respond, Mason gave me a puzzled look. "Don't you want to?"

"I don't know, Mase." I stared down at the floor, avoiding his eyes as I studied the toe of my shoe. "I mean, I don't want Strigoi out there, attacking people either. And I want to stop them in theory . . . but, well, we aren't even close to being ready. I've seen what they can do. . . . I don't know. Rushing in isn't the answer." I shook my head and looked back up. Good grief. I sounded so logical and cautious. I sounded like Dimitri. "It's not important since it's not going to happen anyway. I suppose we should just be excited about the trip, huh?"

Mason's moods were quick to change, and he turned easygoing once more. "Yup. And you'd better try to remember how to ski, because I'm calling you out on knocking down my ego out there. Not that it's going to happen."

I smiled again. "Boy, it sure is going to be sad when I make you cry. I kind of feel guilty already."

He opened his mouth, no doubt to deliver some smartass reply, and then caught sight of something—or rather, someone—behind me. I glanced over and saw Dimitri's tall form approaching from the other side of the gym.

Mason swept me a gallant bow. "Your lord and master. Catch you later, Hathaway. Start planning your ski strategies." He opened the door and disappeared into the frigid darkness. I turned around and joined Dimitri.

Like other dhampir novices, I spent half of my school day on one form or another of guardian training, be it actual physical combat or learning about Strigoi and how to defend against them. Novices also sometimes had practices after school. I, however, was in a unique situation.

I still stood by my decision to run away from St. Vladimir's. Victor Dashkov had posed too much of a threat to Lissa. But our extended vacation had come with consequences. Being away for two years had put me behind in my guardian classes, so the school had declared that I had to make up for it by going to extra practices before *and* after school.

With Dimitri.

Little did they know that they were also giving me lessons in avoiding temptation. But my attraction to him aside, I was a fast learner, and with his help, I had almost caught up to the other seniors.

Since he wasn't wearing a coat, I knew we'd be working inside today, which was good news. It was freezing out. Yet even the happiness I felt over that was nothing compared to what I felt when I saw what exactly he had set up in one of the training rooms.

There were practice dummies arranged on the far wall, dummies that looked amazingly lifelike. No straw-stuffed burlap bags here. There were men and women, wearing ordinary clothes, with rubbery skin and different hair and eye colors. Their expressions ranged from happy to scared to angry. I'd worked with these dummies before in other trainings, using them to practice kicks and punches. But I'd never worked with them while holding what Dimitri held: a silver stake.

"Sweet," I breathed.

It was identical to the one I'd found at the Badica house. It had a hand grip at the bottom, almost like a hilt without the little side flourishes. That was where its resemblance to a dagger ended. Rather than a flat blade, the stake had a thick, rounded body that narrowed to a point, kind of like an ice pick. The entire thing was a little shorter than my forearm.

Dimitri leaned casually against the wall, in an easy stance he always pulled off remarkably well, despite being almost six-seven. With one hand, he tossed the stake into the air. It spun around in a cartwheel a couple of times and then came down. He caught it hilt first.

"Please tell me I get to learn how to do *that* today," I said.

Amusement flashed in the dark depths of his eyes. I think he had a hard time keeping a straight face around me sometimes.

"You'll be lucky if I let you *hold* it today," he said. He flipped the stake into the air again. My eyes followed it longingly. I started to point out that I had already held one, but I knew that line of logic would get me nowhere.

Instead, I tossed my backpack on the floor, threw off my coat, and crossed my arms expectantly. I had on loose pants tied at the waist and a tank top with a hoodie over it. My dark hair was pulled brutally back into a ponytail. I was ready for anything.

"You want me to tell you how they work and why I should always be cautious around them," I announced.

Dimitri stopped flipping the stake and stared at me in astonishment.

"Come on," I laughed. "You don't think I know how you work by now? We've been doing this for almost three months. You always make me talk safety and responsibility before I can do anything fun."

"I see," he said. "Well, I guess you've got it all figured out. By all means, go on with the lesson. I'll just wait over here until you need me again."

He tucked the stake into a leather sheath hanging from his belt and then made himself comfortable against the wall, hands stuffed in pockets. I waited, figuring he was joking, but when he said nothing else, I realized he'd meant his words. With a shrug, I launched into what I knew.

"Silver always has powerful effects on any magical creature—it can help or hurt them if you put enough power into it. These stakes are really hard-core because it takes four different Moroi to make them, and they use each of the elements during the forging." I frowned, suddenly considering something. "Well, except spirit. So these things are supercharged and are about the only non-decapitating weapon that can do damage to a Strigoi—but to kill them, it has to be through the heart."

"Will they hurt *you*?"

I shook my head. "No. I mean, well, yeah, if you drive one through my heart it will, but it won't hurt me like it would a Moroi. Scratch one of them with this, and it'll hit them pretty hard—but not as hard as it'd hit a Strigoi. And they won't hurt humans, either."

I stopped for a moment and stared absentmindedly at the window behind Dimitri. Frost covered the glass in sparkling, crystalline patterns, but I hardly noticed. Mentioning humans and stakes had transported me back to the Badica house. Blood and death flashed through my thoughts.

Seeing Dimitri watching me, I shook off the memories and kept going with the lesson. Dimitri would occasionally give a nod or ask a clarifying question. As the time ticked down, I kept expecting him to tell me I was finished and could start hacking up the dummies. Instead, he waited until almost ten minutes before the end of our session before leading me over to one of them—it was a man with blond hair and a goatee. Dimitri took the stake out from its sheath but didn't hand it to me.

"Where are you going to put this?" he asked.

"In the heart," I replied irritably. "I already told you that like a hundred times. Can I have it now?"

He allowed himself a smile. "Where's the heart?"

I gave him an are-you-serious look. He merely shrugged.

With overdramatic emphasis, I pointed to the left side of the dummy's chest. Dimitri shook his head.

"That's not where the heart is," he told me.

"Sure it is. People put their hands over their hearts when they say the Pledge of Allegiance or sing the national anthem."

He continued to stare at me expectantly.

I turned back to the dummy and studied it. In the back of my brain, I remembered learning CPR and where we had to place our hands. I tapped the center of the dummy's chest.

"Is it here?"

He arched an eyebrow. Normally I thought that was cool. Today it was just annoying. "I don't know," he said. "Is it?"

"That's what I'm asking you!"

"You shouldn't have to ask me. Don't you all have to take physiology?"

"Yeah. Junior year. I was on 'vacation,' remember?" I pointed to the gleaming stake. "Can I please touch it now?"

He flipped the stake again, letting it flash in the light, and then it disappeared in the sheath. "I want you to *tell* me where the heart is the next time we meet. Exactly where. And I want to know what's in the way of it too."

I gave him my fiercest glare, which—judging from his expression—must not have been that fierce. Nine out of ten times, I thought Dimitri was the sexiest thing walking the earth. Then, there were times like this . . .

I headed off to first period, a combat class, in a bad mood.

I didn't like looking incompetent in front of Dimitri, and I'd really, *really* wanted to use one of those stakes. So in class I took out my annoyance on anyone I could punch or kick. By the end of class, no one wanted to spar with me. I'd accidentally hit Meredith—one of the few other girls in my class—so hard that she'd felt it through her shin padding. She was going to have an ugly bruise and kept looking at me as though I'd done it on purpose. I apologized to no avail.

Afterward, Mason found me once again. "Oh, man," he said, studying my face. "Who pissed you off?"

I immediately launched into my tale of silver stake and heart woes.

To my annoyance, he laughed. "How do you not know where the heart is? Especially considering how many of them you've broken?"

I gave him the same ferocious look I'd given Dimitri. This time, it worked. Mason's face paled.

"Belikov is a sick, evil man who should be thrown into a pit of rabid vipers for the great offense he committed against you this morning."

"Thank you." I said primly. Then, I considered. "Can vipers be rabid?"

"I don't see why not. Everything can be. I think." He held the hallway door open for me. "Canadian geese might be worse than vipers, though."

I gave him a sidelong look. "Canadian geese are deadlier than vipers?"

"You ever tried to feed those little bastards?" he asked, attempting seriousness and failing. "They're vicious. You get thrown to vipers, you die quickly. But the geese? That'll go on for days. More suffering."

"Wow. I don't know whether I should be impressed or frightened that you've thought about all this," I remarked.

"Just trying to find creative ways to avenge your honor, that's all."

"You just never struck me as the creative type, Mase."

We stood just outside our second-period classroom. Mason's expression was still light and joking, but there was a suggestive note in his voice when he spoke again. "Rose, when I'm around you, I think of *all sorts* of creative things to do."

I was still giggling about the vipers and abruptly stopped, staring at him in surprise. I'd always thought Mason was cute, but with that serious, smoky look in his eyes, it suddenly occurred to me for the first time that he was actually kind of sexy.

"Oh, look at that," he laughed, noticing how much he'd caught me off guard. "Rose gets rendered speechless. Ashford 1, Hathaway 0."

"Hey, I don't want to make you cry before the trip. It won't be any fun if I've already broken you before we even hit the slopes."

He laughed, and we stepped into the room. This was a class on bodyguard theory, one that took place in an actual classroom instead of the practice field. It was a nice break from all the physical exertion. Today, there were three guardians standing at the front who weren't from the school's regiment. Holiday visitors, I realized. Parents and their guardians had already started coming to campus to accompany their children to the ski resort. My interest was piqued immediately.

One of the guests was a tall guy who looked like he was about a hundred years old but could still kick major ass. The other guy was about Dimitri's age. He had deeply tanned skin and was built well enough that a few of the girls in class looked ready to swoon.

The last guardian was a woman. Her auburn hair was cropped and curly, and her brown eyes were currently narrowed in thought. As I've said, a lot of dhampir women choose to have children rather than follow the guardian path. Since I too was one of the few women in this profession, I was always excited to meet others—like Tamara.

Only, this wasn't Tamara. This was someone I'd known for years, someone who triggered anything but pride and excitement. Instead, I felt resentment. Resentment, anger, and burning outrage.

The woman standing in front of the class was my mother.

FOUR

I COULDN'T BELIEVE IT. JANINE Hathaway. My mother. My insanely famous and stunningly absent mother. She was no Arthur Schoenberg, but she did have a pretty stellar reputation in the guardian world. I hadn't seen her in years because she was always off on same insane mission. And yet . . . here she was at the Academy right now—right *in front* of me—and she hadn't even bothered to let me know she was coming. So much for motherly love.

What the hell was she doing here anyway? The answer came quickly. All the Moroi who came to campus would have their guardians in tow. My mother protected a noble from the Szelsky clan, and several members of that family had shown up for the holidays. Of course she'd be here with him.

I slid into my chair and felt something inside of me shrivel up. I knew she had to have seen me come in, but her attention was focused elsewhere. She had on jeans and a beige T-shirt, covered with what had to be the most boring denim jacket I'd ever seen. At only five feet tall, she was dwarfed by the other guardians, but she had a presence and way of standing that made her seem taller.

Our instructor, Stan, introduced the guests and explained that they were going to share real-life experiences with us.

He paced the front of the room, bushy eyebrows knitting together as he spoke. "I know this is unusual," he explained. "Visiting guardians usually don't have time to stop by our classes. Our three guests, however, have made time to come talk to you today in light of what's happened recently. . . ." He paused a moment, and no one needed to tell us what he was referring to. The Badica attack. He cleared his throat and tried again. "In light of what's happened, we thought it might better prepare you to learn from those currently working in the field."

The class tensed with excitement. Hearing stories—particularly ones with a lot of blood and action—was a hell of a lot more interesting than analyzing theory from a textbook. Apparently some of the other campus guardians thought so too. They often stopped by our classes, but they were present today in a larger-than-usual number. Dimitri stood among them in the back.

The old guy went first. He launched into his story, and I found myself getting hooked in. It described a time when the youngest son of the family he guarded had wandered off in a public place that Strigoi were lurking in.

"The sun was about to set," he told us in a gravelly voice. He swept his hands in a downward motion, apparently to demonstrate how a sunset worked. "There were only two of us, and we had to make a snap decision on how to proceed."

I leaned forward, elbows propped up on my desk. Guardians often worked in pairs. One—the near guard—usually stayed close to those being guarded while the other—the far guard—scouted the area. The far guard still usually stayed within eye contact, so I recognized the dilemma here. Thinking about it, I decided that if I were in that situation, I'd have the near guardian take the rest of the family to a secure location while the other guardian searched for the boy.

"We had the family stay inside a restaurant with my partner while I swept the rest of the area," continued the old guardian. He spread his hands out in a sweeping motion, and I felt smug over having made the correct call. The story ended happily, with a found boy and no Strigoi encounters.

The second guy's anecdote talked about how he'd gotten the drop on a Strigoi stalking some Moroi.

"I wasn't even technically on duty," he said. He was the really cute one, and a girl sitting near me stared at him with wide, adoring eyes. "I was visiting a friend and the family he guarded. As I was leaving their apartment, I saw a Strigoi lurking in the shadows. He never expected a guardian to be out there. I circled the block, came up behind him, and . . ." The man made a staking motion, far more dramatic than the old guy's hand gestures had been. The storyteller even went so far as to mimic twisting the stake into the Strigoi's heart.

And then it was my mother's turn. A scowl spread over my face before she even said a word, a scowl that grew worse once she actually launched into the story. I swear, if I didn't believe her incapable of having the imagination for it—and her bland clothing choices proved she really *didn't* have an imagination—I would have thought she was lying. It was more than a story. It was an epic tale, the kind of thing that gets made into movies and wins Oscars.

She talked about how her charge, Lord Szelsky, and his wife had attended a ball put on by another prominent royal family. Several Strigoi had been lying in wait. My mother discovered one, promptly staked it, and then alerted the other guardians present. With their help, she hunted down the other Strigoi lurking around and performed most of the kills herself.

"It wasn't easy," she explained. From anyone else that statement would have sounded like bragging. Not her. There was a briskness to the way she spoke, an efficient way of stating facts that left no room for flourishes. She'd been raised in Glasgow and some of her words still had a Scottish lilt. "There were three others on the premises. At the time, that was considered an unusually large number to be working together. That's not necessarily true now, considering the Badica massacre." A few people flinched at the casual way she spoke about the attack. Once again, I could see the bodies. "We had to dispatch the remaining Strigoi as quickly and quietly as possible, so as not to alert the others. Now, if you have the element of surprise, the best way to take Strigoi is to come around from behind, break their necks, and then stake them. Breaking their necks won't kill them, of course, but it stuns them and allows you to do the staking before they can make any noise. The most difficult part is actually sneaking up on them, because their hearing is so acute. Since I'm smaller and lighter than most guardians, I can move fairly quietly. So I ended up performing two of the three kills myself."

Again, she used that matter-of-fact tone as she described her own stealthy skills. It was annoying, more so than if she'd been openly haughty about how awesome she was. My classmates' faces shone with wonder; they were clearly more interested in the idea of breaking a Strigoi's neck than analyzing my mother's narrative skills.

She continued with the story. When she and the other guardians had killed the remaining Strigoi, they'd discovered two Moroi had been taken from the party. Such an act wasn't uncommon for Strigoi. Sometimes they wanted to save Moroi for a later "snack"; sometimes lower-ranking Strigoi were dispatched by more powerful ones to bring back prey. Regardless, two Moroi were gone from the ball, and their guardian had been injured.

"Naturally, we couldn't leave those Moroi in Strigoi clutches," she said. "We tracked the Strigoi to their hideout and found several of them living together. I'm sure you can recognize how rare that is."

It was. The evil and selfish nature of Strigoi made them turn on each other as easily as they did their victims. Organizing for attacks—when they had an immediate and bloody goal in mind—was the best they could do. But living together? No. It was almost impossible to imagine.

"We managed to free the two captive Moroi, only to discover that others were being held prisoner," my mother said.

"We couldn't send the ones we'd rescued back by themselves, though, so the guardians who were with me escorted them out and left it to me to get the others."

Yes, of course, I thought. My mother bravely went in alone. Along the way, she got captured but managed to escape and rescue the prisoners. In doing so, she performed what had to be the hat trick of the century, killing Strigoi in all three ways: staking, decapitation, and setting them on fire.

"I had just staked a Strigoi when two more attacked," she explained. "I didn't have time to pull the stake out when the others jumped me. Fortunately, there was an open fireplace nearby, and I pushed one of the Strigoi into it. The last one chased me outside, into an old shed. There was an axe inside and I used that to cut off her head. I then took a can of gasoline and returned to the house. The one I'd thrown into the fireplace hadn't completely burned, but once I doused him in gasoline, he went up pretty quickly."

The classroom was in awe as she spoke. Mouths dropped. Eyes bugged. Not a sound could be heard. Glancing around, I felt like time had frozen for everyone—except me. I appeared to be the only one unimpressed by her harrowing tale, and seeing the awe on everyone's faces enraged me. When she finished, a dozen hands shot up as the class peppered her with questions about her techniques, whether she was scared, etc.

After about the tenth question, I couldn't take it anymore. I raised my hand. It took her a while to notice and call on me. She seemed mildly astonished to find me in class. I considered myself lucky that she even recognized me.

"So, Guardian Hathaway," I began. "Why didn't you guys just secure the place?"

She frowned. I think she'd gone on her guard the moment she called on me. "What do you mean?"

I shrugged and slouched back in my desk, attempting a casual and conversational air. "I don't know. It seems to me like you guys messed up. Why didn't you scope out the place and make sure it was clear of Strigoi in the first place? Seems like you could have saved yourself a lot of trouble."

All eyes in the room turned toward me. My mother was momentarily at a loss for words. "If we hadn't gone through all that 'trouble,' there'd be seven more Strigoi walking the world, *and* those other captured Moroi would be dead or turned by now."

"Yeah, yeah, I get how you guys saved the day and all that, but I'm going back to the principles here. I mean, this is a theory class, right?" I glanced over at Stan who was regarding me with a very stormy look. He and I had a long and unpleasant history of classroom conflicts, and I suspected we were on the verge of another. "So I just want to figure out what went wrong in the beginning."

I'll say this for her—my mother had a hell of a lot more self-control than I did. Had our roles been reversed, I would have walked over and smacked me by now. Her face stayed perfectly calm, however, and a small tightness in the set of her lips was the only sign that I was pissing her off.

"It's not that simple," she replied. "The venue had an extremely complex layout. We went through it initially and found nothing. It's believed the Strigoi came in after the festivities had started—or that there might have been passages and hidden rooms we hadn't been aware of."

The class ooh'ed and ahh'ed over the idea of hidden passages, but I wasn't impressed.

"So what you're saying is that you guys either failed to detect them during your first sweep, or they broke through the 'security' you set up during the party. Seems like someone messed up either way."

The tightness in her lips increased, and her voice grew frosty. "We did the best we could with an unusual situation. I can see how someone at your level might not be able to grasp the intricacies of what I'm describing, but once you've actually learned enough to go beyond *theory*, you'll see how different it is when you're actually out there and lives are in your hands."

"No doubt," I agreed. "Who am I to question your methods? I mean, whatever gets you the *molnija* marks, right?"

"Miss Hathaway." Stan's deep voice rumbled through the room. "Please take your things and go wait outside for the remainder of class."

I stared at him in bewilderment. "Are you serious? Since when is there anything wrong with asking questions?"

"Your attitude is what's wrong." He pointed at the door. "Go."

A silence heavier and deeper than when my mother had

told her story descended over everyone. I did my best not to cower under the stares of guardians and novices alike. This wasn't the first time I'd been kicked out of Stan's class. It wasn't even the first time I'd been kicked out of Stan's class while Dimitri was watching. Slinging my backpack over my shoulder, I crossed the short distance to the door—a distance that felt like miles—and refused to make eye contact with my mother as I passed.

About five minutes before the class let out, she slipped out of the room and walked over to where I sat in the hallway. Looking down on me, she put her hands on her hips in that annoying way that made her seem taller than she was. It wasn't fair that someone over half a foot shorter than me could make me feel so small.

"Well. I see your manners haven't improved over the years."

I stood up and felt a glare snap into place. "Nice to see you too. I'm surprised you even recognized me. In fact, I didn't even think you *remembered* me, seeing as how you never bothered to let me know you were on campus."

She shifted her hands from her hips and crossed her arms across her chest, becoming—if possible—even more impassive. "I couldn't neglect my duty to come coddle you."

"Coddle?" I asked. This woman had never coddled me in her life. I couldn't believe she even knew the word.

"I wouldn't expect you to understand. From what I hear, you don't really know what 'duty' is."

"I know exactly what it is," I retorted. My voice was intentionally haughty. "Better than most people."

Her eyes widened in a sort of mock surprise. I used that sarcastic look on a lot of people and didn't appreciate having it directed toward me. "Oh really? Where were you for the last two years?"

"Where were you for the last five?" I demanded. "Would you have known I was gone if someone hadn't told you?"

"Don't turn this back on me. I was away because I had to be. *You* were away so you could go shopping and stay up late."

My hurt and embarrassment morphed into pure fury. Apparently, I was never going to live down the consequences of running away with Lissa.

"You have *no* idea why I left," I said, my voice's volume rising. "And you have no right to make assumptions about my life when you don't know anything about it."

"I've read reports about what happened. You had reason for concern, but you acted incorrectly." Her words were formal and crisp. She could have been teaching one of my classes. "You should have gone to others for help."

"There was no one I could go to—not when I didn't have hard proof. Besides, we've been learning that we're supposed to think independently."

"Yes," she replied. "Emphasis on *learning*. Something you missed out on for two years. You're hardly in a position to lecture me about guardian protocol."

I wound up in arguments all the time; something in my nature made that inevitable. So I was used to defending myself and having insults slammed at me. I had a tough skin. But somehow, around her—in the brief times I *had* been around her—I always felt like I was three years old. Her attitude humiliated me, and touching on my missed training—already a prickly subject—only made me feel worse. I crossed my arms in a fair imitation of her own stance and managed a smug look.

"Yeah? Well, that's not what my teachers think. Even after missing all that time, I've still caught up with everyone else in my class."

She didn't answer right away. Finally, in a flat voice, she said, "If you hadn't left, you would have surpassed them."

Turning military-style, she walked off down the hall. A minute later, the bell rang, and the rest of Stan's class spilled into the hall.

Even Mason couldn't cheer me up after that. I spent the rest of the day angry and annoyed, sure that everyone was whispering about my mother and me. I skipped lunch and went to the library to read a book about physiology and anatomy.

When it was time for my after-school training with Dimitri, I practically ran up to the practice dummy. With a curled fist, I slapped its chest, very slightly to the left but mostly in the center.

"There," I told him. "The heart is there, and the sternum and ribs are in the way. Can I have the stake now?"

Crossing my arms, I glanced up at him triumphantly, waiting for him to shower me with praise for my new cunning. Instead, he simply nodded in acknowledgment, like I should already have known that. And yeah, I should have.

"And how do you get through the sternum and the ribs?" he asked.

I sighed. I'd figured out the answer to one question, only to be given another. Typical.

We spent a large part of the practice going over that, and he demonstrated several techniques that would yield the quickest kill. Every movement he made was both graceful and deadly. He made it look effortless, but I knew better.

When he suddenly extended his hand and offered the stake to me, I didn't understand at first. "You're giving it to me?"

His eyes sparkled. "I can't believe you're holding back. I figured you'd have taken it and run by now."

"Aren't you always teaching me to hold back?" I asked.

"Not on everything."

"But on *some* things."

I heard the double meaning in my voice and wondered where it had come from. I'd accepted a while ago that there were too many reasons for me to even think about him romantically anymore. Every once in a while, I slipped a little and kind of wished he would too. It'd have been nice to know that he still wanted me, that I still drove him crazy. Studying him now, I realized he might not ever slip because I *didn't* drive him crazy anymore. It was a depressing thought.

"Of course," he said, showing no indication we'd discussed anything other than class matters. "It's like everything else. Balance. Know which things to run forward with—and know which to leave alone." He placed a heavy emphasis on that last statement.

Our eyes met briefly, and I felt electricity race through me. He *did* know what I was talking about. And like always, he was ignoring it and being my teacher—which is exactly what he should have been doing. With a sigh, I pushed my feelings for him out of my head and tried to remember that I was about to touch the weapon I'd been longing for since childhood. The memory of the Badica house came back to me yet again. The Strigoi were out there. I needed to focus.

Hesitantly, almost reverentially, I reached out and curled my fingers around the hilt. The metal was cool and tingled against my skin. It was etched along the hilt for better grip, but in trailing my fingers over the rest of it, I found the surface to be as smooth as glass. I lifted it from his hand and brought it to me, taking a long time to study it and get used to its weight. An anxious part of me wanted to turn around and impale all of the dummies, but instead I looked up at Dimitri and asked, "What should I do first?"

In his typical way, he covered basics first, honing the way I held and moved with the stake. Later on, he finally let me attack one of the dummies, at which point I did indeed discover it was *not* effortless. Evolution had done a smart thing in protecting the heart with the sternum and ribs. Yet through it all, Dimitri never faltered in diligence and patience, guiding me through every step and correcting the finest details.

"Slide *up* through the ribs," he explained, watching me try to fit the stake's point through a gap in the bones. "It'll be easier since you're shorter than most of your attackers. Plus, you can slide along the lower rib's edge."

When practice ended, he took the stake back and nodded his approval.

"Good. Very good."

I glanced at him in surprise. He didn't usually hand out a lot of praise.

"Really?"

"You do it like you've been doing it for years."

I felt a delighted grin creep over my face as we started leaving the practice room. When we neared the door, I noticed a dummy with curly red hair. Suddenly, all the events from Stan's class came tumbling back into my head. I scowled.

"Can I stake that one next time?"

He picked up his coat and put it on. It was long and brown, made of distressed leather. It looked very much like a cowboy duster, though he'd never admit to it. He had a secret fascination with the Old West. I didn't really understand it, but then, I didn't get his weird musical preferences either.

"I don't think that'd be healthy," he said.

"It'd be better than me actually doing it to *her*," I grumbled, slinging my backpack over one shoulder. We headed out to the gym.

"Violence isn't the answer to your problems," he said sagely.

"She's the one with the problem. And I thought the whole point of my education was that violence *is* the answer."

"Only to those who bring it to you first. Your mother isn't assaulting you. You two are just too much alike, that's all."

I stopped walking. "I'm not anything like her! I mean . . . we kind of have the same eyes. But I'm a lot taller. And my hair's completely different." I pointed to my ponytail, just in case he wasn't aware that my thick brown-black hair didn't look like my mother's auburn curls.

He still had kind of an amused expression, but there was something hard in his eyes too. "I'm not talking about your appearances, and you know it."

I looked away from that knowing gaze. My attraction to Dimitri had started almost as soon as we'd met—and it wasn't just because he was so hot, either. I felt like he understood part of me that I didn't understand myself, and sometimes I was pretty sure I understood parts of him that he didn't understand either.

The only problem was that he had the annoying tendency to point out things about myself I didn't *want* to understand.

"You think I'm jealous?"

"Are you?" he asked. I hated it when he answered my questions with questions. "If so, what are you jealous of exactly?"

I glanced back at Dimitri. "I don't know. Maybe I'm jealous of her reputation. Maybe I'm jealous because she's put more time into her reputation than into me. I don't know."

"You don't think what she did was great?"

"Yes. No. I don't know. It just sounded like such a . . . I don't know . . . like she was bragging. Like she did it for the glory." I grimaced. "For the marks." *Molnija* marks were tattoos awarded to guardians when they killed Strigoi. Each one looked like a tiny *x* made of lightning bolts. They went on the backs of our necks and showed how experienced a guardian was.

"You think facing down Strigoi is worth a few marks? I thought you'd learned something from the Badica house."

I felt stupid. "That's not what I—"

"Come on."

I stopped walking. "What?"

We'd been heading toward my dorm, but now he nodded his head toward the opposite side of campus. "I want to show you something."

"What is it?"

"That not all marks are badges of honor."

FIVE

I HAD NO IDEA WHAT Dimitri was talking about, but I followed along obediently.

To my surprise, he led me out of the boundaries of the campus and into the surrounding woods. The Academy owned a lot of land, not all of which was actively used for educational purposes. We were in a remote part of Montana, and at times, it seemed as though the school was just barely holding back the wilderness.

We walked quietly for a while, our feet crunching through thick, unbroken snow. A few birds flitted by, singing their greetings to the rising sun, but mostly all I saw were scraggly, snow-heavy evergreen trees. I had to work to keep up with Dimitri's longer stride, particularly since the snow slowed me down a little. Soon, I discerned a large, dark shape ahead. Some kind of building.

"What is that?" I asked. Before he could answer, I realized it was a small cabin, made out of logs and everything. Closer examination showed that the logs looked worn and rotten in some places. The roof sagged a little.

"Old watch-post," he said. "Guardians used to live on the edge of campus and keep watch for Strigoi."

"Why don't they anymore?"

"We don't have enough guardians to staff it. Besides, Moroi have warded campus with enough protective magic that most don't think it's necessary to have actual people on guard." Provided no humans staked the wards, I thought.

For a few brief moments, I entertained the hope that Dimitri was leading me off to some romantic getaway. Then I heard voices on the opposite side of the building. A familiar hum of feeling coursed into my mind. Lissa was there.

Dimitri and I rounded the corner of the building, coming up on a surprising scene. A small frozen pond lay there, and Christian and Lissa were ice skating on it. A woman I didn't know was with them, but her back was to me. All I could see was a wave of jet-black hair that arced around her when she skated to a graceful stop.

Lissa grinned when she saw me. "Rose!" Christian glanced over at me as she spoke, and I got the distinct impression he felt I was intruding on their romantic moment.

Lissa moved in awkward strides to the pond's edge. She wasn't so adept at skating.

I could only stare in bewilderment—and jealousy. "Thanks for inviting me to the party."

"I figured you were busy," she said. "And this is secret anyway. We aren't supposed to be here." I could have told them that.

Christian skated up beside her, and the strange woman soon followed. "You bringing party crashers, Dimka?" she asked.

I wondered who she was talking to, until I heard Dimitri

laugh. He didn't do it that often, and my surprise increased. "It's impossible to keep Rose away from places she shouldn't be. She always finds them eventually."

The woman grinned and turned around, flipping her long hair over one shoulder, so that I suddenly saw her face full-on. It took every ounce of my already dubiously held self-control not to react. Her heart-shaped face had large eyes exactly the same shade as Christian's, a pale wintry blue. The lips that smiled at me were delicate and lovely, glossed in a shade of pink that set off the rest of her features.

But across her left cheek, marring what would have otherwise been smooth, white skin were raised, purplish scars. Their shape and formation looked very much like someone had bitten into and torn out part of her cheek. Which, I realized, was exactly what had happened.

I swallowed. I suddenly knew who this was. It was Christian's aunt. When his parents had turned Strigoi, they'd come back for him, hoping to hide him away and turn him Strigoi when he was older. I didn't know all the details, but I knew his aunt had fended them off. As I'd observed before, though, Strigoi were deadly. She'd provided enough of a distraction until the guardians showed up, but she hadn't walked away without damage.

She extended her gloved hand to me. "Tasha Ozera," she said. "I've heard a lot about you, Rose."

I gave Christian a dangerous look, and Tasha laughed.

"Don't worry," she said. "It was all good."

"No, it wasn't," he countered.

She shook her head in exasperation. "Honestly, I don't know where he got such horrible social skills. He didn't learn them from me." That was obvious, I thought.

"What are you guys doing out here?" I asked.

"I wanted to spend some time with these two." A small frown wrinkled her forehead. "But I don't really like hanging around the school itself. They aren't always hospitable. . . ."

I didn't get that at first. School officials usually fell all over themselves when royals came to visit. Then I figured it out.

"Because . . . because of what happened . . ."

Considering the way everyone treated Christian because of his parents, I shouldn't have been surprised to find his aunt facing the same discrimination.

Tasha shrugged. "That's the way it is." She rubbed her hands together and exhaled, her breath making a frosty cloud in the air. "But let's not stand out here, not when we can build a fire inside."

I gave a last, wistful glance at the frozen pond and then followed the others inside. The cabin was pretty bare, covered in layers of dust and dirt. It consisted of only one room. There was a narrow bed with no covers in the corner and a few shelves where food had probably once been stored. There was a fireplace, however, and we soon had a blaze going that warmed the small area. The five of us sat down, huddling around its heat, and Tasha produced a bag of marshmallows that we cooked over the flames.

As we feasted on that gooey goodness, Lissa and Christian talked to each other in that easy, comfortable way they always had. To my surprise, Tasha and Dimitri also talked in a familiar and light way. They obviously knew each other from way back when. I'd actually never seen him so animated before. Even when affectionate with me, there'd always been a serious air about him. With Tasha, he bantered and laughed.

The more I listened to her, the more I liked her. Finally, unable to stay out of the conversation, I asked, "So are you coming on the ski trip?"

She nodded. Stifling a yawn, she stretched herself out like a cat. "I haven't been skiing in ages. No time. Been saving all my vacation for this."

"Vacation?" I gave her a curious look. "Do you have . . . a job?"

"Sadly, yes," Tasha said, though she didn't actually sound very sad about it. "I teach martial arts classes."

I stared in astonishment. I couldn't have been more surprised if she'd said she was an astronaut or a telephone psychic.

A lot of royals just didn't work at all, and if they did, it was usually in some sort of investment or other moneymaking business that furthered their family fortunes. And those who *did* work certainly didn't do a lot of martial arts or physically demanding jobs. Moroi had a lot of great attributes: exceptional senses—smell, sight, and hearing—and the power to work magic. But physically, they were tall and slender, often small-boned. They also got weak from being in sunlight. Now, those things weren't enough to prevent someone from becoming a fighter, but they did make it more challenging. An idea had built up among the Moroi over time that their best offense was a good defense, and most shied away from the thought of physical conflict. They hid in well-protected places like the Academy, always relying on stronger, hardier dhampirs to guard them.

"What do you think, Rose?" Christian seemed highly amused by my surprise. "Think you could take her?"

"Hard to say," I said.

Tasha crooked me a grin. "You're being modest. I've seen what you guys can do. This is just a hobby I picked up."

Dimitri chuckled. "Now *you're* being modest. You could teach half the classes around here."

"Not likely," she said. "It'd be pretty embarrassing to be beaten up by a bunch of teenagers."

"I don't think that'd happen," he said. "I seem to remember you doing some damage to Neil Szelsky."

Tasha rolled her eyes. "Throwing my drink in his face wasn't actually damage—unless you consider the damage it did to his suit. And we all know how he is about his clothes."

They both laughed at some private joke the rest of us weren't in on, but I was only half-listening. I was still intrigued about her role with the Strigoi.

The self-control I'd tried to maintain finally slipped. "Did you start learning to fight before or after that happened to your face?"

"Rose!" hissed Lissa.

But Tasha didn't seem upset. Neither did Christian, and he usually grew uncomfortable when the attack with his parents was brought up. She regarded me with a level, thoughtful look. It reminded me of the one I sometimes got from Dimitri if I did something surprising that he approved of.

"After," she said. She didn't lower her gaze or look embarrassed, though I sensed sadness in her. "How much do you know?"

I glanced at Christian. "The basics."

She nodded. "I knew . . . I knew what Lucas and Moira had become, but that still didn't prepare me. Mentally, physically, or emotionally. I think if I had to live through it again, I still wouldn't be ready. But after that night, I looked at myself—figuratively—and realized how defenseless I was. I'd spent my whole life expecting guardians to protect me and take care of me.

"And that's not to say the guardians aren't capable. Like I said, you could probably take me in a fight. But they—Lucas and Moira—cut down our two guardians before we realized what had happened. I stalled them from taking Christian—but just barely. If the others hadn't shown up, I'd be dead, and he'd—" She stopped, frowned, and kept going. "I decided that I didn't want to die that way, not without putting up a real fight and doing everything I could to protect myself and those

I love. So I learned all sorts of self-defense. And after a while, I didn't really, uh, fit in so well with high society around here. So I moved to Minneapolis and made a living from teaching others."

I didn't doubt there were other Moroi living in Minneapolis—though God only knew why—but I could read between the lines. She'd moved there and integrated herself with humans, keeping away from other vampires like Lissa and I had for two years. I started to wonder also if there might have been something else there between the lines. She'd said she'd learned "all sorts of self-defense"—apparently, more than just martial arts. Going along with their offense-defense beliefs, the Moroi didn't think magic should be used as a weapon. Long ago, it had been used that way, and some Moroi still secretly did today. Christian, I knew, was one of them. I suddenly had a good idea of where he might have picked up that kind of thing.

Silence fell. It was hard to follow up a sad story like that. But Tasha, I realized, was one of those people who could always lighten a mood. It made me like her even more, and she spent the rest of the time telling us funny stories. She didn't put on airs like a lot of royals did, so she had lots of dirt on everyone. Dimitri knew a lot of the people she spoke of—honestly, how did someone so antisocial seem to know *everyone* in Moroi and guardian society?—and would occasionally add some small detail. They had us in hysterics until Tasha finally looked at her watch.

"Where's the best place a girl can go shopping around here?" she asked.

Lissa and I exchanged looks. "Missoula," we said in unison.

Tasha sighed. "That's a couple hours away, but if I leave soon, I can probably still get in some time before the stores close. I'm hopelessly behind in Christmas shopping."

I groaned. "I'd kill to go shopping."

"Me too," said Lissa.

"Maybe we could sneak along. . . ." I gave Dimitri a hopeful look.

"No," he said immediately. I gave a sigh of my own.

Tasha yawned again. "I'll have to grab some coffee, so I don't sleep on the drive in."

"Can't one of your guardians drive for you?"

She shook her head. "I don't have any."

"Don't have any . . ." I frowned, parsing her words. "You don't have any guardians?"

"Nope."

I shot up. "But that's not possible! You're royal. You should have at least one. Two, really."

Guardians were distributed among Moroi in a cryptic, micromanaged way by the Guardian Council. It was kind of an unfair system, considering the ratio of guardians to Moroi. Non-royals tended to get them by a lottery system. Royals *always* got them. High-ranking royals often got more than one, but even the lowest-ranking member of royalty wouldn't have been without one.

"The Ozeras aren't exactly first in line when guardians get assigned," said Christian bitterly. "Ever since . . . my parents died . . . there's kind of been a shortage."

My anger flared up. "But that's not fair. They can't punish you for what your parents did."

"It's not punishment, Rose." Tasha didn't seem nearly as enraged as she should have been, in my opinion. "It's just . . . a rearranging of priorities."

"They're leaving you defenseless. You can't go out there by yourself!"

"I'm not defenseless, Rose. I've told you that. And if I really wanted a guardian, I could make a nuisance of myself, but it's a lot of hassle. I'm fine for now."

Dimitri glanced over at her. "You want me to go with you?"

"And keep you up all night?" Tasha shook her head. "I wouldn't do that to you, Dimka."

"He doesn't mind," I said quickly, excited about this solution.

Dimitri seemed amused by me speaking for him, but he didn't contradict me. "I really don't."

She hesitated. "All right. But we should probably go soon."

Our illicit party dispersed. The Moroi went one direction; Dimitri and I went another. He and Tasha made plans to meet up in a half hour.

"So what do you think of her?" he asked when we were alone.

"I like her. She's cool." I thought about her for a moment.

"And I get what you mean about the marks."

"Oh?"

I nodded, watching my footing as we walked along the paths. Even when salted and shoveled, they could still collect hidden patches of ice.

"She didn't do what she did for glory. She did it because she had to. Just like . . . just like my mom did." I hated to admit it, but it was true. Janine Hathaway might be the worst mother ever, but she was a great guardian. "The marks don't matter. *Molnijas* or scars."

"You're a fast learner," he said with approval.

I swelled under his praise. "Why does she call you Dimka?"

He laughed softly. I'd heard a lot of his laughter tonight and decided I'd like to hear more of it.

"It's a nickname for Dimitri."

"That doesn't make any sense. It doesn't sound anything like Dimitri. You should be called, I don't know, Dimi or something."

"That's not how it works in Russian," he said.

"Russian's weird." In Russian, the nickname for Vasilisa was Vasya, which made no sense to me.

"So is English."

I gave him a sly look. "If you'd teach me to swear in Russian, I might have a new appreciation for it."

"You swear too much already."

"I just want to express myself."

"Oh, Roza . . ." He sighed, and I felt a thrill tickle me. "Roza" was my name in Russian. He rarely used it. "You express yourself more than anyone else I know."

I smiled and walked on a bit without saying anything else. My heart skipped a beat, I was so happy to be around him. There was something warm and *right* about us being together.

Even as I floated along, my mind churned over something else that I'd been thinking about. "You know, there's something funny about Tasha's scars."

"What's that?" he asked.

"The scars . . . they mess up her face," I began slowly. I was having trouble putting my thoughts into words. "I mean, it's obvious she used to be really pretty. But even with the scars now . . . I don't know. She's pretty in a different way. It's like . . . like they're part of her. They complete her." It sounded silly, but it was true.

Dimitri didn't say anything, but he gave me a sidelong glance. I returned it, and as our eyes met, I saw the briefest glimpse of the old attraction. It was fleeting and gone too soon, but I'd seen it. Pride and approval replaced it, and they were almost as good.

When he spoke, it was to echo his earlier thoughts. "You're a fast learner, Roza."

SIX

I WAS FEELING PRETTY GOOD about life when I headed to my before-school practice the next day. The secret gathering last night had been super fun, and I felt proudly responsible for fighting the system and encouraging Dimitri to go with Tasha. Better still, I'd gotten my first crack at a silver stake yesterday and had proven I could handle one. High on myself, I couldn't wait to practice even more.

Once I was dressed in my usual workout attire, I practically skipped down to the gym. But when I stuck my head inside the practice room from the day before, I found it dark and quiet. Flipping on the light, I peered around just in case Dimitri was conducting some kind of weird, covert training exercise. Nope. Empty. No staking today.

"Shit," I muttered.

"He's not here."

I yelped and nearly jumped ten feet in the air. Turning around, I looked straight into my mother's narrowed brown eyes.

"What are you doing here?" As soon as the words were out of my mouth, her appearance registered with me. A stretchy spandex shirt with short sleeves. Loose, drawstring workout pants similar to the ones I wore. "Shit," I said again.

"Watch your mouth," she snapped. "You might behave like you have no manners, but at least try not to sound that way."

"Where's Dimitri?"

"*Guardian Belikov* is in bed. He just got back a couple of hours ago and needed to sleep."

Another expletive was on my lips, and I bit it back. Of course Dimitri was asleep. He'd had to drive with Tasha to Missoula during daylight in order to be there during human shopping hours. He'd technically been up all of the Academy's night and had probably only just gotten back. Ugh. I wouldn't have been so quick to encourage him to help her if I'd known it'd result in *this*.

"Well," I said hastily. "I guess that means practice is canceled—"

"Be quiet and put these on." She handed me some training mitts. They were similar to boxing gloves but not as thick and bulky. They shared the same purpose, however: to protect your hands and keep you from gouging your opponent with your nails.

"We've been working on silver stakes," I said sulkily, shoving my hands into the mitts.

"Well, today we're doing this. Come on."

Wishing I'd been hit by a bus on my walk from the dorm today, I followed her out toward the center of the gym. Her curly hair was pinned up to stay out of the way, revealing the back of her neck. The skin there was covered in tattoos. The top one was a serpentine line: the promise mark, given when guardians graduated from academies like St. Vladimir's and agreed to serve. Below that were the *molnija* marks awarded each time a guardian killed a Strigoi. They were shaped like the lightning bolts they took their name from. I couldn't gauge exact numbers, but let's just say it was a wonder my mom had any neck left to tattoo. She'd wielded a lot of death in her time.

When she reached the spot she wanted, she turned toward me and adopted an attack stance. Half expecting her to jump me then and there, I quickly mirrored it.

"What are we doing?" I asked.

"Basic offensive and defensive parrying. Use the red lines."

"That's all?" I asked.

She leapt toward me. I dodged—just barely—and tripped over my own feet in the process. Hastily, I righted myself.

"Well," she said in a voice that *almost* sounded sarcastic. "As you seem so keen on reminding me, I haven't seen you in five years. I have no idea what you can do."

She moved on me again, and again I just barely kept within the lines in escaping her. That quickly became the pattern. She never really gave me the chance to go on the offensive. Or maybe I just didn't have the skills to take the offensive. I spent all my time defending myself—physically, at least. Grudgingly, I had to acknowledge to myself that she was good. *Really* good. But I certainly wasn't going to tell her that.

"So, what?" I asked. "This is your way of making up for maternal negligence?"

"This is my way of making you get rid of that chip on your shoulder. You've had nothing but attitude for me since I arrived. You want to fight?" Her fist shot out and connected with my arm. "Then we'll fight. Point."

"Point," I conceded, backing up to my side. "I don't want to fight. I've just been trying to talk to you."

"Mouthing off to me in class isn't what I'd really call talking. Point."

I grunted from the hit. When I'd first begun training with Dimitri, I'd complained that it wasn't fair for me to fight someone a foot taller than me. He'd pointed out that I'd fight plenty of Strigoi taller than me and that the old adage was true: size doesn't matter. Sometimes I thought he was giving me false hope, but judging from my mom's performance here, I was starting to believe him.

I'd never actually fought anyone smaller than me. As one of the few girls in the novice classes, I accepted that I was almost always going to be shorter and slimmer than my opponents. But my mother was smaller still and clearly had nothing but muscle packed into her petite body.

"I have a unique style of communication, that's all," I said.

"You have a petty teenage delusion that you've somehow been wronged for the last seventeen years." Her foot hit my thigh. "Point. When in reality, you've been treated no differently than any other dhampir. Better, actually. I could have sent you off to live with my cousins. You want to be a blood whore? Is that what you wanted?"

The term "blood whore" always made me flinch. It was a term often applied to the single dhampir mothers who decided to raise their children instead of becoming guardians. These women often had short-term affairs with Moroi men and were looked down on for it—even though there wasn't really anything else they could have done, since Moroi men usually ended up marrying Moroi women. The "blood whore" term came from the fact that some dhampir women let men drink blood from them during sex. In our world, only humans gave blood. A dhampir doing it was dirty and kinky—especially during sex. I suspected only a few dhampir women actually did this, but unfairly, the term tended to get applied to all of them. I had given blood to Lissa when we had run away, and although it had been a necessary act, the stigma still stayed with me.

"No. Of course I don't want to be a blood whore." My breathing was becoming heavy. "And they're not all like that. There're only a few that actually are."

"They bring that reputation on themselves," she growled. I dodged her strike. "They should be doing their duty as guardians, not continuing to fool around and have flings with Moroi."

"They're raising their children," I grunted. I wanted to yell but couldn't waste the oxygen. "Something you'd know nothing about. Besides, aren't you the same as they are? I don't see a ring on your finger. Wasn't my dad just a fling for you?"

Her face turned hard, which is saying something when

you're already beating up your daughter. *"That,"* she said tightly, "is something *you* know nothing about. Point."

I winced at the blow but was happy to see I'd struck a nerve. I had no clue who my dad was. The only bit of information I had was that he was Turkish. I might have my mom's curvy figure and pretty face—though I could smugly say mine was much prettier than hers nowadays—but the rest of my coloring was from him. Lightly tanned skin with dark hair and eyes.

"How'd it happen?" I asked. "Were you on some assignment in Turkey? Meet him at a local bazaar? Or was it even cheaper than that? Did you go all Darwin and select the guy most likely to pass on warrior genes to your offspring? I mean, I know you only had me because it was your *duty*, so I suppose you had to make sure you could give the guardians the best specimen you could."

"Rosemarie," she warned through gritted teeth, "for once in your life, shut up."

"Why? Am I tarnishing your precious reputation? It's just like you told me: you aren't any different from any other dhampir either. You just screwed him and—"

There's a reason they say, "Pride goeth before a fall." I was so caught up in my own cocky triumph that I stopped paying attention to my feet. I was too close to the red line. Going outside of it was another point for her, so I scrambled to stay within and dodge her at the same time. Unfortunately, only one of those could work. Her fist came flying at me, fast and hard—and, perhaps most importantly, a bit higher than the permissable according to rules of this kind of exercise. It smacked me in the face with the power of a small truck, and I flew backward, hitting the hard gym floor back-first and head-second. And I was out of the lines. Damn it.

Pain cracked through the back of my head, and my vision went blurry and sparkly. Within seconds, my mother was leaning over me.

"Rose? Rose? Are you okay?" Her voice sounded hoarse and frantic. The world swam.

At some point after that, other people came, and I somehow wound up in the Academy's med clinic. There, someone shone a light in my eyes and started asking me incredibly idiotic questions.

"What's your name?"

"What?" I asked, squinting at the light.

"Your name." I recognized Dr. Olendzki peering over me.

"You know my name."

"I want you to tell me."

"Rose. Rose Hathaway."

"Do you know your birthday?"

"Of course I do. Why are you asking me such stupid things? Did you lose my records?"

Dr. Olendzki gave an exasperated sigh and walked off, taking the annoying light with her. "I think she's fine," I heard her tell someone. "I want to keep her here for the school day, just to make sure she doesn't have a concussion. I certainly don't want her anywhere near her guardian classes."

I spent the day moving in and out of sleep because Dr. Olendzki kept waking me up to do her tests. She also gave me an ice pack and told me to keep it close to my face. When the Academy's classes let out, she deemed me well enough to leave.

"I swear, Rose, I think you should have a frequent patient's card." There was a small smile on her face. "Short of those with chronic problems like allergies and asthma, I don't think there's any other student I've seen here so often in such a short period of time."

"Thanks," I said, not really sure I wanted the honor. "So, no concussion?"

She shook her head. "No. You're going to have some pain, though. I'll give you something for that before you go." Her smile faded, and suddenly she looked nervous. "To be honest, Rose, I think most of the damage happened to, well, your face."

I shot up from the bed. "What do you mean 'most of the damage happened to my face'?"

She gestured to the mirror above the sink on the far side of the room. I ran over to it and looked at my reflection.

"Son of a bitch!"

Purplish red splotches covered the upper portion of the left side of my face, particularly near the eye. Desperately, I turned around to face her.

"This is going to go away soon, right? If I keep the ice on it?"

She shook her head again. "The ice can help . . . but I'm afraid you're going to have a wicked black eye. It'll probably be at its worst tomorrow but should clear up in a week or so. You'll be back to normal before long."

I left the clinic in a daze that had nothing to do with my head injury. Clear up in a week or so? How could Dr. Olendzki speak so lightly about this? Didn't she realize what was happening? I was going to look like a mutant for Christmas and most of the ski trip. I had a black eye. A freaking black eye.

And my mother had given it to me.

SEVEN

I ANGRILY PUSHED THROUGH THE double doors that led into the Moroi dorm. Snow swirled in behind me, and a few people lingering on the main floor glanced up upon my entrance. Not surprisingly, several of them did double takes. Swallowing, I forced myself not to react. It would be okay. No need to freak out. Novices got injured all the time. It was actually rarer *not* to get injured. Admittedly, this was a more noticeable injury than most, but I could live with it until it healed, right? And it wasn't like anyone would know how I'd received it.

"Hey Rose, is it true your own mother punched you?"

I froze. I'd know that taunting soprano voice anywhere. Turning slowly, I looked into the deep blue eyes of Mia Rinaldi. Curly blond hair framed a face that might have been cute if not for the malicious smirk on it.

A year younger than us, Mia'd taken on Lissa (and me by default) in a war to see who could tear apart the other's life most quickly—a war, I should add, that *she* started. It had involved her stealing Lissa's ex-boyfriend—despite the fact Lissa had decided in the end she didn't want him—and the spreading of all sorts of rumors.

Admittedly, Mia's hatred hadn't been entirely unjustified.

Lissa's older brother, Andre—who had been killed in the same car accident that technically "killed" me—had used Mia pretty badly when she was a freshman. If she weren't such a bitch now, I would have felt sorry for her. It had been wrong of him, and while I could understand her anger, I don't know that it was fair of her to take that out on Lissa in the way she did.

Lissa and I had technically won the war in the end, but Mia had inexplicably bounced back. She didn't run with the same elite that she once had, but she had rebuilt a small contingent of friends. Malicious or not, strong leaders always attract followers.

I'd found that about 90 percent of the time, the most effective response was to ignore her. But we had just crossed over to the other 10 percent, because it's impossible to ignore someone announcing to the world that your mother just punched you—even if it was true. I stopped walking and turned around. Mia stood near a vending machine, knowing she'd drawn me out. I didn't bother asking how she'd found out about my mother giving me the black eye. Things rarely stayed secret around here.

When she caught full sight of my face, her eyes widened in unabashed delight. "Wow. Talk about a face only a mother could love."

Ha. Cute. From anyone else, I would have applauded the joke.

"Well, you're the expert on face injury," I said. "How's your nose?"

Mia's icy smile twitched a little, but she didn't back down. I'd broken her nose about a month ago—at a school dance of all places—and while the nose had since healed, it now sat just the tiniest bit askew. Plastic surgery could probably fix it up, but from my understanding of her family's finances, that wasn't possible just now.

"It's better," she replied primly. "Fortunately, it was only broken by a psychopathic whore and not anyone actually related to me."

I gave her my best psychopathic smile. "Too bad. Family members hit you by accident. Psychopathic whores tend to come back for more."

Threatening physical violence against her was usually a pretty sound tactic, but we had too many people around right now for that to be a legitimate concern for her. And Mia knew it. Not that I was above attacking someone in this kind of setting—hell, I'd done it lots of times—but I *was* trying to work on my impulse control lately.

"Doesn't look like much of an accident to me," she said. "Don't you guys have rules about face punches? I mean, that looks *really* far out of bounds."

I opened my mouth to tell her off, but nothing came out. She had a point. My injury *was* far out of bounds; in that sort of combat, you aren't supposed to hit above the neck. This was *way* above that forbidden line.

Mia saw my hesitation, and it was like Christmas morning had come a week early for her. Until that moment, I don't think there'd ever been a time in our antagonistic relationship in which she'd rendered me speechless.

"Ladies," came a stern, female voice. The Moroi attending the front desk leaned over it and fixed us with a sharp look. "This is a lobby, not a lounge. Either go upstairs or go outside."

For a moment, breaking Mia's nose again sounded like the best idea in the world—to hell with detention or suspension. After a deep breath, I decided retreat was my most dignified action now. I stalked off toward the stairs leading up to the girls' dorm. Over my shoulder, I heard Mia call, "Don't worry, Rose. It'll go away. Besides, it's not your *face* guys are interested in."

Thirty seconds later, I beat on Lissa's door so hard, it was a wonder my fist didn't go through the wood. She opened it slowly and peered around.

"Is it just you out here? I thought there was an army at the—oh my God." Her eyebrows shot up when she noticed the left side of my face. "What happened?"

"You haven't heard already? You're probably the only one in the school who hasn't," I grumbled. "Just let me in."

Sprawling on her bed, I told her about the day's events. She was properly appalled.

"I heard you'd been hurt, but I figured it was one of your normal things," she said.

I stared up at the spackled ceiling, feeling miserable. "The worst part is, Mia was right. It wasn't an accident."

"What, you're saying your mom did it on purpose?" When

I didn't answer, Lissa's voice turned incredulous. "Come on, she wouldn't do that. No way."

"Why? Because she's perfect Janine Hathaway, master of controlling her temper? The thing is, she's also perfect Janine Hathaway, master of fighting and controlling her actions. One way or another, she slipped up."

"Yeah, well," said Lissa, "I think her stumbling and missing her punch is more likely than her doing it on purpose. She'd have to really lose her temper."

"Well, she *was* talking to me. That's enough to make anyone lose their temper. And I accused her of sleeping with my dad because he was the soundest evolutionary choice."

"Rose," groaned Lissa. "You kind of left out that part in your recap. Why'd you say that to her?"

"Because it's probably true."

"But you had to know it'd upset her. Why do you keep provoking her? Why can't you just make peace with her?"

I sat upright. "Make peace with her? *She gave me a black eye.* Probably on purpose! How do I make peace with someone like that?"

Lissa just shook her head and walked over to the mirror to check her makeup. The feelings coming through our bond were ones of frustration and exasperation. Lingering in the back was a bit of anticipation, too. I had the patience to examine her carefully, now that I'd finished my venting. She had on a silky lavender shirt and a knee-length black skirt. Her long hair had the kind of smooth perfection only achieved by spending an hour of your life on it with a hair dryer and flat iron.

"You look nice. What's up?"

Her feelings shifted slightly, her irritation with me dimming a little. "I'm meeting Christian soon."

For a few minutes there, it had felt like the old days with Lissa and me. Just us, hanging out and talking. Her mention of Christian, as well as the realization that she'd have to leave me soon for *him*, stirred up dark feelings in my chest . . . feelings I had to reluctantly admit were jealousy. Naturally, I didn't let on to that.

"Wow. What'd he do to deserve that? Rescue orphans from a burning building? If so, you might want to make sure he didn't set the building on fire in the first place." Christian's element was fire. It was fitting since it was the most destructive one.

Laughing, she turned from the mirror and noticed me gently touching my swollen face with my fingers. Her smile turned kind. "It doesn't look that bad."

"Whatever. I can tell when you're lying, you know. And Dr. Olendzki says it'll be even worse tomorrow." I lay back down on the bed. "There probably isn't enough concealer in the world to cover this, is there? Tasha and I'll have to invest in some *Phantom of the Opera*–style masks."

She sighed and sat on the bed near me. "Too bad I can't just heal it."

I smiled. "That would be nice."

The compulsion and charisma brought on by spirit were great, but really, healing was her coolest ability. The range of things she could achieve was staggering.

Lissa was also thinking about what spirit could do. "I wish there were some other way to control the spirit . . . in a way that still let me use the magic. . . ."

"Yeah," I said. I understood her burning desire to do great things and help people. It radiated off of her. Hell, I would also have liked to have this eye cleared up in an instant rather than days. "I wish there were too."

She sighed again. "And there's more to me than just wishing I could heal and do other stuff with spirit. I also, well, just miss the magic. It's still there; it's just blocked off by the pills. It's burning inside of me. It wants me, and I want it. But there's a wall between us. You just can't imagine it."

"I can, actually."

It was true. Along with having a general sense for her feelings, I could sometimes also "slip into her." It was hard to explain and ever harder to endure. When that happened, I could literally see through her eyes and *feel* what she experienced. During those times, I *was* her. Many times, I'd been in her head while she longed for the magic, and I'd felt the burning need she spoke of. She often woke up at night, yearning for the power she could no longer reach.

"Oh yeah," she said ruefully. "I forget about that sometimes."

A sense of bitterness filled her. It wasn't directed at me

so much as it was the no-win nature of her situation. Anger sparked inside of her. She didn't like feeling helpless any more than I did. The anger and frustration intensified into something darker and uglier, something I didn't like.

"Hey," I said, touching her arm. "You okay?"

She closed her eyes briefly, then opened them. "I just hate it."

The intensity of her feelings reminded me of our conversation, the one we'd had just before I went to the Badica house. "You still feel like the pills might be weakening?"

"I don't know. A little."

"Is it getting worse?"

She shook her head. "No. I still can't use the magic. I feel *closer* to it . . . but it's still blocked off."

"But you still . . . your moods . . ."

"Yeah . . . they're acting up. But don't worry," she said, seeing my face. "I'm not seeing things or trying to hurt myself."

"Good." I was glad to hear it but still worried. Even if she still couldn't touch the magic, I didn't like the idea of her mental state slipping again. Desperately, I hoped the situation would just stabilize on its own. "I'm here," I told her softly, holding her gaze. "If anything happens that's weird . . . you tell me, okay?"

Like that, the dark feelings disappeared within her. As they did, I felt a weird ripple in the bond. I can't explain what it was, but I shuddered from the force. Lissa didn't notice. Her mood perked up again, and she smiled at me.

"Thanks," she said. "I will."

I smiled, happy to see her back to normal. We lapsed into silence, and for the briefest of moments, I wanted to pour my heart out to her. I'd had so much on my mind lately: my mother, Dimitri, and the Badica house. I'd been keeping those feelings locked up, and they were tearing me apart. Now, feeling so comfortable with Lissa for the first time in a long time, I finally felt that I could let her into *my* feelings for a change.

Before I could open my mouth, I felt her thoughts suddenly shift. They became eager and nervous. She had something she wanted to tell me, something she'd been thinking about intently. So much for pouring my heart out. If she wanted to talk, I wouldn't burden her with my problems, so I pushed them aside and waited for her to speak.

"I found something in my research with Ms. Carmack. Something strange . . ."

"Oh?" I asked, instantly curious.

Moroi usually developed their specialized element during adolescence. After that, they were put into magic classes specific to that element. But as the only spirit user on record at the moment, Lissa didn't really have a class she could join. Most people believed she just hadn't specialized, but she and Ms. Carmack—the magic teacher at St. Vladimir's—had been meeting independently to learn what they could about spirit. They researched both current and old records, checking for clues that might lead to other spirit users, now that they knew some of the telltale signs: an inability to specialize, mental instability, etc.

"I didn't find any confirmed spirit users, but I did find . . . reports of, um, unexplained phenomena."

I blinked in surprise. "What kind of stuff?" I asked, pondering what would count as "unexplained phenomena" for vampires. When she and I had lived with humans, *we* would have been considered unexplained phenomena.

"They're scattered reports . . . but, like, I read this one about a guy who could make others see things that weren't there. He could get them to believe they were seeing monsters or other people or whatever."

"That could be compulsion."

"*Really* powerful compulsion. I couldn't do that, and I'm stronger—or used to be—in it than anyone we know. And that power comes from using spirit. . . ."

"So," I finished, "you think this illusion guy must have been a spirit user too." She nodded. "Why not contact him and find out?"

"Because there's no information listed! It's secret. And there are others just as strange. Like someone who could physically drain others. People standing nearby would get weak and lose all their strength. They'd pass out. And there was someone else who could stop things in midair when they were thrown at him." Excitement lit up her features.

"He could have been an air user," I pointed out.

"Maybe," she said. I could feel the curiosity and excitement swirling through her. She desperately wanted to believe there were others out there like her.

I smiled. "Who knew? Moroi have Roswell- and Area 51–type stuff. It's a wonder I'm not being studied somewhere to see if they can figure out the bond."

Lissa's speculative mood turned teasing. "I wish I could see into *your* mind sometimes. I'd like to know how you feel about Mason."

"He's my friend," I said stoutly, surprised at the abrupt change in subject. "That's it."

She tsked. "You used to flirt—and do other stuff—with any guy you could get your hands on."

"Hey!" I said, offended. "I wasn't that bad."

"Okay . . . maybe not. But you don't seem interested in guys anymore."

I *was* interested in guys—well, one guy.

"Mason's really nice," she continued. "And crazy about you."

"He is," I agreed. I thought about Mason, about that brief moment when I'd thought he was sexy outside Stan's class. Plus, Mason was really funny, and we got along beautifully. He wasn't a bad prospect as far as boyfriends went.

"You guys are a lot alike. You're both doing things you shouldn't."

I laughed. That was also true. I recalled Mason's eagerness to take on every Strigoi in the world. I might not be ready for that—despite my outburst in the car—but I shared some of his recklessness. It might be time to give him a shot, I thought. Bantering with him was fun, and it had been a long time since I'd kissed anyone. Dimitri made my heart ache . . . but, well, it wasn't like anything else was going on there.

Lissa watched me appraisingly, like she knew what I was thinking—well, aside from the Dimitri stuff. "I heard Meredith say you were an idiot for not going out with him. She said it's because you think you're too good for him."

"What! That's not true."

"Hey, *I* didn't say it. Anyway, she said she's thinking of going after him."

"Mason and Meredith?" I scoffed. "That's a disaster in the making. They have nothing in common."

It was petty, but I'd gotten used to Mason always doting on me. Suddenly, the thought of someone else getting him irked me.

"You're possessive," Lissa said, again guessing my thoughts. No wonder she got so annoyed at me reading her mind.

"Only a little."

She laughed. "Rose, even if it's not Mason, you really should start dating again. There are lots of guys who would kill to go out with you—guys who are actually nice."

I hadn't always made the best choices when it came to men. Once again, the urge to spill all my worries to her seized me. I'd been hesitant to tell her about Dimitri for so long, even though the secret burned inside of me. Sitting with her here reminded me that she *was* my best friend. I could tell her anything, and she wouldn't judge me. But, just like earlier, I lost the chance to tell her what was on my mind.

She glanced over at her alarm clock and suddenly sprang up from the bed.

"I'm late! I've got to meet Christian!"

Joy filled her, underscored with a bit of nervous anticipation. Love. What could you do? I swallowed back the jealousy that started to raise its ugly head. Once again, Christian had taken her away from me. I wasn't going to be able to unburden myself tonight.

Lissa and I left the dorm, and she practically sprinted away, promising we'd talk tomorrow. I wandered back to my own dorm. When I got to my room, I passed by my mirror and groaned when I saw my face. Dark purple surrounded my eye. In talking to Lissa, I'd almost forgotten about the whole incident with my mother. Stopping to get a closer look, I stared at my face. Maybe it was egotistical, but I knew I looked good. I wore a C-cup and had a body much coveted in a school where most of the girls were supermodel slim. And as I'd noted earlier, my face was pretty too. On a typical day, I was a nine around here—ten on a very good one.

But today? Yeah. I was practically in negative numbers. I was going to look fabulous for the ski trip.

"My mom beat me up," I informed my reflection. It looked back sympathetically.

With a sigh, I decided I might as well get ready for bed. There was nothing else I wanted to do tonight, and maybe extra sleep would speed the healing. I went down the hall to the bathroom to wash my face and brush my hair. When I got back to my room, I slipped on my favorite pajamas, and the feel of soft flannel cheered me up a little.

I was packing my backpack for the next day when a burst of emotion abruptly shot through my bond with Lissa. It caught me unaware and gave me no chance to fight it. It was like being knocked over by a hurricane-force wind, and suddenly, I was no longer looking at my backpack. I was "inside" Lissa, experiencing her world firsthand.

And that's when things got awkward.

Because Lissa was with Christian.

And things were getting . . . hot.

EIGHT

CHRISTIAN WAS KISSING HER, AND wow, was it
a kiss. He wasn't messing around. It was the kind of kiss that
small children shouldn't be allowed to see. Hell, it was the
kind of kiss *no one* should be allowed to see—let alone experience through a psychic link.

As I've noted before, strong emotion from Lissa could
make this phenomenon happen—the one where I got pulled
inside her head. But always, *always*, it was because of some
negative emotion. She'd get upset or angry or depressed, and
that would reach out to me. But this time? She wasn't upset.

She was happy. Very, very happy.

Oh man. I needed to get out of here.

They were up in the attic of the school's chapel or, as I liked
to call it, their love nest. The place had been a regular hangout
for them, back when each of them was feeling antisocial and
wanted to escape. Eventually, they'd decided to be antisocial
together, and one thing had led to another. Since they started
publicly dating, I hadn't known they spent much time here
anymore. Maybe they were back for old time's sake.

And indeed, a celebration did seem to be going on. Little scented candles were set up around the dusty old place,
candles that filled the air with the scent of lilacs. I would

have been a little nervous about setting all those candles in a confined space filled with flammable boxes and books, but Christian probably figured he could control any accidental infernos.

They finally broke that insanely long kiss and pulled back to look at each other. They lay on their sides on the floor. Several blankets had been spread under them.

Christian's face was open and tender as he regarded Lissa, his pale blue eyes aglow with some inner emotion. It was different from the way Mason regarded me. There was certainly adoration with him, but Mason's was a lot like when you walk into a church and fall to your knees in awe and fear of something you worship but don't really understand. Christian clearly worshipped Lissa in his way, but there was a knowing glint to his eyes, a sense that the two of them shared an understanding of each other so perfect and powerful that they didn't even need words to convey it.

"Don't you think we're going to go to hell for this?" asked Lissa.

He reached out and touched her face, trailing his fingers along her cheek and neck and down to the top of her silky shirt. She breathed heavily at that touch, at the way it could be so gentle and small, yet evoke such a strong passion within her.

"For this?" He played with the shirt's edge, letting his finger just barely brush inside of it.

"No," she laughed. "For *this*." She gestured around the

attic. "This is a church. We shouldn't be doing this kind of, um, thing up here."

"Not true," he argued. Gently, he pushed her onto her back and leaned over her. "The church is downstairs. This is just storage. God won't mind."

"You don't believe in God," she chastised. Her hands made their way down his chest. Her movements were as light and deliberate as his, yet they clearly triggered the same powerful response in him.

He sighed happily as her hands slid under his shirt and up his stomach. "I'm humoring you."

"You'd say anything right now," she accused. Her fingers caught the edge of his shirt and pushed it up. He shifted so she could push it all the way off him and then leaned back over her, bare-chested.

"You're right," he agreed. He carefully undid one button on her blouse. Just one. Then he again leaned down and gave her one of those hard, deep kisses. When he came up for air, he continued on as though nothing had happened. "Tell me what you need to hear, and I'll say it." He unfastened another button.

"There's nothing I *need* to hear," she laughed. Another button popped free. "You can tell me whatever you want—it'd just be nice if it were true."

"The truth, huh? No one wants to hear the truth. The truth is never sexy. But you . . ." The last button came undone, and he spread her shirt away. "You are too goddamned sexy to be real."

His words held his trademark snarky tone, but his eyes conveyed a different message entirely. I was witnessing this scene through Lissa's eyes, but I could imagine what he saw. Her smooth, white skin. Slender waist and hips. A lacy white bra. Through her, I could feel that the lace was itchy, but she didn't care.

Feelings both fond and hungry spread over his features. From within Lissa, I could feel her heart race and breathing quicken. Emotions similar to Christian's clouded all other coherent thoughts. Shifting down, he lay on top of her, pressing their bodies together. His mouth sought hers out again, and as their lips and tongues made contact, I knew I *had* to get out of there.

Because I understood it now. I understood why Lissa had dressed up and why the love nest had been decked out like a Yankee Candles showroom. This was it. *The* moment. After a month of dating, they were going to have sex. Lissa, I knew, had done it before with a past boyfriend. I didn't know Christian's past, but I sincerely doubted many girls had fallen prey to his abrasive charm.

But in feeling what Lissa felt, I could tell that none of that mattered. Not in that moment. In that moment, there were only the two of them and the way they felt about each other right now. And in a life filled with more worries than someone her age should have had, Lissa felt absolutely certain about what she was doing now. It was what she wanted. What she'd wanted for a very long time with him.

And I had *no* right to be witnessing it.

Who was I kidding? I didn't *want* to witness it. I took no pleasure in watching other people get it on, and I sure as hell didn't want to experience sex with Christian. It'd be like losing my virginity virtually.

But Jesus Christ, Lissa wasn't making it easy to get out of her head. She had no desire to detach from her feelings and emotions, and the stronger they grew, the stronger they held me. Trying to distance myself from her, I focused my energies on coming back to myself, concentrating as hard as I could.

More clothes disappeared . . .

Come on, come on, I told myself sternly.

The condom came out . . . yikes.

You're your own person, Rose. Get back in your head.

Their limbs intertwined, their bodies moving together . . .

Son of a—

I ripped out of her and back to myself. Once again, I was back in my room, but I no longer had any interest in packing my backpack. My whole world was askew. I felt strange and violated—almost unsure if I was Rose or if I was Lissa. I also felt that resentment toward Christian again. I certainly didn't want to have sex with Lissa, but there was that same pang inside of me, that frustrated feeling that I was no longer the center of her world.

Leaving the backpack untouched, I went right to bed, wrapping my arms around myself and curling into a ball to try to squelch the ache within my chest.

I fell asleep pretty quickly and woke up early as a result. Usually, I had to be dragged out of bed to go meet Dimitri, but today I showed up early enough that I actually beat him to the gym. As I waited, I saw Mason cutting across to one of the buildings that held classrooms.

"Whoa," I called. "Since when are you up this early?"

"Since I had to retake a math test," he said, walking over to me. He gave me his mischievous smile. "Might be worth skipping, though, to hang out with you."

I laughed, remembering my conversation with Lissa. Yes, there were definitely worse things I could do than flirt and start something with Mason.

"Nah. You might get in trouble, then I'd have no real challenge on the slopes."

He rolled his eyes, still smiling. "*I'm* the one with no real challenge, remember?"

"You ready to bet on something yet? Or are you still too afraid?"

"Watch it," he warned, "or I might take back your Christmas present."

"You got me a present?" I hadn't expected that.

"Yup. But if you keep back-talking, I might give it to someone else."

"Like Meredith?" I teased.

"She isn't even in your league, and you know it."

"Even with a black eye?" I asked with a grimace.

"Even with two black eyes."

The look he gave me just then wasn't teasing or even really suggestive. It was just nice. Nice, friendly, and interested. Like he really cared. After all the stress lately, I decided I liked being cared about. And with the neglect I was starting to feel from Lissa, I realized I also kind of liked having someone who wanted to pay so much attention to me.

"What are you doing on Christmas?" I asked.

He shrugged. "Nothing. My mom almost came down but had to cancel at the last minute . . . you know, with everything that happened."

Mason's mother wasn't a guardian. She was a dhampir who'd chosen to just be domestic and have kids. As a result, I knew he saw her quite a bit. It was ironic, I thought, that my mom actually *was* here, but for all intents and purposes, she might as well have been somewhere else.

"Come hang with me," I said on impulse. "I'll be with Lissa and Christian and his aunt. It'll be fun."

"Really?"

"Very fun."

"That's not what I was asking about."

I grinned. "I know. Just be there, okay?"

He swept me one of the gallant bows he liked to make. "Absolutely."

Mason wandered off just as Dimitri showed up for our practice. Talking to Mason had made me feel giddy and happy; I hadn't thought about my face at all with him. But with Dimitri, I suddenly became self-conscious. I didn't want to be anything less than perfect with him, and as we walked inside, I went out of my way to avert my face so he couldn't look at me full-on. Worrying about that brought my mood down, and as it plummeted, all the other things that had been upsetting me came tumbling back.

We returned to the training room with the dummies, and he told me he simply wanted me to practice the maneuvers from two days ago. Happy he wasn't going to bring up the fight, I set to my task with a burning zeal, showing the dummies just what would happen if they messed with Rose Hathaway. I knew my fighting fury was fired up by more than just a simple desire to do well. My feelings were out of control this morning, raw and intense after both the fight with my mother and what I'd witnessed with Lissa and Christian last night. Dimitri sat back and watched me, occasionally critiquing my technique and offering suggestions for new tactics.

"Your hair's in the way," he said at one point. "Not only are you blocking your peripheral vision, you're running the risk of letting your enemy get a handhold."

"If I'm actually in a fight, I'll wear it up." I grunted as I shoved the stake neatly up between the dummy's "ribs." I didn't know what these artificial bones were made of, but they were a bitch to work around. I thought about my mom again and added a little extra force to the jab. "I'm just wearing it down today, that's all."

"Rose," he said warningly. Ignoring him, I plunged again. His voice came more sharply the next time he spoke. "*Rose. Stop.*"

I backed away from the dummy, surprised to find my breathing labored. I hadn't realized I was working that hard. My back hit the wall. With nowhere to go, I looked away from him, directing my eyes toward the ground.

"Look at me," he ordered.

"Dimitri—"

"*Look at me.*"

No matter our close history, he was still my instructor. I couldn't refuse a direct order. Slowly, reluctantly, I turned toward him, still tilting my head slightly down so the hair hung over the sides of my face. Rising from his chair, he walked over and stood before me.

I avoided his eyes but saw his hand move forward to brush back my hair. Then it stopped. As did my breathing. Our short-lived attraction had been filled with questions and reservations, but one thing I'd known for sure: Dimitri had loved my hair. Maybe he still loved it. It was great hair, I'll admit. Long and silky and dark. He used to find excuses to touch it, and he'd counseled me against cutting it as so many female guardians did.

His hand hovered there, and the world stood still as I waited to see what he would do. After what seemed like an eternity, he let his hand gradually fall back to his side. Burning disappointment washed over me, yet at the same time, I'd learned something. He'd hesitated. He'd been afraid to touch me, which maybe—just maybe—meant he still wanted to. He'd had to hold himself back.

I slowly tipped my head back so that we made eye contact. Most of my hair fell back from my face—but not all. His hand trembled again, and I hoped again he'd reach forward. The hand steadied. My excitement dimmed.

"Does it hurt?" he asked. The scent of that aftershave, mingled with his sweat, washed over me. God, I wished he had touched me.

"No," I lied.

"It doesn't look so bad," he told me. "It'll heal."

"I hate her," I said, astonished at just how much venom those three words held. Even while suddenly turned on and wanting Dimitri, I still couldn't drop the grudge I held against my mother.

"No, you don't," he said gently.

"I *do*."

"You don't have time to hate anyone," he advised, his voice still kind. "Not in our profession. You should make peace with her."

Lissa had said exactly the same thing. Outrage joined my other emotions. That darkness within me started to unfurl. "Make peace with her? After she gave me a black eye *on purpose*? Why am I the only one who sees how crazy that is?"

"She absolutely did *not* do it on purpose," he said, voice hard. "No matter how much you resent her, you have to believe that. She wouldn't do that, and anyway, I saw her later that day. She was worried about you."

"Probably more worried someone will bring her up on child abuse charges," I grumbled.

"Don't you think this is the time of year for forgiveness?"

I sighed loudly. "This isn't a Christmas special! This is my life. In the real world, miracles and goodness just don't happen."

He was still eyeing my calmly. "In the real world, you can make your own miracles."

My frustration suddenly hit a breaking point, and I gave up trying to maintain my control. I was so tired of being told reasonable, practical things whenever something went wrong in my life. Somewhere in me, I knew Dimitri only wanted to help, but I just wasn't up for the well-meant words. I wanted comfort for my problems. I didn't want to think about what would make me a better person. I wished he'd just hold me and tell me not to worry.

"Okay, can you just stop this for once?" I demanded, hands on my hips.

"Stop what?"

"The whole profound Zen crap thing. You don't talk to me like a real person. Everything you say is just some wise, life-lesson nonsense. You really do sound like a Christmas special." I knew it wasn't entirely fair to take my anger out on

him, but I found myself practically shouting. "I swear, sometimes it's just like you want to hear yourself talk! And I *know*
you're not always this way. You were perfectly normal when
you talked to Tasha. But with me? You're just going through
the motions. You don't care about me. You're just stuck in
your stupid mentor role."

He stared at me, uncharacteristically surprised. "I don't
care about you?"

"No." I was being petty—very, very petty. And I knew
the truth—that he *did* care and was more than just a mentor. I
couldn't help myself, though. It just kept coming and coming.
I jabbed his chest with my finger. "I'm another student to you.
You just go on and on with your stupid life lessons so that—"

The hand I'd hoped would touch my hair suddenly
reached out and grabbed my pointing hand. He pinned it
to the wall, and I was surprised to see a flare of emotion in
his eyes. It wasn't exactly anger . . . but it was frustration of
another kind.

"*Don't* tell me what I'm feeling," he growled.

I saw then that half of what I'd said was true. He was
almost always calm, always in control—even when fighting.
But he'd also told me how he'd once snapped and beaten up
his Moroi father. He'd actually been like me once—always on
the verge of acting without thinking, doing things he knew he
shouldn't.

"That's it, isn't it?" I asked.

"What?"

"You're always fighting for control. You're the same as me."

"No," he said, still obviously worked up. "I've learned my control."

Something about this new realization emboldened me. "No," I informed him. "You haven't. You put on a good face, and most of the time you do stay in control. But sometimes you can't. And sometimes . . ." I leaned forward, lowering my voice. "Sometimes you don't want to."

"Rose . . ."

I could see his labored breathing and knew his heart was beating as quickly as mine. And he wasn't pulling away. I knew this was wrong—knew all the logical reasons for us staying apart. But right then, I didn't care. I didn't want to control myself. I didn't want to be good.

Before he realized what was happening, I kissed him. Our lips met, and when I felt him kiss me back, I knew I was right. He pressed himself closer, trapping me between him and the wall. He kept holding my hand, but his other one snaked behind my head, sliding into my hair. The kiss was filled with so much intensity; it held anger, passion, release. . . .

He was the one who broke it. He jerked away from me and took several steps back, looking shaken.

"Do *not* do that again," he said stiffly.

"Don't kiss me back then," I retorted.

He stared at me for what seemed like forever. "I don't give 'Zen lessons' to hear myself talk. I don't give them because you're another student. I'm doing this to teach you control."

"You're doing a great job," I said bitterly.

He closed his eyes for half a second, exhaled, and muttered something in Russian. Without another glance at me, he turned and left the room.

NINE

I DIDN'T SEE DIMITRI FOR a while after that. He'd sent a message later that day saying that he thought we should cancel our next two sessions because of the rapidly approaching plans to leave campus. Classes were about to end anyway, he said; taking a break from practice seemed like the reasonable thing.

It was a lame excuse, and I knew that wasn't the reason he was canceling. If he wanted to avoid me, I would have preferred he made up something about how he and the other guardians had to up Moroi security or practice top-secret ninja moves.

Regardless of his story, I knew he was avoiding me because of the kiss. That damned kiss. I didn't regret it, not exactly. God only knew how much I'd been wanting to kiss him. But I'd done it for the wrong reasons. I'd done it because I was upset and frustrated and had simply wanted to prove that I *could*. I was so tired of doing the right thing, the smart thing. I was trying to be more in control lately, but I seemed to be slipping.

I hadn't forgotten the warning that he'd once given me— that us being together wasn't just about age. It would interfere with our jobs. Pushing him into the kiss . . . well, I'd fanned the flames of a problem that could eventually hurt Lissa. I shouldn't have done it. Yesterday, I'd been unable to stop myself. Today I could see more clearly and couldn't believe what I'd done.

Mason met me on Christmas morning, and we went to go hang out with the others. It provided a good opportunity to push Dimitri out of my head. I liked Mason—a lot. And it wasn't like I had to run off and marry him. Like Lissa had said, it would be healthy for me to just date someone again.

Tasha was hosting our Christmas brunch in an elegant parlor in the Academy's guest quarters. Lots of group activities and parties were occurring throughout the school, but I'd quickly noticed that Tasha's presence always created a disturbance. People either secretly stared or went out of their way to avoid her. Sometimes she would challenge them. Sometimes she would just lie low. Today, she'd chosen to stay out of the other royals' way and simply enjoy this small, private party of those who didn't shun her.

Dimitri had been invited to the gathering, and a bit of my resolve faltered when I saw him. He'd actually dressed up for the occasion. Okay, "dressed up" might have been an exaggeration, but it was the closest I'd ever seen him come to that. Usually he just looked a little rough . . . like he could spring into battle at any given moment. Today, his dark hair was tied at the back of his neck, as though he'd actually tried to make it neat. He wore his usual jeans and leather boots, but instead of a T-shirt or thermal shirt, he had on a finely knit black sweater. It was just an ordinary sweater, nothing designer or expensive, but it added a touch of polish I didn't usually see, and good God, did it fit him well.

Dimitri wasn't mean to me or anything, but he certainly didn't go out of his way to make conversation with me. He did talk to Tasha, however, and I watched with fascination as they conversed in that easy way of theirs. I'd since learned that a good friend of his was a distant cousin of Tasha's family; that was how the two of them knew each other.

"Five?" asked Dimitri in surprise. They were discussing the friend's children. "I hadn't heard that."

Tasha nodded. "It's insane. I swear, I don't think his wife's had more than six months off between kids. She's short, too— so she just gets wider and wider."

"When I first met him, he swore he didn't even want kids."

Her eyes widened excitedly. "I *know*! I can't believe it. You should see him now. He just melts around them. I can't even understand him half the time. I swear, he speaks more baby talk than English."

Dimitri smiled his rare smile. "Well . . . children do that to people."

"I can't imagine it happening to *you*," she laughed. "You're always so stoic. Of course . . . I suppose you'd be doing baby talk in Russian, so no one would ever know."

They both laughed at that, and I turned away, grateful Mason was there to talk to. He was a good distraction from everything, because in addition to Dimitri ignoring me, Lissa and Christian were chatting on in their own little world too. Sex appeared to have made them that much more in love, and I wondered if I'd get to spend any time with her at all on the ski trip. She did eventually break away from him to give me my Christmas present.

I opened the box and stared inside. I saw a string of maroon-colored beads, and the scent of roses floated out.

"What the . . ."

I lifted the beads out, and a heavy gold crucifix swung from the end of them. She'd given me a *chotki*. It was similar to a rosary, only smaller. Bracelet-size.

"Are you trying to convert me?" I asked wryly. Lissa wasn't a religious nut or anything, but she believed in God and attended church regularly. Like many Moroi families who'd come from Russia and Eastern Europe, she was an Orthodox Christian.

Me? I was pretty much an Orthodox Agnostic. I figured God probably existed, but I didn't have the time or energy to investigate. Lissa respected that and never tried to push her faith on me, which made the gift that much weirder.

"Flip it over," she said, clearly amused at my shock.

I did. On the back of the cross, a dragon wreathed in flowers had been carved into the gold. The Dragomir crest. I looked up at her, puzzled.

"It's a family heirloom," she said. "One of my dad's good friends has been saving boxes of his stuff. This was in it. It belonged to my great-grandmother's guardian."

"Liss . . ." I said. The chotki took on a whole new meaning. "I can't . . . you can't give me something like this."

"Well, I certainly can't keep it. It's meant for a guardian. My guardian."

I wound the beads around one wrist. The cross felt cool against my skin.

"You know," I teased, "there's a good possibility I'll get kicked out of school before I can become your guardian."

She grinned. "Well, then you can give it back."

Everyone laughed. Tasha started to say something, then stopped when she looked up at the door.

"Janine!"

My mother stood there, looking as stiff and impassive as ever.

"Sorry I'm late," she said. "I had business to take care of."

Business. As always. Even on Christmas.

I felt my stomach turn and heat rise to my cheeks as the details of our fight came rushing back to my mind. She'd never sent one word of communication since it had happened two days ago, not even when I was in the infirmary. No apologies. Nothing. I gritted my teeth.

She sat down with us and soon joined in the conversation. I'd long since discovered she could really only talk about one subject: guardian business. I wondered if she had any hobbies. The Badica attack was on everyone's mind, and this drove her into a conversation about some similar fight she'd been in. To my horror, Mason was riveted by her every word.

"Well, decapitations aren't as easy as they seem," she said in her matter-of-fact way. I'd never thought they were easy at all, but her tone suggested that she believed everyone thought they were cake. "You've got to get through the spinal cord and tendons."

Through the bond, I felt Lissa grow queasy. She wasn't one for gruesome talk.

Mason's eyes lit up. "What's the best weapon to do it with?"

My mother considered. "An axe. You can get more weight behind it." She made a swinging motion by way of illustration.

"Cool," he said. "Man, I hope they let me carry an axe." It was a comical and ludicrous idea, since axes were hardly convenient weapons to carry around. For half a second, the thought of Mason walking down the street with an axe over his shoulder lightened my mood a little. The moment quickly passed.

I honestly couldn't believe we were having this conversation on Christmas. Her presence had soured everything. Fortunately, the gathering eventually dispersed. Christian and Lissa went off to do their own thing, and Dimitri and Tasha apparently had more catching up to do. Mason and I were well on our way to the dhampir dorm when my mother joined us.

None of us said anything. Stars cluttered the black sky, sharp and bright, their glitter matched in the ice and snow around us. I wore my ivory parka with fake fur trimming. It did a good job keeping my body warm, even though it did nothing against the chilly gusts that seared my face. The whole time we walked, I kept expecting my mother to turn off toward the other guardian areas, but she came right inside the dorm with us.

"I've been wanting to talk to you," she finally said. My alarms clicked on. What had I done now?

That was all she said, but Mason picked up on the hint immediately. He was neither stupid nor oblivious to social cues, though at that moment, I kind of wished he was. I also found it ironic that he wanted to fight every Strigoi in the world but was afraid of my mother.

He glanced at me apologetically, shrugged, and said, "Hey, I've got to get, um, somewhere. I'll see you later."

I watched with regret as he left, wishing I could run after him. Probably my mom would only tackle me and punch my other eye if I tried to escape. Better to do things her way and get this over with. Shifting uncomfortably, I looked everywhere but at her and waited for her to speak. Out of the corner of my eye, I noticed a few people glancing over at us. Recalling how everyone in the world seemed to know about her giving me the black eye, I suddenly decided I didn't want witnesses around for whatever lecture she was about to unleash on me.

"You want to, um, go to my room?" I asked.

She looked surprised, almost uncertain. "Sure."

I led her upstairs, keeping a safe distance away as we

walked. Awkward tension built between us. She didn't say anything when we reached my room, but I saw her examine every detail carefully, as though a Strigoi might be lurking in there. I sat on the bed and waited while she paced, unsure what I should do. She ran her fingers over a stack of books on animal behavior and evolution.

"Are these for a report?" she asked.

"No. I'm just interested in it, that's all."

Her eyebrows rose. She hadn't known that. But how would she? She didn't know anything about me. She continued her appraisal, stopping to study little things that apparently surprised her about me. A picture of Lissa and me dressed up like fairies for Halloween. A bag of SweeTarts. It was as though my mother were meeting me for the first time.

Abruptly, she turned and extended her hand toward me. "Here."

Startled, I leaned forward and held my palm out underneath hers. Something small and cool dropped into my hand. It was a round pendant, a small one—not much bigger than a dime in diameter. A base of silver held a flat disc of colored glass circles. Frowning, I ran my thumb over its surface. It was strange, but the circles almost made it look like an eye. The inner one was small, just like a pupil. It was so dark blue that it looked black. Surrounding it was a larger circle of pale blue, which was in turn surrounded by a circle of white. A very, very thin ring of that dark blue color circled the outside.

"Thanks," I said. I hadn't expected anything from her. The gift was weird—why the hell would she give me an eye?—but it *was* a gift. "I . . . I didn't get you anything."

My mom nodded, face blank and unconcerned once more. "It's fine. I don't need anything."

She turned away again and started walking around the room. She didn't have a lot of space to do it, but her shorter height gave her a smaller stride. Each time she passed in front of the window over my bed, the light would catch her auburn hair and light it up. I watched her curiously and realized she was as nervous as me.

She halted in her pacing and glanced back toward me. "How's your eye?"

"Getting better."

"Good." She opened her mouth, and I had a feeling she was on the verge of apologizing. But she didn't.

When she started pacing again, I decided I couldn't stand the inactivity. I began putting my presents away. I'd gotten a pretty nice haul of stuff this morning. One of them was a silk dress from Tasha, red and embroidered with flowers. My mother watched me hang it in the room's tiny closet.

"That was very nice of Tasha."

"Yeah," I agreed. "I didn't know she was going to get me anything. I really like her."

"Me too."

I turned from the closet in surprise and stared at my mom. Her astonishment mirrored mine. If I hadn't known any better,

I'd have said we'd just agreed on something. Maybe Christmas miracles did happen.

"Guardian Belikov will be a good match for her."

"I—" I blinked, not entirely sure what she was talking about. "Dimitri?"

"Guardian Belikov," she corrected sternly, still not approving of my casual way of addressing him.

"What . . . what kind of match?" I asked.

She raised an eyebrow. "You haven't heard? She's asked him to be her guardian—since she doesn't have one."

I felt like I'd been punched again. "But he's . . . assigned here. And to Lissa."

"Arrangements can be made. And regardless of the Ozera reputation . . . she's still royal. If she pushes, she can get her way."

I stared bleakly into space. "Well, I guess they *are* friends and everything."

"More than that—or possibly could be."

Bam! Punched again.

"*What?*"

"Hmm? Oh. She's . . . *interested* in him." By my mother's tone, it was clear that romantic matters actually held no interest for her. "She's willing to have dhampir children, so it's possible they might eventually make an, um, arrangement if he were her guardian."

Oh. My. God.

Time froze.

My heart stopped beating.

I realized my mother was waiting for a response. She was leaning against my desk, watching me. She might be able to hunt down Strigoi, but she was oblivious to my feelings.

"Is . . . is he going to do it? Be her guardian?" I asked weakly.

My mom shrugged. "I don't think he's agreed to it yet, but of course he will. It's a great opportunity."

"Of course," I echoed. Why would Dimitri turn down the chance to be a guardian to a friend of his *and* to have a baby?

I think my mom said something else after that, but I didn't hear it. I didn't hear anything. I kept thinking about Dimitri leaving the Academy, leaving *me*. I thought about the way he and Tasha had gotten along with each other so well. And then, after those recollections, my imagination started improvising future scenarios. Tasha and Dimitri together. Touching. Kissing. Naked. Other things . . .

I squeezed my eyes shut for half a second and then opened them.

"I'm really tired."

My mom stopped mid-sentence. I had no idea what she'd been saying before I interrupted her.

"I'm really tired," I repeated. I could hear the hollowness in my own voice. Empty. No emotion. "Thanks for the eye . . . um, thing, but if you don't mind . . ."

My mother stared at me in surprise, her features open and confused. Then, just like that, her usual wall of cool professionalism slammed back into place. Until that moment, I hadn't realized how much she'd let it up. But she had. For just a brief time, she'd made herself vulnerable with me. That vulnerability was now gone.

"Of course," she said stiffly. "I don't want to bother you."

I wanted to tell her it wasn't that. I wanted to tell her I wasn't kicking her out for any personal reason. And I wanted to tell her that I wished she were the kind of loving, understanding mother you always hear about, one I could confide in. Maybe even a mother I could discuss my troubled love life with.

God. I wished I could tell *anyone* about that, actually. Especially right now.

But I was too caught up in my own personal drama to say a word. I felt like someone had ripped my heart out and tossed it across the other side of the room. There was a burning, agonizing pain in my chest, and I had no idea how it could ever be filled. It was one thing to accept that I couldn't have Dimitri. It was something entirely different to realize someone else *could*.

I didn't say anything else to her because my speech capabilities no longer existed. Fury glinted in her eyes, and her lips flattened out into that tight expression of displeasure she so often wore. Without another word, she turned around and left, slamming the door behind her. That door slam was something I would have done too, actually. I guess we really did share some genes.

But I forgot about her almost immediately. I just kept sitting there and thinking. Thinking and imagining.

I spent the rest of the day doing little more than that. I skipped dinner. I shed a few tears. But mostly, I just sat on my bed thinking and growing more and more depressed. I also discovered that the only thing worse than imagining Dimitri and Tasha together was remembering when he and *I* had been together. He would never touch me again like that, never kiss me again. . . .

This was the worst Christmas ever.

TEN

THE SKI TRIP COULDN'T HAVE come a moment too soon. It was impossible to get the Dimitri and Tasha thing out of my head, but at least packing and getting ready made sure I didn't devote 100 percent of my brain power to him. More like 95 percent.

I had other things to distract me, too. The Academy might—rightfully—be overprotective when it came to us, but sometimes that translated into pretty cool stuff. Example: The Academy had access to a couple of private jets. This meant no Strigoi could attack us at an airport, *and* it also meant we got to travel in style. Each jet was smaller than a commercial plane, but the seats were cushy and had lots of leg room. They extended far enough back that you could practically lie down to sleep. On long flights, we had little consoles in the seats that gave us TV movie options. Sometimes they'd even break out fancy meals. I was betting this flight, however, would be too short for any movies or substantial food.

We left late on the twenty-sixth. When I boarded the jet, I looked around for Lissa, wanting to talk to her. We hadn't really spoken after the Christmas brunch. I wasn't surprised to see her sitting with Christian, and they didn't look like they wanted to be interrupted. I couldn't hear their conversation, but he'd put his arm around her and had that relaxed, flirty expression that only she could bring out. I remained fully convinced that he could never do as good a job as me of taking care of her, but he clearly made her happy. I put on a smile and nodded at them as I passed down the aisle toward where Mason was waving at me. As I did, I also walked by Dimitri and Tasha sitting together. I pointedly ignored them.

"Hey," I said sliding into the seat beside Mason.

He smiled at me. "Hey. You ready for the ski challenge?"

"As ready as I'll ever be."

"Don't worry," he said. "I'll go easy on you."

I scoffed and leaned my head back against the seat. "You're so delusional."

"Sane guys are boring."

To my surprise, he slid his hand over mine. His skin was warm, and I felt my own skin tingle where he touched me. It startled me. I'd convinced myself Dimitri was the only one I'd ever respond to again.

It's time to move on, I thought. *Dimitri obviously has. You should have done it a long time ago.*

I laced my fingers with Mason's, catching him off guard. "I do. This is going to be fun."

And it was.

I tried to keep reminding myself that we were here because of a tragedy, that there were Strigoi and humans out there who might strike again. No one else seemed to remember that, though, and I admit, I was having a difficult time myself.

The resort was gorgeous. It was built to sort of look like a log cabin, but no pioneer cabin could have held hundreds of people or had such luxury accommodations. Three stories of gleaming, golden-colored wood sat among lofty pine trees. The windows were tall and gracefully arched, tinted for Moroi convenience. Crystal lanterns—electric, but shaped to look like torches—hung around all the entrances, giving the entire building a glittering, almost bejeweled look.

Mountains—which my enhanced eyes could just barely make out in the night—surrounded us, and I bet the view would have been breathtaking when it was light out. One side of the grounds led off to the skiing area, complete with steep hills and moguls, as well as lifts and tow ropes. Another side of the lodge had an ice rink, which delighted me since I'd missed out that one day by the cabin. Near that, smooth hills were reserved for sledding.

And that was just the outside.

Inside, all sorts of arrangements had been made to cater to Moroi needs. Feeders stayed on hand, ready to serve twenty-four hours a day. The slopes ran on a nocturnal schedule. Wards and guardians circled the entire place. Everything a living vampire could want.

The main lobby had a cathedral ceiling and an enormous chandelier hanging over it. Its floor was intricately tiled marble, and the front desk stayed open around the clock, ready to indulge our every need. The rest of the lodge, hallways and lounges, had a red, black, and gold color scheme. The deep shade of red dominated over the other hues, and I wondered if its resemblance to blood was a coincidence. Mirrors and art adorned the walls, and little ornamental tables had been placed here and there. They held vases of pale green, purple-spotted orchids that filled the air with a spicy scent.

The room I shared with Lissa was bigger than our dorm rooms put together and had the same rich colors as the rest of the lodge. The carpet was so plush and deep that I imme-diately shed my shoes at the door and walked in barefoot, luxuriating in the way my feet sank into that softness. We had king-size beds, covered in feather duvets and set with so many pillows that I swore a person could get lost in them all and never be seen again. French doors opened on to a spa-cious balcony, which, considering we were on the top floor, would have been cool if not for the fact it was freezing out-side. I suspected the two-person hot tub on the far end would go a long way to make up for the cold.

Drowning in so much luxury, I reached an overload point where the rest of the accommodations started swimming together. The jetted marble bathtub. The plasma-screen TV. The basket of chocolate and other snacks. When we finally decided to go skiing, I had to practically drag myself from the room. I could probably have spent the rest of my vacation lounging in there and been perfectly content.

But we finally ventured outside, and once I managed to push Dimitri and my mother out of my head, I started to enjoy myself. It helped that the lodge was so enormous; there was little chance of running into them.

For the first time in weeks, I was able to finally focus on Mason and realize just how much fun he was. I also got to hang out with Lissa more than I had in a while, which put me in an even better mood.

With Lissa, Christian, Mason, and me, we were able to get kind of a double-date thing going. The four of us spent almost all of the first day skiing, though the two Moroi had a bit of trouble keeping up. Considering what Mason and I went through in our classes, he and I weren't afraid to try daring stunts. Our competitive natures made us eager to go out of our way to outdo each other.

"You guys are suicidal," remarked Christian at one point. It was dark outside, and tall light posts illuminated his bemused face.

He and Lissa had been waiting at the bottom of the mogul hill, watching Mason and me come down. We'd been moving at insane speeds. The part of me that had been trying to learn control and wisdom from Dimitri knew it was dangerous, but the rest of me liked embracing that recklessness. That dark streak of rebelliousness still hadn't let me go.

Mason grinned as we skidded to a halt, sending up a spray of snow. "Nah, this is just a warm-up. I mean, Rose has been able to keep up with me the whole time. Kid stuff."

Lissa shook her head. "Aren't you guys taking this too far?"

Mason and I looked at each other. "No."

She shook her head. "Well, we're going inside. Try not to kill yourselves."

She and Christian left, arm and arm. I watched them go, then turned back to Mason. "I'm good for a while longer. You?"

"Absolutely."

We took a lift back up to the top of the hill. When we were just about to head down, Mason pointed.

"Okay, how about this? Hit those moguls there, then jump over that ridge, swing back with a hairpin turn, dodge those trees, and land there."

I followed his finger as he pointed out a jagged path down one of the biggest slopes. I frowned.

"That one really is insane, Mase."

"Ah," he said triumphantly. "She finally cracks."

I glowered. "She does not." After another survey of his crazy route, I conceded. "Okay. Let's do it."

He gestured. "You first."

I took a deep breath and leapt off. My skis slid smoothly over the snow, and piercing wind blasted into my face. I made the first jump neatly and precisely, but as the next part of the course sped forward, I realized just how dangerous it really was. In that split second, I had a decision to make. If I didn't do it, I'd never hear the end of it from Mason—and I *really* wanted to show him up. If I did manage it, I could feel pretty secure about my awesomeness. But if I tried and messed up . . . I could break my neck.

Somewhere in my head, a voice that sounded suspiciously

like Dimitri's started talking about wise choices and learning when to show restraint.

I decided to ignore that voice and went for it.

This course was as hard as I'd feared, but I pulled it off flawlessly, one insane move after another. Snow flew up around me as I made each sharp, dangerous turn. When I safely reached bottom, I looked up and saw Mason gesturing wildly. I couldn't make out his expression or words, but I could imagine his cheers. I waved back and waited for him to follow suit.

But he didn't. Because when Mason got halfway down, he wasn't able to pull off one of the jumps. His skis caught, and his legs twisted. Down he went.

I reached him at about the same time some of the resort staff did. To everyone's relief, Mason hadn't broken his neck or anything else. His ankle did appear to have a nasty sprain, however, which was probably going to limit his skiing for the rest of the trip.

One of the instructors monitoring the slopes ran forward, fury all over her face.

"What were you kids thinking?" she exclaimed. She turned on me. "I couldn't believe it when you did those stupid stunts!" Her glare fixed on Mason next. "And then *you* had to go ahead and copy her!"

I wanted to argue that it had all been his idea, but blame didn't matter at this point. I was just glad he was all right. But as we all went inside, guilt began to gnaw at me. I *had* acted irresponsibly. What if he'd been seriously injured? Horrible visions danced through my mind. Mason with a broken leg . . . a broken neck . . .

What had I been thinking? No one had made me do that course. Mason had suggested it . . . but I hadn't fought back. Goodness knew I probably could have. I might have had to endure some mockery, but Mason was crazy enough about me that feminine wiles probably would have stopped this madness. I'd gotten caught up in the excitement and the risk—much as I had in kissing Dimitri—not giving enough thought to the consequences because secretly, inside of me, that impulsive desire to be wild still lurked. Mason had it too, and his called to me.

That mental Dimitri voice chastised me once more.

After Mason was safely returned to the lodge and had ice on his ankle, I carried our equipment back outside toward the storage buildings. When I went back inside, I went through a different doorway than I normally used. This entrance was set behind a huge, open porch with an ornate wooden railing. The porch was built into the side of the mountain and had a breathtaking view of the other peaks and valleys around us— if you felt like standing around long enough in freezing temperatures to admire it. Which most people didn't.

I walked up the steps to the porch, stomping snow off my boots as I did. A thick scent, both spicy and sweet, hung in the air. Something about it felt familiar, but before I could identify it, a voice suddenly spoke to me out of the shadows.

"Hey, little dhampir."

Startled, I realized someone was indeed standing on the porch. A guy—a Moroi—leaned against the wall not far from the door. He brought a cigarette up to his mouth, took a long drag, and then dropped it to the floor. He stamped the butt out and crooked me a smile. That was the scent, I realized. Clove cigarettes.

Warily, I stopped and crossed my arms as I took him in. He was a little shorter than Dimitri but wasn't as lanky as some Moroi guys ended up looking. A long, charcoal coat—probably made out of some insanely expensive cashmere-wool blend—fit his body exceptionally well, and the leather dress shoes he wore indicated more money still. He had brown hair that looked like it had been purposely styled to appear a little unkempt, and his eyes were either blue or green—I didn't have quite enough light to know for sure. His face was cute, I supposed, and I pegged him to be a couple years older than me. He looked like he'd just come from a dinner party.

"Yeah?" I asked.

His eyes swept over my body. I was used to attention from Moroi guys. It just usually wasn't so obvious. And I usually wasn't bundled up in winter clothing and sporting a black eye.

He shrugged. "Just saying hi, that's all."

I waited for more, but all he did was stuff his hands into the coat's pockets. With a shrug of my own, I took a couple steps forward.

"You smell good, you know," he suddenly said.

I stopped walking again and gave him a puzzled look, which only made his sly smile grow a little bigger.

"I . . . um, what?"

"You smell good," he repeated.

"Are you joking? I've been sweating all day. I'm disgusting." I wanted to walk away, but there was something eerily compelling about this guy. Like a train wreck. I didn't find him attractive per se; I was just suddenly interested in talking to him.

"Sweat isn't a bad thing," he said, leaning his head against the wall and looking upward thoughtfully. "Some of the best things in life happen while sweating. Yeah, if you get too much of it and it gets old and stale, it turns pretty gross. But on a beautiful woman? Intoxicating. If you could smell things like a vampire does, you'd know what I'm talking about. Most people mess it all up and drown themselves in perfume. Perfume can be good . . . especially if you get one that goes with your chemistry. But you only need a hint. Mix about 20 percent of that with 80 percent of your own perspiration . . . mmm." He tilted his head to the side and looked at me. "Dead sexy."

I suddenly remembered Dimitri and his aftershave. Yeah. *That* had been dead sexy, but I certainly wasn't going to tell this guy about it.

"Well, thanks for the hygiene lesson," I said. "But I don't own any perfume, *and* I'm going to go shower all this hot sweaty action off me. Sorry."

He pulled out a pack of cigarettes and offered it to me. He moved only a step closer, but it was enough for me to smell something else on him. Alcohol. I shook my head at the cigarettes, and he tapped one out for himself.

"Bad habit," I said, watching him light it.

"One of many," he replied. He inhaled deeply. "You here with St. Vlad's?"

"Yup."

"So you're going to be a guardian when you grow up."

"Obviously."

He exhaled smoke, and I watched it drift away into the night. Heightened vampire senses or no, it was a wonder he could smell anything around those cloves.

"How long until you grow up?" he asked. "I might need a guardian."

"I graduate in the spring. But I'm already spoken for. Sorry."

Surprise flickered in his eyes. "Yeah? Who is he?"

"*She's* Vasilisa Dragomir."

"Ah." His face split into a huge grin. "I knew you were trouble as soon as I saw you. You're Janine Hathaway's daughter."

"I'm Rose Hathaway," I corrected, not wanting to be defined by my mother.

"Nice to meet you, Rose Hathaway." He extended a gloved hand to me that I hesitantly took. "Adrian Ivashkov."

"And you think *I'm* trouble," I muttered. The Ivashkovs were a royal family, one of the wealthiest and most powerful. They were the kind of people who thought they could get anything they wanted and walked over those in their way. No wonder he was so arrogant.

He laughed. He had a nice laugh, rich and almost melodious. It made me think of warm caramel, dripping from a spoon. "Handy, huh? Each of our reputations precedes us."

I shook my head. "You don't know anything about me. And I only know of your *family*. I don't know anything about you."

"Want to?" he asked tauntingly.

"Sorry. I'm not into older guys."

"I'm twenty-one. Not that much older."

"I have a boyfriend." It was a small lie. Mason certainly wasn't my boyfriend yet, but I hoped Adrian would leave me alone if he thought I was taken.

"Funny you didn't mention that right away," Adrian mused. "He didn't give you that black eye, did he?"

I felt myself blushing, even in the cold. I'd been hoping he wouldn't notice the eye, which was stupid. With his vampire eyes, he'd probably noticed as soon as I stepped onto the porch.

"He wouldn't be alive if he did. I got it during . . . practice. I mean, I'm training to be a guardian. Our classes are always rough."

"That's pretty hot," he said. He dropped this second cigarette to the ground and put it out with his foot.

"Punching me in the eye?"

"Well, no. Of course not. I meant that the idea of getting

rough with you is hot. I'm a big fan of full-contact sports."

"I'm sure you are," I said dryly. He was arrogant and presumptuous, yet I still couldn't quite force myself to leave.

The sound of footsteps behind me made me turn. Mia came around the path and walked up the steps. When she saw us, she stopped suddenly.

"Hey, Mia."

She glanced between the two of us.

"*Another* guy?" she asked. From her tone, you would have thought I had my own harem of men.

Adrian gave me a questioning, amused look. I gritted my teeth and decided not to dignify that with a response. I opted for uncharacteristic politeness.

"Mia, this is Adrian Ivashkov."

Adrian turned on the same charm he'd used on me. He shook her hand. "Always a pleasure to meet a friend of Rose's, especially a pretty one." He spoke like he and I had known each other since childhood.

"We aren't friends," I said. So much for politeness.

"Rose only hangs out with guys and psychopaths," said Mia. Her voice carried the usual scorn she harbored for me, but there was a look on her face that showed Adrian had clearly caught her interest.

"Well," he said cheerfully, "since I'm both a psychopath and a guy, that would explain why we're such good friends."

"You and I aren't friends either," I told him.

He laughed. "Always playing hard to get, huh?"

"She's not that hard to get," said Mia, clearly upset that Adrian was paying more attention to me. "Just ask half the guys at our school."

"Yeah," I retorted, "and you can ask the other half about Mia. If you can do a favor for her, she'll do *lots* of favors for you." When she'd declared war on Lissa and me, Mia had managed to get a couple of guys to tell everyone at school that I'd done some pretty awful things with them. The ironic thing was that she'd gotten them to lie for her by sleeping with them herself.

A flicker of embarrassment passed over her face, but she held her ground.

"Well," she said, "at least I don't do them for free."

Adrian made some cat noises.

"Are you done?" I asked. "It's past your bedtime, and the grown-ups would like to talk now." Mia's youthful looks were a sore point with her, one I frequently enjoyed exploiting.

"Sure," she said crisply. Her cheeks turned pink, intensifying her porcelain-doll appearance. "I have better things to do anyway." She turned toward the door, then paused with her hand resting on it. She glanced toward Adrian. "Her mom gave her that black eye, you know."

She went inside. The fancy glass doors swung shut behind her.

Adrian and I stood there in silence. Finally, he took out the cigarettes again and lit another. "Your mom?"

"Shut up."

"You're one of those people who either has soul mates or mortal enemies, aren't you? No in-between. You and Vasilisa are probably like sisters, huh?"

"I guess."

"How is she?"

"Huh? What do you mean?"

He shrugged, and if I didn't know better, I'd have said he was overdoing casualness. "I don't know. I mean, I know you guys ran away . . . and there was that stuff with her family and Victor Dashkov. . . ."

I stiffened at the reference to Victor. "So?"

"Dunno. Just figured it might be a lot for her to, you know, handle."

I studied him carefully, wondering what he was getting at. There had been a brief leak about Lissa's fragile mental health, but it had been well-contained. Most people had forgotten about it or assumed it was a lie.

"I've got to go." I decided avoidance was the best tactic just now.

"Are you sure?" He sounded only mildly disappointed. Mostly he seemed as cocky and amused as before. Something about him still intrigued me, but whatever it was, it wasn't enough to combat everything else I was feeling, or to risk discussing Lissa. "I thought it was time for the grown-ups to talk. Lots of grown-up things I'd like to talk about."

"It's late, I'm tired, and your cigarettes are giving me a headache," I growled.

"I suppose that's fair." He drew in on the cigarette and let out the smoke. "Some women think they make me look sexy."

"I think you smoke them so you have something to do while thinking up your next witty line."

He choked on the smoke, caught between inhaling and laughing. "Rose Hathaway, I can't wait to see you again. If you're this charming while tired and annoyed *and* this gorgeous while bruised and in ski clothes, you must be devastating at your peak."

"If by 'devastating' you mean that you should fear for your life, then yeah. You're right." I jerked open the door. "Good night, Adrian."

"I'll see you soon."

"Not likely. I told you, I'm not into older guys."

I walked into the lodge. As the door closed, I just barely heard him call behind me, "Sure, you aren't."

ELEVEN

LISSA WAS UP AND GONE before I even stirred the next morning, which meant I had the bathroom to myself while I got ready for the day. I loved that bathroom. It was enormous. My king-size bed would have fit comfortably inside it. A scalding shower with three different nozzles woke me up, though my muscles ached from yesterday. As I stood in front of the full-length mirror and combed my hair, I saw with some disappointment that the bruise was still there. It was significantly lighter, however, and had turned yellowish. Some concealer and powder almost entirely covered it up.

I headed downstairs in search of food. The dining room was just shutting down breakfast, but one of the waitresses gave me a couple of peach marzipan scones to go. Munching on one as I walked, I expanded my senses to get a feel for where Lissa was. After a couple of moments, I sensed her on the other side of the lodge, away from the student rooms. I followed the trail until I arrived at a room on the third floor. I knocked.

Christian opened the door. "Sleeping Beauty arrives. Welcome."

He ushered me inside. Lissa sat cross-legged on the room's bed and smiled when she saw me. The room was as sumptuous as mine, but most of the furniture had been shoved aside to make space, and in that open area, Tasha stood.

"Good morning," she said.

"Hey," I said. So much for avoiding her.

Lissa patted a spot beside her. "You've got to see this."

"What's going on?" I sat down on the bed and finished the last of the scone.

"Bad things," she said mischievously. "You'll approve."

Christian walked over to the empty space and faced Tasha. They regarded each other, forgetting about Lissa and me. I'd apparently interrupted something.

"So why can't I just stick with the consuming spell?" asked Christian.

"Because it uses a lot of energy," she told him. Even with jeans and a ponytail—*and* the scar—she managed to look ridiculously cute. "Plus, it'll most likely kill your opponent."

He scoffed. "Why wouldn't I want to kill a Strigoi?"

"You might not always be fighting one. Or maybe you need information from them. Regardless, you should be prepared either way."

They were practicing offensive magic, I realized. Excitement and interest replaced the sullenness I'd acquired upon seeing Tasha. Lissa hadn't been kidding about them doing "bad things." I'd always suspected they were practicing offensive magic, but . . . wow. Thinking about it and actually seeing it were two very different things. Using magic as a weapon was forbidden. A punishable offense. A student experimenting with it might be forgiven and simply disciplined, but for an adult to actively be teaching a minor . . . yeah. That could get Tasha in *major* trouble. For half a second, I toyed with the idea of turning her in. Immediately, I dismissed the notion. I might hate her for making moves on Dimitri, but part of me sort of believed in what she and Christian were doing. Plus, it was just cool.

"A distracting spell is almost as useful," she continued.

Her blue eyes took on the intense focus I often saw Moroi get while using magic. Her wrist flicked forward, and a streak of fire snaked past Christian's face. It didn't touch him, but from the way he flinched, I suspected it had been close enough for him to feel the heat.

"Try it," she told him.

Christian hesitated for only a moment and then made the same hand motion she had. Fire streaked out, but it had none of the finely tuned control hers had had. He also didn't have her aim. It went straight for her face, but before it could touch her, it parted and split around her, almost like it had hit an invisible shield. She'd deflected it with her own magic.

"Not bad—aside from the fact you would have burned my face off."

Even I wouldn't want her face burned off. But her hair . . . ah, yes. We'd see how pretty she was without that raven-black mane.

She and Christian practiced a while longer. He improved

as time went by, though he clearly had a ways to go before he had Tasha's skill. My interest grew and grew as they went on, and I found myself pondering all the possibilities this kind of magic could offer.

They wrapped up their lesson when Tasha said she had to go. Christian sighed, clearly frustrated that he hadn't been able to master the spell in an hour. His competitive nature was almost as strong as mine.

"I still think it'd be easier to just burn them entirely," he argued.

Tasha smiled as she brushed her hair into a tighter ponytail. Yeah. She could *definitely* do without that hair, particularly since I knew how much Dimitri liked long hair.

"Easier because it involves less focus. It's sloppy. Your magic'll be stronger in the long run if you can learn this. And, like I said, it has its uses."

I didn't want to agree with her, but I couldn't help it.

"It could be really useful if you were fighting with a guardian," I said excitedly. "Especially if completely burning a Strigoi takes so much energy. This way, you use just a quick burst of your strength to distract the Strigoi. And it *will* distract one since they hate fire so much. Then that's all the time a guardian would need to stake them. You could take down a whole bunch of Strigoi that way."

Tasha grinned at me. Some Moroi—like Lissa and Adrian— smiled without showing their teeth. Tasha always showed hers, including the fangs.

"Exactly. You and I'll have to go Strigoi hunting someday," she teased.

"I don't think so," I replied.

The words in and of themselves weren't that bad, but the tone I used to deliver them certainly was. Cold. Unfriendly. Tasha looked momentarily surprised at my abrupt change in attitude but shrugged it off. Shock from Lissa traveled to me through the bond.

Tasha didn't seem bothered, however. She chatted with us a bit longer and made plans to see Christian for dinner. Lissa gave me a sharp look as she, Christian, and I walked down the elaborate spiral staircase leading back down to the lobby.

"What was *that* about?" she asked.

"What was what about?" I asked innocently.

"Rose," she said meaningfully. It was hard to play dumb when your friend knew you could read her mind. I knew exactly what she was talking about. "You being a bitch to Tasha."

"I wasn't that much of a bitch."

"You were rude," she exclaimed, stepping out of the way of a bunch of Moroi children who came tearing through the lobby. They were bundled up in parkas, and a weary-looking Moroi ski instructor followed them.

I put my hands on my hips. "Look, I'm just grumpy, okay? Didn't get much sleep. Besides, I'm not like you. I don't have to be polite all the time."

As happened so often lately, I couldn't believe what I'd just said. Lissa stared at me, more astonished than hurt. Christian glowered, on the verge of snapping back at me, when Mason mercifully approached us. He hadn't needed a cast or anything, but he had a slight limp to his walk.

"Hey there, Hop-Along," I said, sliding my hand into his.

Christian put his anger for me on hold and turned to Mason. "Is it true your suicidal moves finally caught up with you?"

Mason's eyes were on me. "Is it true you were hanging out with Adrian Ivashkov?"

"I—what?"

"I heard you guys got drunk last night."

"You did?" asked Lissa, startled.

I looked between both their faces. "No, of course not! I barely know him."

"But you *do* know him," pushed Mason.

"Barely."

"He's got a bad reputation," warned Lissa.

"Yeah," said Christian. "He goes through a lot of girls."

I couldn't believe this. "Will you guys lay off? I talked to him for, like, five minutes! And that's only because he was blocking my way inside. Where are you getting all this?" Immediately, I answered my own question. "Mia."

Mason nodded and had the grace to look embarrassed.

"Since when do you talk to her?" I asked.

"I just ran into her, that's all," he told me.

"And you believed her? You know she lies half the time."

"Yeah, but there's usually some truth in the lies. And you *did* talk to him."

"Yes. *Talk*. That's it."

I really had been trying to give some serious thought about dating Mason, so I didn't appreciate him not believing me. He had actually helped me unravel Mia's lies earlier in the school year, so I was surprised he'd be so paranoid about them now. Maybe if his feelings really had grown for me, he was more susceptible to jealousy.

Surprisingly, it was Christian who came to the rescue and changed the subject. "I suppose there's no skiing today, huh?" He pointed to Mason's ankle, immediately triggering an indignant response.

"What, you think this is going to slow me down?" asked Mason.

His anger diminished, replaced by that burning need to prove himself—the need he and I both shared. Lissa and Christian looked at him like he was crazy, but I knew nothing we said would stop him.

"You guys want to come with us?" I asked Lissa and Christian.

Lissa shook her head. "We can't. We have to go to this luncheon being hosted by the Contas."

Christian groaned. "Well, *you* have to go."

She elbowed him. "So do you. The invitation said I get to bring a guest. Besides, this is just a warm-up for the *big* one."

"Which one is that?" asked Mason.

"Priscilla Voda's huge dinner," sighed Christian. Seeing him look so pained made me smile. "The queen's best friend. All the snobbiest royals will be there, *and* I'll have to wear a suit."

Mason flashed me a grin. His earlier antagonism was gone. "Skiing's sounding better and better, huh? Less of a dress code."

We left the Moroi behind and went outside. Mason couldn't compete with me in the same way he had yesterday; his movements were slow and awkward. Still, he did remarkably well when one considered everything. The injury wasn't as bad as we'd feared, but he had the prudence to stick to extremely easy runs.

The full moon hung in the blankness, a glowing sphere of silvery white. The electric lights overpowered most of its illumination on the ground, but here and there, in the shadows, the moon just barely managed to cast its glow. I wished it were bright enough to reveal the surrounding mountain range, but those peaks stayed shrouded in darkness. I'd forgotten to look at them when it was light out earlier.

The runs were super simple for me, but I stayed with Mason and only occasionally teased him about how his remedial skiing was putting me to sleep. Boring runs or no, it was just nice to be outside with my friends, and the activity stirred my blood enough to warm me against the chill air. The light posts lit up the snow, turning it into a vast sea of white, the flakes' crystals sparkling faintly. And if I managed to turn away and block the lights from my field of vision, I could look up and see the stars spilling over the sky. They stood out stark and crystalline in the clear, freezing air. We stayed out for most of the day again, but this time, I called it quits early, pretending to be tired so Mason could get a break. He might manage easy skiing with his tender ankle, but I could tell it was starting to hurt him.

Mason and I headed back toward the lodge walking very close to each other, laughing about something we'd seen earlier. Suddenly, I saw a streak of white in my peripheral vision, and a snowball smashed into Mason's face. I immediately went on the defensive, jerking backward and peering around. Whoops and cries sounded from an area of the resort grounds that held storage sheds and was interspersed with looming pines.

"Too slow, Ashford," someone called. "Doesn't pay to be in love."

More laughs. Mason's best friend, Eddie Castile, and a few other novices from school materialized from behind a cluster of trees. Beyond them, I heard more shouts.

"We'll still take you in, though, if you want to be on our team," said Eddie. "Even if you do dodge like a girl."

"Team?" I asked excitedly.

Back at the Academy, throwing snowballs was strictly prohibited. School officials were inexplicably afraid that we'd throw snowballs packed with glass shards or razor blades, though I had no clue how they thought we'd get a hold of that kind of stuff in the first place.

Not that a snowball fight was *that* rebellious, but after all the stress I'd been through recently, throwing objects at other people suddenly sounded like the best idea I'd heard in a while. Mason and I dashed off with the others, the prospect of forbidden fighting giving him new energy and causing him to forget the pain in his ankle. We set to the fight with a die-hard zeal.

The fight soon became a matter of nailing as many people as possible while dodging attacks from others. I was exceptional at both and furthered the immaturity by catcalling and shouting silly insults at my victims.

By the time someone noticed what we were doing and yelled at us, we were all laughing and covered with snow. Mason and I once again started back for the lodge, and our mood was so high, I knew the Adrian thing was long forgotten.

Indeed, Mason looked at me just before we went inside. "Sorry I, uh, jumped all over you about Adrian earlier."

I squeezed his hand. "It's okay. I know Mia can tell some pretty convincing stories."

"Yeah . . . but even if you were with him . . . it's not like I have any right . . ."

I stared at him, surprised to see his usual brash countenance turn shy. "Don't you?" I asked.

A smile turned up his lips. "Do I?"

Smiling back, I stepped forward and kissed him. His lips felt amazingly warm in the freezing air. It wasn't like the earth-shattering kiss I'd had with Dimitri before the trip, but it was sweet and nice—a friendly sort of kiss that *maybe* could turn into more. At least, that was how I saw it. From the look on Mason's face, it appeared his whole world had been rocked.

"Wow," he said, eyes wide. The moonlight made his eyes look silvery blue.

"You see?" I said. "Nothing to worry about. Not Adrian, not anybody."

We kissed again—a bit longer this time—before finally dragging ourselves apart. Mason was clearly in a better mood, as well as he should have been, and I dropped into bed with a smile on my face. I wasn't technically sure if Mason and I were a couple now, but we were very close to it.

But when I slept, I dreamed about Adrian Ivashkov.

I stood with him on the porch again, only it was summer. The air was balmy and warm, and the sun hung bright in the sky, coating everything in golden light. I hadn't been in this much sun since living among humans. All around, the mountains and valleys were green and alive. Birds sang everywhere.

Adrian leaned against the porch's railing, glanced over, and did a double-take when he saw me. "Oh. Didn't expect to see you here." He smiled. "I was right. You *are* devastating when you're cleaned up."

Instinctively, I touched the skin around my eye.

"It's gone," he said.

Even without being able to see it, I somehow knew he was right. "You aren't smoking."

"Bad habit," he said. He nodded toward me. "You scared? You're wearing a lot of protection."

I frowned, then looked down. I hadn't noticed my clothing. I wore a pair of embroidered jeans I'd seen once but had been unable to afford. My T-shirt was cropped, showing off my stomach, and I wore a belly-button ring. I'd always wanted to get my belly button pierced but had never been able to afford it. The charm I now wore here was a little silver dangly one, and hanging at the end of it was that weird blue eye pendant my mom had given me. Lissa's chotki was wound around my wrist.

I looked back up at Adrian, studying the way the sun shone off his brown hair. Here, in full daylight, I could see that his eyes were indeed green—a deep emerald as opposed to Lissa's pale jade. Something startling suddenly occurred to me.

"Doesn't all this sun bother you?"

He gave a lazy shrug. "Nah. It's my dream."

"No, it's *my* dream."

"Are you sure?" His smile returned.

I felt confused. "I . . . I don't know."

He chuckled, but a moment later, the laugher faded. For the first time since I'd met him, he looked serious. "Why do you have so much darkness around you?"

I frowned. "What?"

"You're surrounded in blackness." His eyes studied me shrewdly, but not in a checking-me-out sort of way. "I've never seen anyone like you. Shadows everywhere. I never would have guessed it. Even while you're standing here, the shadows keep growing."

I looked down at my hands but saw nothing out of the ordinary. I glanced back up. "I'm shadow-kissed. . . ."

"What's that mean?"

"I died once." I'd never talked to anyone other than Lissa and Victor Dashkov about that, but this was a dream. It didn't matter. "And I came back."

Wonder lit his face. "Ah, interesting . . ."

I woke up.

Someone was shaking me. It was Lissa. Her feelings hit me so hard through the bond that I briefly snapped into her mind and found myself looking at me. "Weird" didn't begin to cover it. I pulled back into myself, trying to sift through the terror and alarm coming from her.

"What's wrong?"

"There's been another Strigoi attack."

TWELVE

I WAS OUT OF BED in a flash. We found the entire lodge abuzz with the news. People clustered in small groups in the halls. Family members sought each other out. Some conversations were conducted in terrified whispers; some were loud and easy to overhear. I stopped a few people, trying to get the story straight. Everyone had a different version of what had happened, though, and some wouldn't even pause to talk. They hurried past, either seeking out loved ones or preparing to leave the resort, convinced there might be a safer place elsewhere.

Frustrated with the differing stories, I finally—reluctantly—knew I had to seek out one of the two sources who would give me solid information. My mother or Dimitri. It was like flipping a coin. I wasn't really thrilled with either one of them right now. I debated momentarily and finally decided on my mother, seeing as how she wasn't getting it on with Tasha Ozera.

The door to my mother's room was ajar, and as Lissa and I entered, I saw that a sort of makeshift headquarters had been established here. Lots of guardians were milling around, moving in and out, and discussing strategy. A few gave us odd looks, but no one stopped or questioned us. Lissa and I slid onto a small sofa to listen to a conversation my mother was having.

She stood with a group of guardians, one of whom was Dimitri. So much for avoiding him. His brown eyes glanced at me briefly, and I averted my gaze. I didn't want to deal with my troubled feelings for him right now.

Lissa and I soon discerned the details. Eight Moroi had been killed along with their five guardians. Three Moroi were missing, either dead or turned Strigoi. The attack hadn't really happened near here; it had been somewhere in northern California. Nonetheless, a tragedy like this couldn't help but reverberate within the Moroi world, and for some, two states away was far too close. People were terrified, and I soon learned what in particular made this attack so notable.

"There had to be more than last time," said my mother.

"More?" exclaimed one of the other guardians. "That last group was unheard of. I still can't believe nine Strigoi managed to work together—you expect me to believe they managed to get more organized still?"

"Yes," snapped my mother.

"Any evidence of humans?" someone else asked.

My mother hesitated, then: "Yes. More broken wards. And the way it was all conducted . . . it's identical to the Badica attack."

Her voice was hard, but there was a kind of weariness in it, too. It wasn't physical exhaustion, though. It was mental, I realized. Strain and hurt over what they were talking about.

I always thought of my mother as some sort of unfeeling killing machine, but this was clearly hard for her. It was a hard, ugly matter to discuss—but at the same time, she was tackling it without hesitation. It was her duty.

A lump formed in my throat that I quickly swallowed down. Humans. Identical to the Badica attack. Ever since that massacre, we'd extensively analyzed the oddity of such a large group of Strigoi teaming up and recruiting humans. We'd spoken in vague terms about "if something like this ever happens again . . ." But no one had seriously talked about *this* group—the Badica killers—doing it again. One time was a fluke—maybe a bunch of Strigoi had happened to gather and impulsively decided to go on a raid. It was horrible, but we could write that off.

But now . . . now it looked as though that group of Strigoi hadn't been a random occurrence. They'd united with purpose, utilized humans strategically, and had attacked again. We now had what could be a pattern: Strigoi actively seeking out large groups of prey. Serial killings. We could no longer trust the protective magic of the wards. We couldn't even trust sunlight. Humans could move around in the day, scouting and sabotaging. The light was no longer safe.

I remembered what I'd said to Dimitri at the Badica house: *This changes everything, doesn't it?*

My mother flipped through some papers on a clipboard. "They don't have forensic details yet, but the same number of Strigoi couldn't have done this. None of the Drozdovs or their staff escaped. With five guardians, seven Strigoi would have been preoccupied—at least temporarily—for some to escape. We're looking at nine or ten, maybe."

"Janine's right," said Dimitri. "And if you look at the venue . . . it's too big. Seven couldn't have covered it."

The Drozdovs were one of the twelve royal families. They were large and prosperous, not like Lissa's dying clan. They had plenty of family members to go around, but obviously, an attack like this was still horrible. Furthermore, something about them tickled my brain. There was something I should remember . . . something I should know about the Drozdovs.

While part of my mind puzzled that out, I watched my mother with fascination. I'd listened to her tell her stories. I'd seen and *felt* her fight. But really, truly, I'd never seen her in action in a real-life crisis. She showed every bit of that hard control she did around me, but here, I could see how necessary it was. A situation like this created panic. Even among the guardians, I could sense those who were so keyed up that they wanted to do something drastic. My mother was a voice of reason, a reminder that they had to stay focused and fully assess the situation. Her composure calmed everybody; her strong manner inspired them. This, I realized, was how a leader behaved.

Dimitri was just as collected as she was, but he deferred to her to run things. I had to remind myself sometimes that he was young as far as guardians went. They discussed the attack more, how the Drozdovs had been having a belated

Christmas party in a banquet hall when they were attacked.

"First Badicas, now Drozdovs," muttered one guardian. "They're going after royals."

"They're going after Moroi," said Dimitri flatly. "Royal. Non-royal. It doesn't matter."

Royal. Non-royal. I suddenly knew why the Drozdovs were important. My spontaneous instincts wanted me to jump up and ask a question right now, but I knew better. This was the real deal. This was no time for irrational behavior. I wanted to be as strong as my mother and Dimitri, so I waited for the discussion to end.

When the group started to break up, I leapt up off the sofa and pushed my way toward my mother.

"Rose," she said, surprised. Like in Stan's class, she hadn't noticed me in the room. "What are you doing here?"

It was such a stupid question, I didn't try to answer it. What did she think I was doing here? This was one of the biggest things to happen to the Moroi.

I pointed to her clipboard. "Who else was killed?"

Irritation wrinkled her forehead. "Drozdovs."

"But who else?"

"Rose, we don't have time—"

"They had staff, right? Dimitri said non-royals. Who were they?"

Again, I saw the weariness in her. She took these deaths hard. "I don't know all the names." Flipping through a few pages, she turned the clipboard toward me. "There."

I scanned the list. My heart sank.

"Okay," I told her. "Thanks."

Lissa and I left them to go about their business. I wished I could have helped, but the guardians ran smoothly and efficiently on their own; they had no need for novices underfoot.

"What was that about?" asked Lissa, once we were heading back to the main part of the lodge.

"The Drozdovs' staff," I said. "Mia's mom worked for them. . . ."

Lissa gasped. "And?"

I sighed. "And her name was on the list."

"Oh God." Lissa stopped walking. She stared off into space, blinking back tears. "Oh God," she repeated.

I moved in front of her and placed my hands on her shoulders. She was shaking.

"It's okay," I said. Her fear came to me in waves, but it was a numbed fear. Shock. "This is going to be okay."

"You heard them," she said. "There's a band of Strigoi organizing and attacking us! How many? Are they coming here?"

"No," I said firmly. I had no evidence of that, of course. "We're safe here."

"Poor Mia . . ."

There was nothing I could say to that. I thought Mia was an absolute bitch, but I wouldn't wish this on anyone, not even my worst enemy—which, technically, she was. Immediately, I corrected that thought. Mia wasn't my worst enemy.

I couldn't bear to leave Lissa's side for the rest of the day. I knew there were no Strigoi lurking in the lodge, but my protective instincts ran too strong. Guardians protected their Moroi. Like usual, I also worried about her being anxious and upset, so I did my best to diffuse those feelings.

The other guardians provided reassurance for Moroi too. They didn't walk side by side with the Moroi, but they reinforced lodge security and stayed in constant communication with guardians at the scene of the attack. Information flowed in all day about the grisly specifics, as well as speculation about where the band of Strigoi was. Little of this was shared with novices, of course.

While the guardians did what they did best, the Moroi also did what they—unfortunately—did best: *talk*.

With so many royals and other important Moroi at the lodge, a meeting was organized that night to discuss what had happened and what might be done in the future. Nothing official would be decided here; the Moroi had a queen and a governing council elsewhere for those types of decisions. Everyone knew, though, that opinions gathered here would make their way up the chain of command. Our future safety could very well depend on what was discussed in this meeting.

It was held in an enormous banquet hall inside the lodge, one with a podium and plenty of seating. Despite the businesslike atmosphere, you could tell this room had been designed for things other than meetings about massacres and defense. The carpet had the texture of velvet and showed an ornate floral design in shades of silver and black. The chairs were made of black polished wood and had high backs, clearly intended for fancy dining. Paintings of long-dead Moroi royalty hung on the walls. I stared briefly at one of a queen whose name I didn't know. She wore an old-fashioned dress—too heavy on lace for my tastes—and had pale hair like Lissa's.

Some guy I didn't know was in charge of moderating and stood at the podium. Most of the royals on hand gathered at the front of the room. Everyone else, including students, took seats wherever they could. Christian and Mason had found Lissa and me by that point, and we all started to sit in the back when Lissa suddenly shook her head.

"I'm going to sit in the front."

The three of us stared at her. I was too dumbfounded to probe her mind.

"Look." She pointed. "The royals are sitting up there, sitting by family."

It was true. Members of the same clans had clustered near each other: Badicas, Ivashkovs, Zekloses, etc. Tasha sat there as well, but she was by herself. Christian was the only other Ozera there.

"I need to be up there," said Lissa.

"No one expects you to be there," I told her.

"I have to represent the Dragomirs."

Christian scoffed. "It's all a bunch of royal bullshit."

Her face set into a determined expression. "I need to be up there."

I opened myself up to Lissa's feelings and liked what I found. She'd spent most of the day quiet and afraid, much as she had when we'd found out about Mia's mom. That fear was within her still, but it was overpowered by a steady confidence and determination. She recognized that she was one of the ruling Moroi, and as much as the idea of roving bands of Strigoi scared her, she wanted to do her part.

"You should do it," I said softly. I also liked the idea of her defying Christian.

Lissa met my eyes and smiled. She knew what I had sensed. A moment later, she turned to Christian. "You should join your aunt."

Christian opened his mouth to protest. If not for the horribleness of the situation, seeing Lissa order him around would have been funny. He was always stubborn and difficult; those who tried to push him didn't succeed. Watching his face, I saw the same realization I'd had about Lissa come over him. He liked seeing her strong too. He pressed his lips together in a grimace.

"Okay." He caught her hand, and the two of them walked off toward the front.

Mason and I sat down. Just before things started, Dimitri sat down on the other side of me, hair tied behind his neck and the leather coat draping around him as he settled in the chair. I glanced at him in surprise but said nothing. There were few guardians at this gathering; most were too busy doing damage control. It would figure. There I was, stuck between both of my men.

The meeting kicked off shortly thereafter. Everyone was eager to talk about how they thought the Moroi should be saved, but really, two theories got the most attention.

"The answer's all around us," said one royal, once he'd been given leave to speak. He stood by his chair and looked around the room. "*Here*. In places like this lodge. And St. Vladimir's. We send our children to safe places, places where they have safety in numbers and can be easily guarded. And look how many of us made it here, children and adults alike. Why don't we live this way all the time?"

"Plenty of us already do," someone shouted back.

The man waved that off. "A couple of families here and there. Or a town with a large Moroi population. But those Moroi are still decentralized. Most don't pool their resources—their guardians, their magic. If we could emulate this model . . ." He spread his hands out. ". . . we'd never have to worry about Strigoi again."

"And Moroi could never interact with the rest of the world again," I muttered. "Well, until humans discovered secret vampire cities sprouting up in the wilderness. Then we'd have *lots* of interactions."

The other theory about how to protect the Moroi involved fewer logistical problems but had greater personal impact— particularly for me.

"The problem is simply that we don't have enough guardians." This plan's advocate was some woman from the Szelsky clan. "And so, the answer is simple: *get more.* The Drozdovs had five guardians, and that wasn't enough. Only six to protect over a dozen Moroi! That's unacceptable. It's no wonder these kinds of things keep happening."

"Where do you propose getting more guardians from?" asked the man who'd been in favor of Moroi banding together. "They're kind of a limited resource."

She pointed to where I and a few other novices sat. "We've got plenty already. I've watched them train. They're deadly. Why are we waiting until they turn eighteen? If we accelerated the training program and focused more on combat training than bookwork, we could turn out new guardians when they're sixteen."

Dimitri made a sound low in his throat that didn't seem happy. Leaning forward, he placed his elbows on his knees and rested his chin in his hands, eyes narrowed in thought.

"Not only that, we have plenty of potential guardians going to waste. Where are all the dhampir women? Our races are intertwined. The Moroi are doing their part to help the dhampirs survive. Why aren't these women doing theirs? Why aren't they here?"

A long, sultry laugh came as an answer. All eyes turned toward Tasha Ozera. Whereas many of the other royals had dressed up, she was easy and casual. She wore her usual jeans, a white tank top that showed a bit of midriff, and a blue, lacy knit cardigan that came to her knees.

Glancing at the moderator, she asked, "May I?"

He nodded. The Szelsky woman sat down; Tasha stood up. Unlike the other speakers, she strode right up to the podium, so she could be clearly seen by everyone. Her glossy black hair was pulled back into a ponytail, completely exposing her scars in a way I suspected was intentional. Her face was bold and defiant. Beautiful.

"Those women aren't here, Monica, because they're too busy raising their children—you know, the ones you want to start sending out to the fronts as soon as they can walk. And please don't insult us all by acting like the Moroi do a huge favor to the dhampirs by helping them reproduce. Maybe it's different in your family, but for the rest of us, sex is fun. The Moroi doing it with dhampirs aren't really making that big of a sacrifice."

Dimitri had straightened up now, his expression no longer angry. Probably he was excited that his new girlfriend had mentioned sex. Irritation shot through me, and I hoped that if I had a homicidal look on my face, people would assume it was for Strigoi and not the woman currently addressing us.

Beyond Dimitri, I suddenly noticed Mia sitting by herself, farther down the row. I hadn't realized she was here. She was slumped in her seat. Her eyes were red-rimmed, her face paler than usual. A funny ache burned in my chest, one I'd never expected her to bring about.

"And the reason we're waiting for these guardians to turn

eighteen is so that we can allow them to enjoy some pretense of a life before forcing them to spend the rest of their days in constant danger. They need those extra years to develop mentally as well as physically. Pull them out before they're ready, treat them like they're parts on an assembly line—and you're just creating Strigoi fodder."

A few people gasped at Tasha's callous choice of words, but she succeeded in getting everyone's attention.

"You create more fodder still if you try making the other dhampir women become guardians. You can't force them into that life if they don't want it. This entire plan of yours to get more guardians relies on throwing children and the unwilling into harm's way, just so you can—barely—stay one step ahead of the enemy. I would have said it's the stupidest plan I've ever heard, if I hadn't already had to listen to his."

She pointed at the first speaker, the one who had wanted Moroi compounds. Embarrassment clouded his features.

"Enlighten us then, Natasha," he said. "Tell us what *you* think we should do, seeing as you have so much experience with Strigoi."

A thin smile played on Tasha's lips, but she didn't rise to the insult. "What do I think?" She strode closer to the stage's front, gazing at us as she answered his question. "I think we should stop coming up with plans that involve us relying on someone or something to protect us. You think there are too few guardians? That's not the problem. The problem is there are too many Strigoi. And we've let them multiply and become more powerful because we do nothing about them except have stupid arguments like this. We run and hide behind the dhampirs and let the Strigoi go unchecked. It's our fault. *We* are the reason those Drozdovs died. You want an army? Well, here we are. Dhampirs aren't the only ones who can learn to fight. The question, Monica, isn't where the dhampir women are in this fight. The question is: *Where are we?*"

Tasha was shouting by now, and the exertion turned her cheeks pink. Her eyes shone with her impassioned feelings, and when combined with the rest of her pretty features—and even with the scar—she made a striking figure. Most people couldn't take their eyes off her. Lissa watched Tasha with wonder, inspired by her words. Mason looked hypnotized. Dimitri looked impressed. And farther past him . . .

Farther past him was Mia. Mia no longer hunched in her chair. She was sitting up straight, straight as a stick, her eyes as wide as they could go. She stared at Tasha as though she alone held all the answers to life.

Monica Szelsky looked less awed, and she fixed her gaze on Tasha. "Surely you aren't suggesting the Moroi fight alongside the guardians when the Strigoi come?"

Tasha regarded her levelly. "No. I'm suggesting the Moroi and the guardians go fight the Strigoi *before* they come."

A guy in his twenties who looked like a Ralph Lauren spokesmodel shot up. I would have wagered money he was royal. No one else could have afforded blond highlights that perfect. He untied an expensive sweater from around his waist and draped it over the back of his chair. "Oh," he said in a mocking voice, speaking out of turn. "So, you're going to just give us clubs and stakes and send us off to do battle?"

Tasha shrugged. "If that's what it takes, Andrew, then sure." A sly smile crossed her pretty lips. "But there are other weapons we can learn to use, too. Ones the guardians can't."

The look on his face showed how insane he thought that idea was. He rolled his eyes. "Oh yeah? Like what?"

Her smile turned into a full-fledged grin. "Like this."

She waved her hand, and the sweater he'd placed on the back of his chair burst into flames.

He yelped in surprise and knocked it to the floor, stamping it out with his feet.

There was a brief, collective intake of breath throughout the room. And then . . . chaos broke out.

THIRTEEN

PEOPLE STOOD UP AND SHOUTED, everyone wanting their opinion to be heard. As it was, most of them held the same view: Tasha was wrong. They told her she was crazy. They told her that in sending out Moroi and dhampirs to fight the Strigoi, she'd be expediting the extinction of both races. They even had the nerve to suggest that that was Tasha's plan all along—that she was somehow collaborating with the Strigoi in all of this.

Dimitri stood up, disgust all over his features as he surveyed the chaos. "You might as well leave. Nothing useful's going to happen now."

Mason and I rose, but he shook his head when I started to follow Dimitri out.

"You go on," said Mason. "I want to check something out."

I glanced at the standing, arguing people. I shrugged. "Good luck."

I couldn't believe it had only been a few days since I'd spoken to Dimitri. Stepping out into the hall with him, I felt like it'd been years. Being with Mason these last couple of days had been fantastic, but seeing Dimitri again, all of my old feelings for him came rushing back. Suddenly, Mason seemed like a child. My distress over the Tasha situation also came back, and stupid words fell out of my mouth before I could stop them.

"Shouldn't you be in there protecting Tasha?" I asked. "Before the mob gets her? She's going to get in big trouble for using magic like that."

He raised an eyebrow. "She can take care of herself."

"Yeah, yeah, because she's a badass karate magic user. I get all that. I just figured since you're going to be her guardian and all . . ."

"Where did you hear that?"

"I have my sources." Somehow, saying I'd heard it from my mom sounded less cool. "You've decided to, right? I mean, it sounds like a good deal, seeing as she's going to give you fringe benefits. . . ."

He gave me a level look. "What happens between her and me is none of your business," he replied crisply.

The words *between her and me* stung. It sounded like he and Tasha were a done deal. And, as often happened when I was hurt, my temper and attitude took over.

"Well, I'm sure you guys'll be happy together. She's just your type, too—I know how much you like women who aren't your own age. I mean, she's what, six years older than you? Seven? And I'm seven years younger than you."

"Yes," he said after several moments of silence. "You are. And every second this conversation goes on, you only prove how young you really are."

Whoa. My jaw almost hit the floor. Not even my mother

punching me had hurt as badly as that. For a heartbeat, I thought I saw regret in his eyes, like he too realized just how harsh his words had been. But the moment passed, and his expression was hard once more.

"Little dhampir," a voice suddenly said nearby.

Slowly, still stunned, I turned toward Adrian Ivashkov. He grinned at me and gave a brief nod of acknowledgment to Dimitri. I suspected my face was bright red. How much had Adrian heard?

He held up his hands in a casual gesture. "I don't want to interrupt or anything. Just wanted to talk to you when you have time."

I wanted to tell Adrian I didn't have time to play whatever game he was into now, but Dimitri's words still smarted. He was looking at Adrian now in a very disapproving way. I suspected he, like everyone else, had heard about Adrian's bad reputation. *Good*, I thought. I suddenly wanted him to be jealous. I wanted to hurt him as much as he'd hurt me lately.

Swallowing my pain, I unearthed my man-eating smile, one I hadn't used to full effect in sometime. I walked over to Adrian and put a hand on his arm.

"I've got time now." I gave a nod of my own to Dimitri and steered Adrian away, walking close to him. "See you later, Guardian Belikov."

Dimitri's dark eyes followed us stonily. Then I turned away and didn't look back.

"Not into older guys, huh?" asked Adrian once we were alone.

"You're imagining things," I said. "Clearly, my stunning beauty has clouded your mind."

He laughed that nice laugh of his. "That's entirely possible."

I started to step back, but he tossed an arm around me. "No, no, you wanted to play chummy with me—now you've got to see it through."

I rolled my eyes at him and let the arm stay. I could smell alcohol on him as well as the perpetual smell of cloves. I wondered if he was drunk now. I had the feeling that there was probably little difference between his attitudes drunk or sober.

"What do you want?" I asked.

He studied me for a moment. "I want you to grab Vasilisa and come with me. We're going to have some fun. You'll probably want a swimsuit too." He seemed disappointed by the admission of this. "Unless you want to go naked."

"What? A bunch of Moroi and dhampirs just got slaughtered, and you want to go swimming and 'have fun'?"

"It's not just swimming," he said patiently. "Besides, that slaughter is exactly why you should go do this."

Before I could argue that, I saw my friends round the corner: Lissa, Mason, and Christian. Eddie Castile was with the group, which shouldn't have surprised me, but Mia was as well—which certainly did surprise me. They were deep in conversation, though they all stopped talking when they saw me.

"There you are," said Lissa, a puzzled look on her face.

I remembered Adrian's arm was still around me. I stepped out of it. "Hey, guys," I said. A moment of awkwardness hung around us, and I was pretty sure I heard a low chuckle from Adrian. I beamed at him and then my friends. "Adrian invited us to go swimming."

They stared at me in surprise, and I could almost see the wheels of speculation turning in their heads. Mason's face darkened a little, but like the others, he said nothing. I stifled a groan.

Adrian took me inviting the others to his secret interlude pretty well. With his easygoing attitude, I hadn't really expected anything else. Once we had swimsuits, we followed his directions to a doorway in one of the far wings of the lodge. It held a staircase that led down—and down and down. I nearly got dizzy as we wound around and around. Electric lights hung in the walls, but as we went farther, the painted walls changed to carved stone.

When we reached our destination, we discovered Adrian had been right—it wasn't just swimming. We were in a special spa area of the resort, one used only for the most elite Moroi. In this case, it was reserved for a bunch of royals I assumed were Adrian's friends. There were about thirty others, all his age or older, who bore the marks of wealth and elitism.

The spa consisted of a series of hot mineral pools. Maybe once they'd been in a cave or something, but the lodge builders had long since gotten rid of any sort of rustic surroundings.

The black stone walls and ceiling were as polished and beautiful as anything else in the resort. It was like being in a cave—a
really nice, designer cave. Racks of towels lined the walls, as
did tables full of exotic food. The baths matched the rest of the
room's hewn-out décor: stone-lined pools containing hot water
that was heated from some underground source. Steam filled
the room, and a faint, metallic smell hung in the air. Sounds of
partygoers laughing and splashing echoed around us.

"Why is Mia with you?" I asked Lissa softly. We were
winding our way through the room, looking for a pool that
wasn't occupied.

"She was talking to Mason when we were getting ready
to leave," she returned. She kept her voice just as quiet. "It
seemed mean to just . . . I don't know . . . leave her . . ."

Even I agreed with that. Obvious signs of grief were written all over her face, but Mia seemed at least momentarily dis-
tracted by whatever Mason was telling her.

"I thought you didn't know Adrian," Lissa added. Disap-
proval hung in her voice and in the bond. We finally found
a large pool, a little out of the way. A guy and a girl were on
the opposite side, all over each other, but there was plenty of
room for the rest of us. They were easy to ignore.

I put a foot into the water and pulled it back immediately.

"I don't," I told her. Cautiously, I inched the foot back in,
slowly followed by the rest of my body. When I got to my
stomach, I grimaced. I had on a maroon bikini, and the scalding water caught my stomach by surprise.

"You must know him a little. He invited you to a party."

"Yeah, but do you see him with us now?"

She followed my gaze. Adrian stood on the far side of the room with a group of girls in bikinis much smaller than mine. One was a Betsey Johnson suit I'd seen in a magazine and coveted. I sighed and looked away.

We'd all slipped into the water by then. It was so hot I felt like I was in a soup kettle. Now that Lissa seemed convinced of my innocence with Adrian, I tuned into the others' discussion.

"What are you talking about?" I interrupted. It was easier than listening and figuring it out myself.

"The meeting," said Mason excitedly. Apparently, he'd gotten over seeing me and Adrian together.

Christian had settled onto a small shelf in the pool. Lissa curled up beside him. Putting a proprietary arm around her, he tipped his back so it rested on the edge.

"Your boyfriend wants to lead an army against the Strigoi," he told me. I could tell he was saying it to provoke me.

I looked at Mason questioningly. It wasn't worth the effort to challenge the "boyfriend" comment.

"Hey, it was *your* aunt who suggested it," Mason reminded Christian.

"She only said we should find the Strigoi before they find us again," countered Christian. "She wasn't pushing for novices fighting. That was Monica Szelsky."

A waitress came by then with a tray of pink drinks. These were in elegant, long-stemmed crystal glasses with sugared rims. I had a strong suspicion the drinks were alcoholic, but I doubted anyone who made it into this party was going to get carded. I had no idea what they were. Most of my experiences with alcohol had involved cheap beer. I took a glass and turned back to Mason.

"You think that's a good idea?" I asked him. I sipped the drink, cautiously. As a guardian in training, I felt like I should always be on alert, but tonight I once again felt like being rebellious. The drink tasted like punch. Grapefruit juice. Something sweet, like strawberries. I was still pretty sure there was alcohol in it, but it didn't appear strong enough for me to lose sleep over.

Another waitress soon appeared with a tray of food. I eyed it and recognized almost nothing. There was something that looked vaguely like mushrooms stuffed with cheese, as well as something else that looked little round patties of meat or sausage. As a good carnivore, I reached for one, thinking it couldn't be that bad.

"It's foie gras," said Christian. There was a smile on his face I didn't like.

I eyed him warily. "What's that?"

"You don't know?" His tone was cocky, and for once in his life, he sounded like a true royal touting his elite knowledge over us underlings. He shrugged. "Take a chance. Find out."

Lissa sighed in exasperation. "It's goose liver."

I jerked my hand back. The waitress moved on, and Christian laughed. I glared at him.

Meanwhile, Mason was still hung up on my question about whether novices going to battle before graduation was a good idea.

"What else are we doing?" he asked indignantly. "What are *you* doing? You run laps with Belikov every morning. What's that doing for you? For the Moroi?"

What was that doing for me? Making my heart race and my mind have indecent thoughts.

"We aren't ready," I said instead.

"We've only got six more months," piped in Eddie.

Mason nodded his agreement. "Yeah. How much more can we learn?"

"Plenty," I said, thinking of how much I'd picked up from my tutoring sessions with Dimitri. I finished my drink. "Besides, where does it stop? Let's say they end school six months early, then send us off. What next? They decide to push back further and cut our senior year? Our junior year?"

He shrugged. "I'm not afraid to fight. I could have taken on Strigoi when I was a sophomore."

"Yeah," I said dryly. "Just like you did skiing on that slope."

Mason's face, already flushed from the heat, turned redder still. I immediately regretted my words, particularly when Christian started laughing.

"Never thought I'd live to see the day when I agreed with you, Rose. But sadly, I do." The cocktail waitress came by again, and both Christian and I took new drinks. "The Moroi have got to start helping us defend *themselves*."

"With magic?" asked Mia suddenly.

It was the first time she'd spoken since we'd got here. Silence met her. I think Mason and Eddie didn't respond because they knew nothing about fighting with magic. Lissa, Christian, and I did—and were trying very hard to act like we didn't. There was a funny sort of hope in Mia's eyes, though, and I could only imagine what she'd gone through today. She'd woken up to learn her mother was dead and then been subjected to hours and hours of political bantering and battle strategies. The fact that she was sitting here at all seeming semi-composed was a miracle. I assumed people who actually liked their mothers would barely be able to function in that situation.

When no one else looked like they were going to answer her, I finally said, "I suppose. But . . . I don't know much about that."

I finished the rest of my drink and averted my eyes, hoping someone else would take up the conversation. They didn't. Mia looked disappointed but said no more when Mason switched back to the Strigoi debate.

I took a third drink and sank into the water as far as I reasonably could and still hold the glass. This drink was different. It looked chocolatey and had whipped cream on top. I took a taste and definitely detected the bite of alcohol. Still, I figured the chocolate probably diluted it.

When I was ready for a fourth drink, the waitress was nowhere in sight. Mason seemed really, really cute to me all of a sudden. I would have liked a little romantic attention from him, but he was still going on about Strigoi and the logistics of leading a strike in the middle of the day. Mia and Eddie were nodding along with him eagerly, and I got the feeling that if he decided to hunt Strigoi right now, they'd follow. Christian was actually joining the talk, but it was more to play devil's advocate. Typical. He thought a sort of preemptive strike would require guardians *and* Moroi, much as Tasha had said. Mason, Mia, and Eddie argued that if the Moroi weren't up to it, the guardians should take matters into their own hands.

I confess, their enthusiasm was kind of contagious. I rather liked the idea of getting the drop on Strigoi. But in the Badica and Drozdov attacks, all of the guardians had been killed. Admittedly the Strigoi had organized into huge groups and had help, but all that told me was that our side needed to be extra careful.

His cuteness aside, I didn't want to listen to Mason talk about his battle skills anymore. I wanted another drink. I stood up and climbed over the edge of the pool. To my astonishment, the world started spinning. I'd had that happen before when I got out of baths or hot tubs too quickly, but when things didn't right themselves, I realized those drinks might have been stronger than I thought.

I also decided a fourth wasn't such a good idea, but I didn't want to get back in and let everyone know I was drunk. I headed off toward a side room I'd seen the waitress disappear into. I hoped maybe there was a secret stash of desserts somewhere, chocolate mousse instead of goose liver. As I walked, I paid special attention to the slippery floor, thinking that falling into one of the pools and cracking my skull would definitely cost me coolness points.

I was paying so much attention to my feet and trying not to stagger that I walked into someone. To my credit, it'd been his fault; he'd backed into me.

"Hey, watch it," I said, steadying myself.

But he wasn't paying attention to me. His eyes were on another guy, a guy with a bloody nose.

I'd walked right into the middle of a fight.

FOURTEEN

TWO GUYS I'D NEVER MET before were squaring off against each other. They looked to be in their twenties, and neither noticed me. The one who'd bumped into me shoved the other one hard, forcing him to stagger back considerably.

"You're afraid!" yelled the guy by me. He had on green swimming trunks, and his black hair was slicked back with water. "You're all afraid. You just want to hole up in your mansions and let the guardians do your dirty work. What are you going to do when they're all dead? Who'll protect you then?"

The other guy wiped the blood off his face with the back of his hand. I suddenly recognized him—thanks to his blond highlights. He was the royal who'd yelled at Tasha about wanting to lead Moroi to battle. She'd called him Andrew. He tried to land a hit and failed; his technique was all wrong. "This is the safest way. Listen to that Strigoi-lover, and we'll *all* be dead. She's trying to kill our whole race off!"

"She's trying to save us!"

"She's trying to get us to use black magic!"

The "Strigoi-lover" had to be Tasha. The non-royal guy was the first person outside of my little circle whom I'd ever heard speak in her favor. I wondered how many others out there shared his view. He punched Andrew again, and my base instincts—or maybe the punch—made me leap into action.

I sprang forward and wedged myself between them. I was still dizzy and a bit unsteady. If they hadn't been standing so close, I probably would have fallen over. They both hesitated, clearly caught off guard.

"Get out of here," snapped Andrew.

Being male and Moroi, they had greater height and weight than I, but I was probably stronger than either one alone. Hoping I could make the most of that, I grabbed each of them by the arm, pulled them toward me, and then shoved them away as hard as I could. They staggered, not having expected my strength. I staggered a little too.

The non-royal glared and took a step toward me. I was counting on the fact that he'd be old-fashioned and not hit a girl. "What are you doing?" he exclaimed. Several people had gathered and were watching excitedly.

I returned his glare. "I'm trying to stop you guys from being any more idiotic than you already are! You want to help? Stop fighting each other! Ripping each other's heads off isn't going to save the Moroi unless you're trying to thin stupidity out of the gene pool." I pointed at Andrew. "Tasha Ozera is *not* trying to kill everyone off. She's trying to get you to stop being a victim." I turned to the other guy. "And as for you, you've got a long ways to go if you think this is the way to get your point across. Magic—especially offensive magic—takes a lot of self-control, and so far, you aren't impressing me with yours. *I* have more than you do, and if you knew me at all, you'd know how crazy that is."

The two guys stared at me, stunned. I was apparently more effective than a taser. Well, at least for several seconds I was. Because once the shock of my words wore off, they went at each other again. I got caught in the crossfire and shoved away, nearly falling in the process. Suddenly, from behind me, Mason came to my defense. He punched the first guy he could—the non-royal.

The guy flew backward, falling into one of the pools with a splash. I yelped, remembering my earlier fear about skull-cracking, but a moment later, he found his feet and rubbed water out of his eyes.

I grabbed Mason's arm, trying to hold him back, but he shrugged me off and went after Andrew. He shoved Andrew hard, pushing him into several Moroi—Andrew's friends, I suspected—who seemed to be trying to break up the fight. The guy in the pool climbed out, fury written all over his face, and made moves toward Andrew. This time, both Mason and I blocked his way. He glared at all of us.

"Don't," I warned him.

The guy clenched his fists and looked as though he might try to take us on. But we were intimidating, and he didn't appear to have an entourage of friends here like Andrew— who was shouting obscenities and being led away—did. With a few muttered threats, the non-royal backed off.

As soon as he was gone, I turned on Mason. "Are you out of your mind?"

"Huh?" he asked.

"Jumping into the middle of that!"

"You jumped in too," he said.

I started to argue, then realized he was right. "It's different," I grumbled.

He leaned forward. "Are you drunk?"

"*No.* Of course not. I'm just trying to keep you from doing something stupid. Just because you have delusions of being able to kill a Strigoi doesn't mean you have to take it out on everyone else."

"Delusions?" he asked stiffly.

I started to feel kind of nauseous just then. My head spinning, I continued toward the side room, hoping I didn't stumble.

But when I reached it, I saw that it wasn't some kind of dessert or drink room after all. Well, at least not in the way I'd been thinking. It was a feeder room. Several humans reclined on satin-covered chaise lounges with Moroi by their sides. Jasmine incense burned in the air. Stunned, I watched with an eerie fascination as a blond Moroi guy leaned forward and bit into the neck of a very pretty redhead. All of these feeders were exceptionally good-looking, I realized just then. Like actresses or models. Only the best for royalty.

The guy drank long and deep, and the girl closed her eyes and parted her lips, an expression of pure bliss on her face as Moroi endorphins flooded into her bloodstream. I shivered, taken back to when I too had experienced that same kind of euphoria. In my alcohol-hazed mind, the whole thing suddenly seemed startlingly erotic. In fact, I almost felt intrusive—like I was watching people have sex. When the Moroi finished and licked the last of the blood away, he brushed his lips against her cheek in a soft kiss.

"Want to volunteer?"

Light fingertips brushed my neck, and I jumped. I turned around and saw Adrian's green eyes and knowing smirk.

"Don't do that," I told him, knocking his hand away.

"Then what are you doing in here?" he asked.

I gestured around me. "I'm lost."

He peered at me. "Are you drunk?"

"*No*. Of course not . . . but . . ." The nausea had settled a little, but I still didn't feel right. "I think I should sit down."

He took my arm. "Well, don't do it in here. Someone might get the wrong idea. Let's go somewhere quiet."

He steered me off into a different room, and I looked around with interest. It was a massage area. Several Moroi lay back on tables and were getting back and foot massages from hotel staff. The oil they used smelled like rosemary and lavender. Under any other circumstances, a massage would have sounded great, but lying on my stomach seemed like the worst idea just now.

I sat down on the carpeted floor, leaning back against the wall. Adrian walked away and returned with a glass of water. Sitting down as well, he handed it to me.

"Drink this. It'll help."

"I told you, I'm not drunk," I mumbled. But I downed the water anyway.

"Uh-huh." He smiled at me. "You did nice work with that fight. Who was the other guy that helped you?"

"My boyfriend," I said. "Sort of."

"Mia was right. You do have a lot of guys in your life."

"It's not like that."

"Okay." He was still smiling. "Where's Vasilisa? I figured she'd be attached to you."

"She's with *her* boyfriend." I studied him.

"What's with the tone? Jealous? You want him for yourself?"

"God, no. I just don't like him."

"Does he treat her badly?" he asked.

"No," I admitted. "He adores her. He's just kind of a jerk."

Adrian was clearly enjoying this. "Ah, you *are* jealous. Does she spend more time with him than you?"

I ignored that. "Why do you keep asking about her? Are you interested in her?"

He laughed. "Rest easy, I'm not interested in her in the same way I am you."

"But you are interested."

"I just want to talk to her."

He left to fetch me more water. "Feeling better?" he asked, handing the glass to me. It was crystal and intricately carved. It seemed too fancy for plain water.

"Yeah . . . I didn't think those drinks were that strong."

"That's the beauty of them," he chuckled. "And speaking of beauty . . . that's a great color on you."

I shifted. I might not have been showing as much skin as those other girls, but I was showing more than I really wanted to with Adrian. Or was I? There was something weird about him. His arrogant manner annoyed me . . . but I still liked being around him. Maybe the smartass in me recognized a kindred spirit.

Somewhere in the back of my drunken mind, a light clicked on. But I couldn't quite get to it. I drank more water.

"You haven't had a cigarette in, like, ten minutes," I pointed out, wanting to change the subject.

He made a face. "No smoking in here."

"I'm sure you've made up for it in punch."

His smile returned. "Well, *some* of us can hold our liquor. You aren't going to be sick, are you?"

I still felt tipsy but no longer nauseous. "No."

"Good."

I thought back to when I'd dreamed about him. It *had* been just a dream, but it had stuck with me, particularly the talk about me being surrounded in darkness. I wanted to ask him about it . . . even though I knew it was stupid. It had been my dream, not his.

"Adrian . . ."

He turned his green eyes on me. "Yes, darling?"

I couldn't bring myself to ask. "Never mind."

He started to retort, then tilted his head toward the door. "Ah, here she comes."

"Who—"

Lissa stepped into the room, eyes scanning around. When she spotted us, I saw relief break over her. I couldn't feel it, though. Intoxicants like alcohol numbed the bond. It was another reason I shouldn't have taken such a stupid chance tonight.

"There you are," she said, kneeling beside me. Glancing at Adrian, she gave him a nod. "Hey."

"Hey yourself, cousin," he returned, using the family terms royals sometimes used around each other.

"You okay?" Lissa asked me. "When I saw how drunk you were, I thought you might have fallen in somewhere and drowned."

"I'm not—" I gave up trying to deny it. "I'm fine."

Adrian's usual expression had turned serious as he studied Lissa. It again reminded me of the dream. "How'd you find her?"

Lissa gave him a puzzled look. "I, um, checked all the rooms."

"Oh." He looked disappointed. "I thought you might have used your bond."

Both she and I stared.

"How do you know about that?" I demanded. Only a few

people at school knew about it. Adrian had spoken about it as casually as he might have my hair color.

"Hey, I can't reveal all my secrets, can I?" he asked mysteriously. "And besides, there's a certain way you two act around each other . . . it's hard to explain. It's pretty cool . . . all the old myths are true."

Lissa regarded him warily. "The bond only works one way. Rose can sense what I'm feeling and thinking, but I can't do it back to her."

"Ah." We sat in silence a few moments, and I drank more water. Adrian spoke again. "What'd you specialize in anyway, cousin?"

She looked embarrassed. We both knew it was important to keep her spirit powers secret from others who might abuse her healing, but her cover story of not having specialized always bothered her.

"I haven't," she said.

"Do they think you're going to? Late bloomer?"

"No."

"You're probably higher in the other elements, though, right? Just not strong enough to really master any?" He reached out to pat her shoulder in an exaggerated show of comfort.

"Yeah, how'd you—"

The instant his fingers touched her, she gasped. It was as though a bolt of lightning had struck her. The strangest look crossed her face. Even drunk, I felt the flood of joy that came pouring through the bond. She stared at Adrian in wonder. His eyes were locked onto hers too. I didn't understand why they were looking at each other like that, but it bothered me.

"Hey," I said. "Stop that. I told you, she has a boyfriend."

"I know," he said, still watching her. A small smile turned his lips. "We need to have a chat someday, cousin."

"Yes," she agreed.

"Hey." I was more confused than ever. "*You* have a boyfriend. And there he is."

She blinked back to reality. All three of us turned toward the doorway. Christian and the others stood there. I suddenly had a flashback to when they'd found me with Adrian's arm around me. This wasn't much better. Lissa and I were sitting on either side of him, very close.

She sprang up, looking mildly guilty. Christian was regarding her curiously.

"We're getting ready to leave," he said.

"Okay," she told him. She looked down at me. "Ready?"

I nodded and started to clamber to my feet. Adrian caught my arm as I did and helped me up. He smiled at Lissa. "Nice talking to you." To me, he murmured very quietly, "Don't worry. I told you, I'm not interested in her in that way. She doesn't look as good in a bathing suit. Probably not as good out of one either."

I pulled my arm away. "Well, you'll never find out."

"It's okay," he said. "I have a good imagination."

I joined the others, and we headed back toward the main part of the lodge. Mason gave me as strange a look as Christian had given Lissa and stayed away from me, walking toward the front with Eddie. To my surprise and discomfort, I found myself walking beside Mia. She looked miserable.

"I . . . I'm really sorry about what happened," I said finally.

"You don't have to act like you care, Rose."

"No, no. I mean it. It's horrible. . . . I'm so sorry." She wouldn't look at me. "Is . . . that is, are you going to see your dad soon?"

"Whenever they have the memorial," she said stiffly.

"Oh."

I didn't know what else to say and gave up, instead turning my attention to the stairs as we climbed back up to the lodge's main level. Unexpectedly, Mia was the one who continued the conversation.

"I watched you break up that fight . . ." she said slowly. "You mentioned offensive magic. Like you knew about it."

Oh. Great. She was going to make a play at blackmail . . . or was she? At the moment, she seemed almost civil.

"I was just guessing," I said. No way was I going to bust Tasha and Christian. "I don't really know that much. Just stories I've heard."

"Oh." Her face fell. "What kind of stories?"

"Um, well . . ." I tried to think of something neither too vague nor too specific. "Like I told those guys . . . the concentration thing is big. Because if you're in a battle with Strigoi, all sorts of things can distract you. So you've got to keep control."

That was actually a basic guardian rule, but it must have been new to Mia. Her eyes widened with eagerness. "What else? What kind of spells do people use?"

I shook my head. "I don't know. I don't really even know how spells work, and like I said, these are just . . . stories I've heard. My guess is you just find ways to use your element as a weapon. Like . . . fire users really have an advantage because fire'll kill Strigoi, so it's easy for them. And air users can suffocate people." I'd actually experienced that last one vicariously through Lissa. It had been horrible.

Mia's eyes grew wider still. "What about a water user?" she asked. "How could water hurt a Strigoi?"

I paused. "I, uh, never heard any stories about water users. Sorry."

"Do you have any ideas, though? Ways that, like, someone like me could learn to fight?"

Ah. So that's what this was about. It actually wasn't all that crazy. I remembered how excited she'd looked at the meeting when Tasha had talked about attacking Strigoi. Mia wanted to take revenge on the Strigoi for her mother's death. No wonder she and Mason had been getting along so well.

"Mia," I said gently, catching hold of the door to let her pass. We were almost at the lobby now. "I know how you must want to . . . do something. But I think you're better off just sort of letting yourself, um, grieve."

She reddened, and suddenly, I was seeing the normal and angry Mia. "Don't talk down to me," she said.

"Hey, I'm not. I'm serious. I'm just saying you shouldn't do anything rash while you're still upset. Besides . . ." I bit off my words.

She narrowed her eyes. "What?"

Screw it. She needed to know. "Well, I don't really know what good a water user would be against a Strigoi. It's probably the least useful element to use on one of them."

Outrage filled her features. "You're a real bitch, you know that?"

"I'm just telling you the truth."

"Well, let me tell *you* the truth. You're a total idiot when it comes to guys."

I thought about Dimitri. She wasn't entirely off base.

"Mason's great," she continued. "One of the nicest guys I know—and you don't even notice! He'd do anything for you, and you were off throwing yourself at Adrian Ivashkov."

Her words surprised me. Could Mia have a crush on Mason? And while I certainly hadn't been throwing myself at Adrian, I could see how it might have looked that way. And even if it weren't true, that wouldn't have stopped Mason from feeling hurt and betrayed.

"You're right," I said.

Mia stared at me, so astonished I'd agreed with her that she didn't say anything else for the rest of the walk.

We reached the part of the lodge that split off into different wings for guys and girls. I grabbed a hold of Mason's arm as the others walked off.

"Hang on," I told him. I badly needed to reassure him about Adrian, but a tiny part of me wondered if I was doing it because I actually wanted Mason or because I just liked the idea of him wanting me and selfishly didn't want to lose that. He stopped and looked at me. His face was wary. "I wanted to tell you I'm sorry. I shouldn't have yelled at you after the fight—I know you were just trying to help. And with Adrian . . . nothing happened. I mean it."

"It didn't look that way," Mason said. But the anger on his face had faded.

"I know, but believe me, it's all him. He's got some kind of stupid crush on me."

My tone must have been convincing because Mason smiled. "Well. Hard not to."

"I'm not interested in him," I continued. "Or anyone else." It was a small lie, but I didn't think it mattered just then. I was going to be over Dimitri soon, and Mia had been right about Mason. He was wonderful and sweet and cute. I would be an idiot not to pursue this . . . right?

My hand was still on his arm, and I pulled him toward me. He didn't need much more of a signal. He leaned down and kissed me, and in the process, I found myself pressed up against the wall—very much like with Dimitri in the practice room. Of course, it felt nothing like how it had with Dimitri, but it was still nice in its way. I put my arms around Mason and started to pull him closer.

"We could go . . . somewhere," I said.

He pushed back and laughed. "Not when you're drunk."

"I'm not . . . that . . . drunk anymore," I said, trying to pull him back.

Giving me a small kiss on the lips, he stepped back. "Drunk enough. Look, this isn't easy, believe me. But if you still want me tomorrow—when you're sober—then we'll talk."

He leaned down and kissed me again. I tried to wrap my arms around him, but he broke away once more.

"Easy there, girl," he teased, backing toward his hallway.

I glared at him, but he only laughed and turned around. As he walked away, my glare faded, and I headed back to my room with a smile on my face.

FIFTEEN

I WAS TRYING TO PAINT my toenails the next morning—not easy with such a god-awful hangover—when I heard a knock at the door. Lissa had been gone when I woke up, so I staggered across the room, trying not to ruin my wet nail polish. Opening up the door, I saw one of the hotel staff standing outside with a large box in both arms. He shifted it slightly so that he could peer around and look at me.

"I'm looking for Rose Hathaway."

"That's me."

I took the box from him. It was big but not all that heavy. With a quick thank-you, I shut the door, wondering if I should have tipped him. Oh well.

I sat on the floor with the box. It had no markings on it and was sealed with packing tape. I found a pen and stabbed at the tape. Once I'd hacked off enough, I opened the box and peered inside.

It was filled with perfume.

There had to be at least thirty little bottles of perfume packed into the box. Some I'd heard of, some I hadn't. They ranged from crazy expensive, movie-star caliber to cheap kinds I'd seen in drugstores. *Eternity. Angel. Vanilla Fields. Jade Blossom. Michael Kors. Poison. Hypnotic Poison. Pure Poi-*

son. Happy. Light Blue. Jōvan Musk. Pink Sugar. Vera Wang. One by one, I picked up the boxes, read the descriptions, and then pulled out the bottles for a sniff.

I was about halfway through when reality hit. These had to be from Adrian.

I didn't know how he'd managed to get all of these delivered to the hotel in such a short amount of time, but money can make almost anything happen. Still, I didn't need the attention of a rich, spoiled Moroi; apparently he hadn't picked up on my signals. Regretfully, I started to place the perfumes back in the box—then stopped. Of course I'd return them . . . but there was no harm in sniffing the rest before I did.

Once more, I started pulling out bottle after bottle. Some I just sniffed the cap of; others I sprayed in the air. *Serendipity. Dolce & Gabbana. Shalimar. Daisy.* Note after note hit me: rose, violet, sandalwood, orange, vanilla, orchid . . .

By the time I was finished, my nose barely worked anymore. All of these had been designed for humans. They had a weaker sense of smell than vampires and even dhampirs, so these scents were extra strong. I had a new appreciation for what Adrian had meant about only a splash of perfume being necessary. If all these bottles were making me dizzy, I could only imagine what a Moroi would smell. The sensory overload wasn't really helping the headache I'd woken up with either.

I packed up the perfume for real this time, stopping only

when I came to a certain kind that I really liked. I hesitated, holding the little box in my hand. Then, I took the red bottle out and re-sniffed it. It was a crisp, sweet fragrance. There was some kind of fruit—but not a candied or sugary fruit. I racked my brain for a scent I'd once smelled on a girl I knew in my dorm. She'd told me the name. It was like a cherry . . . but sharper. Currant, that's what it was. And here it was in this perfume, mixed with some florals: lily of the valley and others I couldn't identify. Whatever the blend, something about it appealed to me. Sweet—but not *too* sweet. I read the box, looking for the name. *Amor Amor.*

"Fitting," I muttered, seeing how many love problems I seemed to have lately. But I kept the perfume anyway and repacked the rest.

Hoisting the box up in my arms, I took it down to the front desk and acquired some packing tape to reseal it. I also got directions to Adrian's room. Apparently, the Ivashkovs practically had their own wing. It wasn't too far from Tasha's room.

Feeling like a delivery girl, I walked down the hall and stopped in front of his door. Before I could manage to knock, it opened up, and Adrian stood before me. He looked as surprised as I felt.

"Little dhampir," he said cordially. "Didn't expect to see you here."

"I'm returning these." I hoisted the box toward him before he could protest. Clumsily, he caught it, staggering a bit in surprise. Once he had a good grip, he took a few steps back and set it on the floor.

"Didn't you like any of them?" he asked. "You want me to get you some more?"

"Don't send me any more gifts."

"It isn't a gift. It's a public service. What woman doesn't own perfume?"

"Don't do it again," I said firmly.

Suddenly, a voice behind him asked, "Rose? Is that you?"

I peered beyond him. Lissa.

"What are you doing here?"

Between my headache and what I had assumed was some interlude with Christian, I'd blocked her out as best I could this morning. Normally I would have known the instant I approached that she was inside the room. I opened myself up again, letting her shock run into me. She hadn't expected me to show up here.

"What are *you* doing here?" she asked.

"Ladies, ladies," he said teasingly. "No need to fight over me."

I glared. "We're not. I just want to know what's going on here."

A breath of aftershave hit me, and then I heard a voice behind me: "Me too."

I jumped. Spinning around, I saw Dimitri standing in the hallway. I had no clue what he was doing in the Ivashkov wing.

On his way to Tasha's room, a voice inside me suggested.

Dimitri no doubt always expected me to get into all sorts of trouble, but I think seeing Lissa there caught him off guard. He stepped past me and came into the room, looking between the three of us.

"Male and female students aren't supposed to be in each other's rooms."

I knew pointing out that Adrian wasn't technically a student wasn't going to get us out of trouble here. We weren't supposed to be in any guy's room.

"How do you keep doing this?" I asked Adrian, frustrated.

"Do what?"

"Keep making us look bad!"

He chuckled. "You guys are the ones who came here."

"You shouldn't have let them in," scolded Dimitri. "I'm sure you know the rules at St. Vladimir's."

Adrian shrugged. "Yeah, but I don't have to follow any school's stupid rules."

"Perhaps not," said Dimitri coldly. "But I would have thought you'd still respect those rules."

Adrian rolled his eyes. "I'm kind of surprised to find *you* lecturing about underage girls."

I saw the anger kindle in Dimitri's eyes, and for a moment, I thought I might have seen the loss of control I'd teased him about. But he stayed composed, and only his clenched fists showed how angry he was.

"Besides," continued Adrian, "nothing sordid was going on. We were just hanging out."

"If you want to 'hang out' with young girls, do it at one of the public areas."

I didn't really like Dimitri calling us 'young girls,' and I kind of felt like he was overreacting here. I also suspected part of his reaction had to do with the fact that *I* was here.

Adrian laughed just then, a weird kind of laugh that made my skin crawl. "Young girls? *Young* girls? Sure. Young and old at the same time. They've barely seen anything in life, yet they've already seen too much. One's marked with life, and one's marked with death . . . but *they're* the ones you're worried about? Worry about yourself, dhampir. Worry about you, and worry about me. We're the ones who are young."

The rest of us just sort of stared. I don't think anyone had expected Adrian to suddenly take an abrupt trip to Crazyville.

Adrian was calm and looked perfectly normal again. He turned away and strolled toward the window, glancing casually back at the rest of us as he pulled out his cigarettes.

"You ladies should probably go. He's right. I am a bad influence."

I exchanged looks with Lissa. Hurriedly, we both left and followed Dimitri down the hall toward the lobby.

"That was . . . strange," I said a couple of minutes later. It was stating the obvious, but, well, someone had to.

"Very," said Dimitri. He didn't sound angry so much as puzzled.

When we reached the lobby, I started to follow Lissa back toward our room, but Dimitri called to me.

"Rose," he said. "Can I talk to you?"

I felt a sympathetic rush of feeling from Lissa. I turned toward Dimitri and stepped off to the side of the room, out of the way of those passing through. A party of Moroi in diamonds and fur swept past us, anxious looks on their faces. Bellhops followed with luggage. People were still leaving in search of safer places. The Strigoi paranoia was far from over.

Dimitri's voice snapped my attention back to him. "That's Adrian Ivashkov." He said the name the same way everyone else did.

"Yeah, I know."

"This is the second time I've seen you with him."

"Yeah," I replied glibly. "We hang out sometimes."

Dimitri arched an eyebrow, then jerked his head back toward where we'd come from. "You hang out in his room a lot?"

Several retorts popped into my head, and then a golden one took precedence. "What happens between him and me is none of your business." I managed a tone very similar to the one he'd used on me when making a similar comment about him and Tasha.

"Actually, as long as you're at the Academy, what you do *is* my business."

"Not my personal life. You don't have any say in that."

"You're not an adult yet."

"I'm close enough. Besides, it's not like I'll magically become an adult on my eighteenth birthday."

"Clearly," he said.

I blushed. "That's not what I meant. I meant—"

"I know what you meant. And the technicalities don't matter right now. You're an Academy student. I'm your instructor. It's my job to help you and to keep you safe. Being in the bedroom of someone like *him* . . . well, that's not safe."

"I can handle Adrian Ivashkov," I muttered. "He's weird—really weird, apparently—but harmless."

I secretly wondered if Dimitri's problem might be that he was jealous. He hadn't pulled Lissa aside to yell at her. The thought made me slightly happy, but then I remembered my earlier curiosity about why Dimitri had even wandered by.

"Speaking of personal lives . . . I suppose you were off visiting Tasha, huh?"

I knew it was petty, and I expected a "none of your business" response. Instead he replied, "Actually, I was visiting your mother."

"You going to hook up with her too?" I knew of course that he wasn't, but the quip seemed too good to pass up.

He seemed to know that too and merely gave me a weary glance. "No, we were looking over some new data about the Strigoi in the Drozdov attack."

My anger and snarkiness dried up. The Drozdovs. The

Badicas. Suddenly, everything that had happened this morning seemed incredibly trivial. How could I have stood there arguing with Dimitri about romances that might or might not be happening when he and the other guardians were trying to protect us?

"What'd you find out?" I asked quietly.

"We've managed to track some of the Strigoi," he said. "Or at least the humans with them. There were witnesses who lived nearby who spotted a few of the cars the group used. The plates were all from different states—the group appears to have split up, probably to make it harder for us. But one of the witnesses did catch one plate number. It's registered to an address in Spokane."

"Spokane?" I asked incredulously. "Spokane, *Washington*? Who makes Spokane their hideout?" I'd been there once. It was about as boring as every other backwoods northwest city.

"Strigoi, apparently," he said, deadpan. "The address was fake, but other evidence shows they really are there. There's a kind of shopping plaza that has some underground tunnels. There've been Strigoi sightings around that area."

"Then . . ." I frowned. "Are you going to go after them? Is somebody going to? I mean, this is what Tasha's been saying all along. . . . If we know where they are . . ."

He shook his head. "The guardians can't do anything without permission from higher up. That's not going to happen anytime soon."

I sighed. "Because the Moroi talk too much."

"They're being cautious," he said.

I felt myself getting worked up again. "Come *on*. Even you can't want to be careful on this one. You actually know where Strigoi are hiding out. Strigoi who massacred children. Don't you want to go after them when they don't expect it?" I sounded like Mason now.

"It's not that easy," he said. "We answer to the Guardian Council and the Moroi government. We can't just run off and act on impulse. And anyway, we don't know everything yet. You should never walk into any situation without knowing all the details."

"Zen life lessons again," I sighed. I ran a hand through my hair, tucking it behind my ears. "Why'd you tell me this, anyway? This is guardian stuff. Not the kind of thing you let novices in on."

He considered his words, and his expression softened. He always looked amazing, but I liked him best like this. "I've said a few things . . . the other day and today . . . that I shouldn't have. Things that insulted your age. You're seventeen . . . but you're capable of handling and processing the same things those much older than you do."

My chest grew light and fluttery. "Really?"

He nodded. "You're still really young in a lot of ways—and act young—but the only way to really change that is to treat you like an adult. I need to do that more. I know you'll take this information and understand how important it is and keep it to yourself."

I didn't love being told I acted young, but I liked the idea that he would talk to me like an equal.

"Dimka," came a voice. Tasha Ozera walked up to us. She smiled when she saw me. "Hello, Rose."

There went my mood. "Hey," I said flatly.

She placed a hand on Dimitri's forearm, sliding her fingers over the leather of his coat. I eyed those fingers angrily. How dare they touch him?

"You've got that look," she told him.

"What look?" he asked. The stern look he'd worn with me vanished. There was a small, knowing smile on his lips. Almost a playful one.

"That look that says you're going to be on duty all day."

"Really? I have a look like that?" There was a teasing, mocking tone to his voice.

She nodded. "When does your shift technically end?"

Dimitri actually looked—I swear—sheepish. "An hour ago."

"You can't keep doing this," she groaned. "You need a break."

"Well . . . if you consider that I'm always Lissa's guardian . . ."

"For now," she said knowingly. I felt sicker than I had last night. "There's a big pool tournament going on upstairs."

"I can't," he said, but the smile was still on his face. "Even though I haven't played in a long time . . ."

What the—? Dimitri played *pool*?

Suddenly, it didn't matter that we'd just had a discussion about him treating me like an adult. Some small part of me did know what a compliment that was—but the rest of me wanted him to treat me like he did Tasha. Playful. Teasing. Casual. They were so familiar with each other, so completely at ease.

"Come on, then," she begged. "Just one round! We could take them all."

"I can't," he repeated. He sounded regretful. "Not with everything going on."

She sobered a little. "No. I suppose not." Glancing at me, she said teasingly, "I hope you realize what a hard-core role model you have here. He's never off duty."

"Well," I said, copying her lilting tone from earlier, *"for now*, at least."

Tasha looked puzzled. I don't think it occurred to her I'd be making fun of her. Dimitri's dark look told me he knew exactly what I was doing. I immediately realized I'd just killed whatever progress I'd made as an adult.

"We're finished here, Rose. Remember what I said."

"Yeah," I said, turning away. I suddenly wanted to go to my room and veg for a while. This day was making me tired already. "Definitely."

I hadn't gotten far when I ran into Mason. Good God. Men everywhere.

"You're mad," he said as soon as he looked at my face. He had a knack for discovering my moods. "What happened?"

"Some . . . authority problems. It's been a weird morning."

I sighed, unable to get Dimitri off the brain. Looking at Mason, I remembered how I'd been convinced I wanted to get serious with him last night. I was a head case. I couldn't make up my mind about anyone. Deciding the best way to banish one guy was to pay attention to another, I grabbed Mason's hand and steered him away.

"Come on. Wasn't the deal to go somewhere . . . um, private today?"

"I figured you weren't drunk anymore," he joked. But his eyes looked very, very serious. And interested. "I assumed it was all off."

"Hey, I stand by my claims, no matter what." Opening my mind, I searched for Lissa. She was no longer in our room. She'd gone off to some other royal event, no doubt still practicing for Priscilla Voda's big dinner. "Come on," I told Mason. "We'll go to my room."

Aside from when Dimitri inconveniently happened to be passing by someone's room, nobody was really enforcing the mixed-gender rule. It was practically like being back in my Academy dorms. As Mason and I went upstairs, I related to him what Dimitri had told me about the Strigoi in Spokane. Dimitri had told me to keep it to myself, but I was mad at him again, and I didn't see any harm in telling Mason. I knew he'd be interested in this.

I was right. Mason got really worked up.

"What?" he exclaimed as we walked into my room. "They're not *doing* anything?"

I shrugged and sat on my bed. "Dimitri said—"

"I know, I know . . . I heard you. About being careful and all that." Mason paced around my room angrily. "But if those Strigoi go after another Moroi . . . another family . . . damn it! They're going to wish they weren't so careful then."

"Forget about it," I said. I felt kind of miffed that me on a bed wasn't enough to deter him from crazy battle plans. "There's nothing we can do."

He stopped walking. "*We* could go."

"Go where?" I asked stupidly.

"To Spokane. There are buses you can catch in town."

"I . . . wait. You want us to go to Spokane and take on Strigoi?"

"Sure. Eddie'd do it too . . . we could go to that mall. They wouldn't be organized or anything, so we could wait and pick them off one by one . . ."

I could only stare. "When did you get so dumb?"

"Oh, I see. Thanks for the vote of confidence."

"It's not about confidence," I argued, standing up and approaching him. "You kick major ass. I've seen it. But this . . . this isn't the way. We can't go get Eddie and take on Strigoi. We need more people. More planning. More information."

I rested my hands on his chest. He placed his over them and smiled. The fire of battle was still in his eyes, but I could tell his mind was shifting to more immediate concerns. Like me.

"I didn't mean to call you dumb," I told him. "I'm sorry."

"You're just saying that now because you want to have your way with me."

"Of course I am," I laughed, happy to see him relax. The nature of this conversation reminded me a little of the one Christian and Lissa had had in the chapel.

"Well," he said, "I don't think I'm going to be too hard to take advantage of."

"Good. Because there are *lots* of things I want to do."

I slid my hands up and around his neck. His skin was warm beneath my fingers, and I remembered how much I'd enjoyed kissing him last night.

Suddenly, out of nowhere, he said, "You really are his student."

"Whose?"

"Belikov's. I was just thinking about when you mentioned needing more information and stuff. You act just like him. You've gotten all serious since you've been hanging out with him."

"No, I haven't."

Mason had pulled me closer, but now I suddenly didn't feel so romantic. I'd wanted to make out and *forget* Dimitri for a while, not have a conversation about him. Where had this come from? Mason was supposed to be distracting me.

He didn't notice anything was wrong. "You've just changed, that's all. It's not bad . . . just different."

Something about that made me angry, but before I could snap back, his mouth met mine in a kiss. Reasonable discussions sort of vanished. A bit of that dark temper started to rise in me, but I simply channeled that intensity into physicality as Mason and I fell on top of each other. I yanked him down on the bed, managing to do so without stopping the kissing. I was nothing if not a multitasker. I dug my nails into his back while his hands slid up the back of my neck and released the ponytail I'd just made minutes ago. Running his fingers through the unbound hair, he shifted his mouth down and kissed my neck.

"You are . . . amazing," he told me. And I could tell that he meant it. His whole face glowed with affection for me.

I arched upward, letting his lips press harder against my skin while his hands slipped under the bottom of my shirt. They trailed upward along my stomach, just barely tracing the edge of my bra.

Considering we'd just been having an argument a minute ago, I was surprised to see things escalating so quickly. Honestly, though . . . I didn't mind. This was the way I lived my life. Everything was always fast and intense with me. The night Dimitri and I had fallen victim to Victor Dashkov's lust charm, there'd been some pretty furious passion going on too. Dimitri had controlled it, though, so sometimes we'd taken things slowly . . . and that had been wonderful in its own way. But most of the time, we hadn't been able to hold ourselves back. I could feel it all over again. The ways his hands had run over my body. The deep, powerful kisses.

It was then that I realized something.

I was kissing Mason, but in my head, I was with Dimitri. And it wasn't like I was simply remembering either. I was actually imagining I was with Dimitri—right *now*—reliving that night all over again. With my eyes closed, it was easy to pretend.

But when I opened them and saw Mason's eyes, I knew he was with *me*. He adored me and had wanted me for a long time. For me to do this . . . to be with him and pretend I was with someone else . . .

It wasn't right.

I wiggled out of his reach. "No . . . don't."

Mason stopped immediately because that's the kind of guy he was.

"Too much?" he asked. I nodded. "That's okay. We don't have to do that."

He reached for me again, and I moved farther away. "No, I just don't . . . I don't know. Let's call it quits, okay?"

"I . . ." He was speechless for a moment. "What happened to the 'lots of things' you wanted to do?"

Yeah . . . it looked pretty bad, but what could I say? *I can't get physical with you because when I do, I just think about the other guy I actually want. You're just a stand-in.*

I swallowed, feeling stupid. "I'm sorry, Mase. I just can't."

He sat up and ran a hand over his hair. "Okay. All right."

I could hear the hardness in his voice. "You're mad."

He glanced over at me, a stormy expression on his face. "I'm just confused. I can't read your signals. One moment you're hot, the next you're cold. You tell me you want me, you tell me you don't. If you picked one, that'd be fine, but you keep making me think one thing and then you end up going in a completely different direction. Not just now—all the time."

It was true. I had gone back and forth with him. Sometimes I was flirty, other times I completely ignored him.

"Is there something you want me to do?" he asked when I didn't say anything. "Something that'll . . . I don't know. Make you feel better about me?"

"I don't know," I said weakly.

He sighed. "Then what do you want in general?"

Dimitri, I thought. Instead, I repeated myself. "I don't know."

With a groan, he stood up and headed for the door. "Rose, for someone who claims she wants to gather as much information as possible, you really have a lot to learn about yourself."

The door slammed behind him. The noise made me flinch, and as I stared at where Mason had just stood, I realized he was right. I did have a lot to learn.

SIXTEEN

LISSA FOUND ME LATER IN the day. I'd fallen asleep after Mason left, too dejected to leave the bed. Her slamming of the door jolted me awake.

I was happy to see her. I needed to spill about the fumbled thing with Mason, but before I could, I read her feelings. They were as troubled as mine. So, as always, I put her first.

"What happened?"

She sat on her bed, sinking into the feather duvet, her feelings both furious and sad. "Christian."

"Really?" I'd never known them to fight. They teased each other a lot, but it was hardly the kind of thing that could nearly bring her to tears.

"He found out . . . I was with Adrian this morning."

"Oh, wow," I said. "Yeah. That might be a problem." Standing up, I walked over to the dresser and found my brush. Wincing, I stood in front of the gilt-framed mirror and began brushing out the snarls acquired during my nap.

She groaned. "But nothing happened! Christian's freaking out over nothing. I can't believe he doesn't trust me."

"He trusts you. The whole thing's just weird, that's all." I thought about Dimitri and Tasha. "Jealousy makes people do and say stupid things."

"But nothing happened," she repeated. "I mean, you were there and—hey, I never found out. What *were* you doing there?"

"Adrian sent me a bunch of perfume."

"He—you mean that giant box you were carrying?"

I nodded.

"Whoa."

"Yeah. I came to return it," I said. "The question is, what were you doing there?"

"Just talking," she said. She started to light up, on the verge of telling me something, but then she paused. I felt the thought almost reach the front of her mind and then get shoved back. "I've got a lot to tell you, but first tell me what's up with you."

"Nothing's up with me."

"Whatever, Rose. I'm not psychic like you, but I know when you're pissed off about something. You've been kind of down since Christmas. What's up?"

Now wasn't the time to get into what had happened on Christmas when my mom told me about Tasha and Dimitri. But I did tell Lissa the story about Mason—editing out why I had stopped—and simply driving home how I had.

"Well . . ." she said when I finished. "That was your right."

"I know. But I kind of led him on. I can see why he'd be upset."

"You guys can probably fix it, though. Go talk to him. He's crazy about you."

It was more than miscommunication. Things with Mason and me couldn't be patched up so easily. "I don't know," I told her. "Not everyone's like you and Christian."

Her face darkened. "Christian. I still can't believe he's being so stupid about this."

I didn't mean to, but I laughed. "Liss, you guys'll kiss and make up in like a day. More than kiss, probably."

It slipped out before I could stop it. Her eyes widened. "You know." She shook her head in exasperation. "Of *course* you know."

"Sorry," I said. I hadn't meant to let her know I knew about the sex thing, not until she told me herself.

She eyed me. "How much do you know?"

"Um, not much," I lied. I'd finished brushing my hair but began playing with the brush's handle in order to avoid her eyes.

"I have *got* to learn to keep you out of my mind," she muttered.

"Only way I can 'talk' to you lately." Another slipup.

"What's that supposed to mean?" she demanded.

"Nothing . . . I . . ." She was giving me a sharp look. "I . . . I don't know. I just feel like we don't talk as much anymore."

"Takes two to fix that," she said, voice kind again.

"You're right," I said, not pointing out that two could fix that only if one wasn't always with her boyfriend. True, I was guilty in my own way of locking things up—but I *had* wanted to talk to her a number of times lately. The timing just never seemed to be right—not even now. "You know, I never thought you'd be first. Or I guess I never thought I'd be a senior and still be a virgin."

"Yeah," she said dryly. "Me either."

"Hey! What's *that* supposed to mean?"

She grinned, then caught sight of her watch. Her smile fell. "Ugh. I've got to go to Priscilla's banquet. Christian was supposed to go with me, but he's off being an idiot. . . ." Her eyes focused hopefully on me.

"What? No. Please, Liss. You know how I hate those formal royal things."

"Oh, come on," she begged. "Christian flaked out. You can't throw me to the wolves. And didn't you just say we needed to talk more?" I groaned. "Besides, when you're my guardian, you'll have to do these things all the time."

"I know," I said darkly. "I thought I could maybe enjoy my last six months of freedom."

But in the end, she conned me into going with her, as we'd both known she would.

We didn't have much time, and I had to do a rush shower, blow-dry, and makeup job. I'd brought Tasha's dress on a whim, and while I still wanted her to suffer horribly for being attracted to Dimitri, I was grateful for her present now. I pulled on the silken material, happy to see the shade of red was just as killer on me as I'd imagined. It was a long, Asian-style dress with flowers embroidered into the silk. The high neck and long hem covered a lot of skin, but the material clung to me and looked sexy in a different kind of way than showing a lot of skin did. My black eye was practically nonexistent by now.

Lissa, as always, looked amazing. She wore a deep purple dress by Johnna Raski, a well-known Moroi designer. It was sleeveless and made of satin. The tiny amethyst-like crystals set into the straps sparkled against her pale skin. She wore her hair up in a loose, artfully styled bun.

When we reached the banquet room, we drew a few eyes. I don't think the royals had expected the Dragomir princess to bring her dhampir friend to this highly anticipated, invitation-only dinner. But hey, Lissa's invite had said "and guest." She and I took our places at one of the tables with some royals whose names I promptly forgot. They were happy to ignore me, and I was happy to be ignored.

Besides, it wasn't like there weren't plenty of other distractions. This room was done all in silver and blue. Midnight blue silk cloths covered the tables, so shiny and smooth that I was terrified to eat on them. Sconces of beeswax candles hung all over the walls, and a fireplace decorated with stained glass crackled away in one corner. The effect was a spectacular panorama of color and light, dizzying to the eye. In the corner, a slim Moroi woman played soft cello music, her face dreamy as she focused on the song. The clinking of crystal wineglasses complemented the strings' low, sweet notes.

Dinner was equally amazing. The food was elaborate, but I recognized everything on my plate (china, of course) and liked

all of it. No foie gras here. Salmon in a sauce of shiitake mushrooms. A salad with pears and goat cheese. Delicate almond-
stuffed pastries for dessert. My only complaint was that the
portions were small. The food seemed more like it was there
to simply decorate the plates, and I swear, I finished it in ten
bites. Moroi might still need food along with their blood, but
they didn't need as much as a human—or, say, a growing
dhamphir girl—needed.

Still, the food alone could have justified me coming along
on this venture, I decided. Except, when the meal ended, Lissa
told me we couldn't leave.

"We have to mingle," she whispered.

Mingle?

Lissa laughed at my discomfort. "You're the social one."

It was true. In most circumstances, I was the one who put
myself out there and wasn't afraid to talk to people. Lissa
tended to be shyer. Only, with this group, the tables were
turned. This was her element, not mine, and it amazed me
to see just how well she could interact with royal high society now. She was perfect, polished and polite. Everyone was
eager to talk to her, and she always seemed to know the right
thing to say. She wasn't using compulsion, exactly, but she definitely put out an air that drew others to her. I think it might
have been an unconscious effect of spirit. Even with the meds,
her magical and natural charisma came through. Whereas
intense social interactions had once been forced and stress-
ful for her, she now conducted them with ease. I was proud

of her. Most of the conversation stayed pretty light: fashion, royal love lives, etc. No one seemed to want to spoil the atmosphere with ugly Strigoi talk.

So I clung to her side for the rest of the night. I tried to tell myself it was just practice for the future, when I'd follow her around like a quiet shadow anyway. The truth was, I just felt too uncomfortable with this group and knew my usual snarky defense mechanisms really weren't useful here. Plus, I was painfully aware that I was the only dhampir dinner guest. There were other dhampirs, yes, but they were in formal guardian mode, hovering on the periphery of the room.

As Lissa worked the crowd, we drifted over to a small group of Moroi whose voices were growing louder. One of them I recognized. He was the guy from the fight that I'd helped break up, only this time he wore a striking black tuxedo instead of a swimsuit. He glanced up at our approach, blatantly checked us out, but apparently didn't remember me. Ignoring us, he continued on with his argument. Not surprisingly, Moroi protection was the topic. He was the one who'd been in favor of Moroi going on the offensive against the Strigoi.

"What part of 'suicide' don't you understand?" asked one of the men standing nearby. He had silvery hair and a bushy mustache. He wore a tux too, but the younger guy looked better in one. "Moroi training as soldiers will be the end of our race."

"It's not suicide," exclaimed the young guy. "It's the right thing to do. We have to start looking out for ourselves. Learning to fight and use our magic is our greatest asset, other than the guardians."

"Yes, but with the guardians, we don't need other assets," said Silver Hair. "You've been listening to non-royals. They don't have any guardians of their own, so of course they're scared. But that's no reason to drag *us* down and put *our* lives at risk."

"Then don't," said Lissa suddenly. Her voice was soft, but everyone in the little group stopped and looked at her. "When you talk about Moroi learning how to fight, you make it sound like an all-or-nothing matter. It's not. If you don't want to fight, then you shouldn't have to. I completely understand." The man looked slightly mollified. "But, that's because you *can* rely on your guardians. A lot of Moroi can't. And if they want to learn self-defense, there's no reason why they shouldn't do it on their own."

The younger guy grinned triumphantly at his adversary. "There, you see?"

"It's not that easy," countered Silver Hair. "If it was just a matter of you crazy people wanting to get yourselves killed, then fine. Go do it. But where are you going to learn all these so-called fighting skills?"

"We'll figure the magic out on our own. Guardians will teach us actual physical fighting."

"Yes, see? I knew that was where this was going. Even if

the rest of us don't take part in your suicide mission, you still want to strip us of our guardians to train up your pretend army."

The young guy scowled at the word *pretend*, and I wondered if more fists would fly. "You owe it to us."

"No, they don't," said Lissa.

Intrigued gazes turned her way again. This time, it was Silver Hair who regarded her triumphantly. The younger guy's features flushed with anger.

"Guardians are the best battle resources we have."

"They are," she agreed, "but that doesn't give you the right to take them away from their duty." Silver Hair practically glowed.

"Then how are we supposed to learn?" demanded the other guy.

"The same way guardians do," Lissa informed him. "If you want to learn to fight, go to the academies. Form classes and start at the beginning, the same way the novices do. That way, you won't be taking guardians away from active protection. It's a safe environment, and the guardians there specialize in teaching students anyway." She paused thoughtfully. "You could even start making defense part of the standard curriculum for Moroi students already there."

Astonished stares fell on her, mine included. It was such an elegant solution, and everyone else around us realized it. It gave no party 100 percent of its demands, but it met most in a way that didn't really harm the other side. Pure genius. The other Moroi studied her with wonder and fascination.

Suddenly, everyone started talking at once, excited about the idea. They drew Lissa in, and soon there was a passionate conversation going on about her plan. I got shuffled to the edges and decided that was just fine. Then I retreated altogether and sought out a corner near a door.

Along the way, I passed a server with a tray of hors d'oeuvres. Still hungry, I eyed them suspiciously but saw nothing that looked like the foie gras from the other day. I gestured to one that looked like some sort of braised, rare meat.

"Is that goose liver?" I asked.

She shook her head. "Sweetbread."

That didn't sound bad. I reached for it.

"It's pancreas," said a voice behind me. I jerked back.

"What?" I squeaked. The waitress took my shock for rejection and moved on.

Adrian Ivashkov moved into my line of sight, looking immensely pleased with himself.

"Are you messing with me?" I asked. "'Sweetbread' is *pancreas*?" I don't know why that shocked me so much. Moroi consumed blood. Why not internal organs? Still, I repressed a shudder.

Adrian shrugged. "It's really good."

I shook my head in disgust. "Oh, man. Rich people suck."

His amusement continued. "What are you doing here, little dhampir? Are you following me around?"

"Of course not," I scoffed. He was dressed to perfection, as always. "Especially not after all the trouble you've gotten us into."

He flashed one of his tantalizing smiles, and despite how much he annoyed me, I again felt that overwhelming urge to be near him. What was up with that?

"I don't know," he teased. He looked perfectly sane now, exhibiting no trace of the weird behavior I'd witnessed in his room. And yeah, he looked *a lot* better in a tuxedo than any guy I'd seen in there so far. "As many times as we keep seeing each other? This is, what, the fifth time? It's starting to look suspicious. Don't worry, though. I won't tell your boyfriend. Either of them."

I opened my mouth to protest, then remembered he'd seen me with Dimitri earlier. I refused to blush. "I only have *one* boyfriend. Sort of. Maybe not anymore. And anyway, there's nothing to tell. I don't even like you."

"No?" asked Adrian, still smiling. He leaned toward me, like he had a secret to share. "Then why are you wearing my perfume?"

This time, I did blush. I took a step back. "I'm not."

He laughed. "Of course you are. I counted the boxes after you left. Besides, I can smell it on you. It's nice. Sharp . . . but still sweet—just like I'm sure you are deep down inside. And you got it right, you know. Just enough to add an edge . . . but not enough to drown your own scent." The way he said "scent" made it sound like a dirty word.

Royal Moroi might make me uncomfortable, but smartass

guys hitting on me didn't. I dealt with them on a regular basis. I shook off my shyness and remembered who I was.

"Hey," I said, tossing my hair back. "I had every right to take one. You offered them. Your mistake is in assuming me taking one means anything. It doesn't. Except that maybe you should be more careful with where you dump all that money of yours."

"Ooh, Rose Hathaway is here to play, folks." He paused and took a glass of what looked like champagne from a passing waiter. "You want one?"

"I don't drink."

"Right." Adrian handed me a glass anyway, then shooed the waiter away and took a drink of the champagne. I had a feeling it wasn't his first of the night. "So. Sounds like our Vasilisa put my dad in his place."

"Your . . ." I glanced back at the group I'd just left. Silver Hair still stood there, gesticulating wildly. "That guy's your dad?"

"That's what my mom says."

"You agree with him? About how Moroi fighting would be suicide?"

Adrian shrugged and took another sip. "I don't really have an opinion on that."

"That's not possible. How can you not feel one way or another?"

"Dunno. Just not something I think about. I've got better things to do."

"Like stalk me," I suggested. "And Lissa." I still wanted to know why she'd been in his room.

He smiled again. "I told you, you're the one following me."

"Yeah, yeah, I know. Five times—" I stopped. "Five times?"

He nodded.

"No, it's only been four." With my free hand, I ticked them off. "There was that first night, the night at the spa, then when I came to your room, and now tonight."

The smile turned secretive. "If you say so."

"I *do* say so. . . ." Again, my words trailed off. I had talked to Adrian one other time. Sort of. "You can't mean . . ."

"Mean what?" A curious, eager expression lit his eyes. It was more hopeful than presumptuous.

I swallowed, recalling the dream. "Nothing." Without thinking about it, I took a drink of champagne. Across the room, Lissa's feelings burned back to me, calm and content. Good.

"Why are you smiling?" Adrian asked.

"Because Lissa's still over there, working that crowd."

"No surprise there. She's one of those people who can charm anyone she wants if she tries hard enough. Even people who hate her."

I gave him a wry look. "I feel that way when I talk to you."

"But you don't hate me," he said, finishing the last of his champagne. "Not really."

"I don't like you either."

"So you keep saying." He took a step toward me, not threatening, just making the space between us more intimate. "But I can live with that."

"Rose!"

The sharpness of my mother's voice cut through the air. A few people within earshot glanced over at us. My mother—all five angry feet of her—stormed up to us.

SEVENTEEN

"WHAT DO YOU THINK YOU'RE doing?" she demanded. Her voice was still too loud as far as I was concerned.

"Nothing, I—"

"Excuse us, Lord Ivashkov," she growled. Then, like I was five years old, she grabbed me by my arm and jerked me out of the room. Champagne sloshed out of my glass and splashed onto the skirt of my dress.

"What do you think *you're* doing?" I exclaimed, once we were out in the hall. Mournfully, I looked down at my dress. "This is *silk*. You could have ruined it."

She grabbed the champagne flute and set it down on a nearby table. "Good. Maybe it'll stop you from dressing up like a cheap whore."

"Whoa," I said, shocked. "That's kind of harsh. And where do you get off turning motherly all of a sudden?" I gestured to the dress. "This isn't exactly cheap. You thought it was nice of Tasha to give it to me."

"That's because I didn't expect you to wear it out with Moroi and make a spectacle of yourself."

"I'm not making a spectacle of myself. And anyway, it covers everything up."

"A dress that tight might as well be showing everything," she retorted. She, of course, was dressed in guardian black: tailored black linen pants and a matching blazer. She had a few curves of her own, but the clothing hid them.

"Especially when you're with a group like that. Your body's . . . conspicuous. And flirting with Moroi doesn't really help."

"I wasn't flirting with him."

The accusation made me angry because I felt I'd been on really good behavior lately. I used to flirt all the time—and do other things—with Moroi guys, but after a few talks and one embarrassing incident with Dimitri, I'd realized how stupid that was. Dhampir girls did have to be careful with Moroi guys, and I kept that in mind all the time now.

Something petty occurred to me. "Besides," I said mockingly, "isn't that what I'm supposed to do? Hook up with a Moroi and further my race? It's what *you* did."

She glowered. "Not when I was your age."

"You were only a few years older than me."

"Don't do anything stupid, Rose," she said. "You're too young for a baby. You don't have the life experience for it—you haven't even lived your own life yet. You won't be able to do the kind of job you wish you could."

I groaned, mortified. "Are we really even discussing this? How did we go from me allegedly flirting to suddenly having a litter? I'm not having sex with him or anyone else, and even if I were, I know about birth control. Why are you talking to me like I'm a child?"

"Because you act like one." It was remarkably like what Dimitri had told me.

I glared. "So you're going to send me to my room now?"

"No, Rose." She suddenly looked tired. "You don't have to go to your room, but don't go back in there, either. Hopefully you didn't draw too much attention."

"You make it sound like I was giving a lap dance in there," I told her. "I just had dinner with Lissa."

"You'd be surprised what things can spark rumors," she warned. "Especially with Adrian Ivashkov."

With that, she turned and headed off down the hall. Watching her, I felt anger and resentment burn through me. Overreact much? I hadn't done anything wrong. I knew she had her whole blood-whore paranoia, but this was extreme, even for her. Worst of all, she'd dragged me out of there, and several people had witnessed it. For someone who supposedly didn't want me attracting attention, she'd kind of messed that one up.

A couple of Moroi who'd been standing near Adrian and me walked out of the room. They glanced in my direction and then whispered something as they passed.

"Thanks, Mom," I muttered to myself.

Humiliated, I stalked off in the opposite direction, not really sure where I was going. I headed out toward the back of the lodge, away from all the activity.

The hall eventually ended, but a door leading to some stairs sat on the left. The door was unlocked, so I followed the stairs upward to another door. To my pleasure, it opened up onto a small rooftop deck that didn't appear to see much use. A blanket of snow lay over it all, but it was early morning out here, and the sun shone brightly, making everything glitter.

I brushed snow off of a large, box-like object that looked to be part of the ventilation system. Heedless of my dress, I sat down on it. Wrapping my arms around myself, I stared off, taking in the view and the sun I rarely got to enjoy.

I was startled when the door opened a few minutes later. When I looked back I was even more startled still to see Dimitri emerge. My heart gave a small flutter, and I turned away, unsure what to think. His boots crunched in the snow as he walked over to where I was sitting. A moment later, he took off his long coat and draped it over my shoulders.

He sat down beside me. "You must be freezing."

I was, but I didn't want to admit it. "The sun's out."

He tipped his head back, looking up at the perfect blue sky. I knew he missed the sun as much as I did sometimes. "It is. But we're still on a mountain in the middle of winter."

I didn't answer. We sat there in a comfortable silence for a while. Occasionally, a light wind blew clouds of snow around. It was night for Moroi, and most would be going to bed soon, so the ski runs were quiet.

"My life is a disaster," I finally said.

"It's not a disaster," he said automatically.

"Did you follow me from the party?"

"Yes."

"I didn't even know you were there." His dark clothes indicated he must have been on guardian duty at the party. "So you saw the illustrious Janine cause a commotion by dragging me out."

"It wasn't a commotion. Hardly anyone noticed. I saw because I was watching you."

I refused to let myself get excited over that. "That's not what she said," I told him. "I might as well have been working a corner as far as she was concerned."

I relayed the conversation from the hallway.

"She's just worried about you," Dimitri said when I finished.

"She overreacted."

"Sometimes mothers are overprotective."

I stared at him. "Yeah, but this is *my* mother. And she didn't seem that protective, really. I think she was more worried I'd embarrass her or something. And all that becoming-a-mother-too-young stuff was stupid. I'm not going to do anything like that."

"Maybe she wasn't talking about you," he said.

More silence. My jaw fell open.

You don't have the life experience for it—you haven't even lived your own life yet. You won't be able to do the kind of job you wish you could.

My mom had been twenty when I was born. Growing up, that had always seemed really old to me. But now . . . that was only a few years off for me. Not old at all. Did she think she'd had me too soon? Had she done a shoddy job raising me simply because she didn't know any better at the time? Did she regret the way things had turned out between us? And was it . . . was it *maybe* possible that she'd had some personal experience of her own with Moroi men and people spreading rumors about her? I'd had inherited a lot of her features. I mean, I'd even noticed tonight what a nice figure she had. She had a pretty face, too—for a nearly forty-year-old, I mean. She'd probably been really, really good-looking when she was younger. . . .

I sighed. I didn't want to think about that. If I did, I might have to reevaluate my relationship with her—maybe even acknowledge my mother as a real person—and I already had too many relationships stressing me. Lissa always worried me, even though she seemed to be okay for a change. My so-called romance with Mason was in shambles. And then, of course, there was Dimitri. . . .

"We aren't fighting right now." I blurted out.

He gave me a sidelong look. "Do you want to fight?"

"No. I hate fighting with you. Verbally, I mean. I don't mind in the gym."

I thought I detected the hint of a smile. Always a half-smile for me. Rarely a full one. "I don't like fighting with you either."

Sitting next to him there, I marveled at the warm and happy emotions springing up inside of me. There was something about being around him that felt so good, that moved me in a way Mason couldn't. You can't force love, I realized. It's there or it isn't. If it's not there, you've got to be able to admit it. If it is there, you've got to do whatever it takes to protect the ones you love.

The next words that came out of my mouth astonished me, both because they were completely unselfish and because I actually meant them.

"You should take it."

He flinched. "What?"

"Tasha's offer. You should take her up on it. It's a really great chance."

I remembered my mom's words about being ready for children. I wasn't. Maybe she hadn't been. But Tasha was. And I knew Dimitri was too. They got along really well. He could go be her guardian, have some kids with her . . . it would be a good deal for both of them.

"I never expected to hear you say anything like that," he told me, voice tight. "Especially after—"

"What a bitch I've been? Yeah." I tugged his coat tighter against the cold. It smelled like him. It was intoxicating, and I could half-imagine being wrapped in his embrace. Adrian might have been onto something about the power of scent. "Well. Like I said, I don't want to fight anymore. I don't want us to hate each other. And . . . well . . ." I squeezed my eyes shut and then opened them. "No matter how I feel about *us* . . . I want you to be happy."

Silence yet again. I noticed then that my chest hurt.

Dimitri reached out and put his arm around me. He pulled me to him, and I rested my head on his chest. "Roza," was all he said.

It was the first time he'd *really* touched me since the night of the lust charm. The practice room had been something different . . . more animal. This wasn't even about sex. It was just about being close to someone you cared about, about the emotion that kind of connection flooded you with.

Dimitri might run off with Tasha, but I would still love him. I would probably always love him.

I cared about Mason. But I would probably never love him.

I sighed into Dimitri, just wishing I could stay like that forever. It felt right being with him. And—no matter how much the thought of him and Tasha made me ache—doing what was best for him felt right. Now, I knew, it was time to stop being a coward and do something else that was right. Mason had said I needed to learn something about myself. I just had.

Reluctantly, I pulled away and handed Dimitri his coat. I stood up. He regarded me curiously, sensing my unease.

"Where you going?" he asked.

"To break someone's heart," I replied.

I admired Dimitri for a heartbeat more—the dark, knowing eyes and silken hair. Then I headed inside. I had to apologize to Mason . . . and tell him there'd never be anything between us.

EIGHTEEN

THE HIGH HEELS WERE STARTING to hurt me, so I took them off when I went back inside, walking barefoot through the lodge. I hadn't been to Mason's room, but I remembered him mentioning the number once and found it without difficulty.

Shane, Mason's roommate, opened the door a few moments after I knocked. "Hey, Rose."

He stepped aside for me, and I walked in, peering around. Some infomercial was playing on the TV—one downside of a nocturnal life was a shortage of good programming—and empty soda cans covered nearly every flat surface. There was no sign of Mason anywhere.

"Where is he?" I asked.

Shane stifled a yawn. "I thought he was with you."

"I haven't seen him all day."

He yawned again, then frowned in thought. "He was throwing some stuff in a bag earlier. I figured you guys were running off for some crazy romantic getaway. Picnic or something. Hey, nice dress."

"Thanks," I murmured, feeling a frown of my own coming on.

Packing a bag? That didn't make any sense. There was

nowhere to go. There was no *way* to go, either. This resort was as tightly guarded as the Academy. Lissa and I had only managed to break out of that place with compulsion, and it had still been a pain in the ass. Yet, why on earth would Mason pack a bag if he wasn't leaving?

I asked Shane a few more questions and decided to follow up on the possibility, crazy as it seemed. I found the guardian in charge of security and scheduling. He gave me the names of those guardians who'd been on duty around the resort's borders when Mason had last been seen. Most of the names I knew, and most were off duty now, making them easy to find.

Unfortunately, the first couple hadn't seen Mason around today. When they asked why I wanted to know, I gave vague answers and hurried off. The third person on my list was a guy named Alan, a guardian who usually worked the Academy's lower campus. He was just coming in after skiing, taking his equipment off near the door. Recognizing me, he smiled as I approached.

"Sure, I saw him," he said, bending down to his boots.

Relief flooded over me. Until then, I hadn't realized how worried I'd been.

"Do you know where he is?"

"Nope. Let him and Eddie Castile . . . and, what's her name, the Rinaldi girl, out through the north gate and didn't see them after that."

I stared. Alan continued unhooking his skis as though we were discussing slope conditions.

"You let Mason and Eddie . . . and *Mia* out?"

"Yup."

"Um . . . why?"

He finished and looked back up at me, a kind of happy and bemused look on his face. "Because they asked me."

An icy feeling started creeping through me. I found out which guardian had watched the north gate with Alan and immediately sought him out. That guardian gave me the same response. He'd let Mason, Eddie, and Mia out, no questions asked. And, like Alan, he didn't seem to think there was anything wrong with that. He appeared almost dazed. It was a look I'd seen before . . . a look that came over people when Lissa used compulsion.

In particular, I'd seen it happen when Lissa didn't want people to remember something very well. She could bury the memory in them, either erasing it all together or planting it for later. She was so good at compulsion, though, that she could just make people forget completely. For them to still have some memories meant someone who wasn't as good at compulsion had worked on them.

Someone, say, like Mia.

I wasn't the fainting type, but for just a moment, I felt like I could keel over. The world spun, and I closed my eyes and took a deep breath. When I could see again, my surroundings stayed stable. Okay. No problem. I would reason this out.

Mason, Eddie, and Mia had left the resort earlier today. Not only that, they had done it by using compulsion—which was utterly forbidden. They hadn't told anyone. They'd left through the north gate. I'd seen a map of the resort. The north gate guarded a driveway that connected to the only semi-major road in the area, a small highway that led to a little town about twelve miles away. The town Mason had mentioned that had buses.

To Spokane.

Spokane—where this traveling pack of Strigoi and their humans might be living.

Spokane—where Mason could fulfill all his crazy dreams of slaying Strigoi.

Spokane—which he only knew about because of *me*.

"No, no, no," I murmured to myself, almost running toward my room.

There, I stripped off the dress and changed into heavy winter clothes: boots, jeans, and a sweater. Grabbing my coat and gloves, I hurried back toward the door and then paused. I was acting without thinking. What was I actually going to do? I needed to tell someone, obviously . . . but that would get the trio in a lot of trouble. It would also tip Dimitri off that I'd gone and gossiped about the Spokane Strigoi information he'd told me in confidence as a sign of respecting my maturity.

I studied the time. It would take a while for anyone around the resort to know we were missing. *If* I could actually get out of the resort.

A few minutes later, I found myself knocking on Christian's door. He answered, looking sleepy and cynical as usual.

"If you've come to apologize for her," he told me loftily, "you can just go ahead and—"

"Oh, shut up," I snapped. "This isn't about you."

Hastily, I relayed the details of what was going on. Even Christian didn't have a witty response for that one.

"So . . . Mason, Eddie, and Mia went to Spokane to hunt Strigoi?"

"Yes."

"Holy shit. Why didn't you go with them? Seems like something you'd do."

I resisted the urge to smack him. "Because I'm not insane! But I'm going to go get them before they do something even stupider."

That was when Christian caught on. "And what do you need from me?"

"I need to get off the resort's property. They got Mia to use compulsion on the guards. I need you to do the same thing. I know you've practiced it."

"I have," he agreed. "But . . . well . . ." For the first time ever, he looked embarrassed. "I'm not very good at it. And doing it on dhampirs is nearly impossible. Liss is a hundred times better than me. Or probably any Moroi."

"I know. But I don't want her to get in trouble."

He snorted. "But you don't mind if I do?"

I shrugged. "Not really."

"You're a piece of work, you know that?"

"Yeah. I do, actually."

So, five minutes later, he and I found ourselves trekking out to the north gate. The sun was coming up, so most everyone was inside. This was a good thing, and I hoped it'd make our escape that much easier.

Stupid, stupid, I kept thinking. This was going to blow up in our faces. Why had Mason done this? I knew he'd had this whole crazy vigilante attitude . . . and he'd certainly seemed upset that the guardians hadn't done anything about the recent attack. But still. Was he really that unhinged? He *had* to know how dangerous this was. Was it possible . . . was it possible *I'd* upset him so much with the making-out disaster that he'd gone off the deep end? Enough to go do this and get Mia and Eddie to join him? Not that those two would be hard to convince. Eddie would follow Mason anywhere, and Mia was almost as gung ho as Mason to kill every Strigoi in the world.

Yet, out of all the questions I had about this, one thing was definitely clear. I'd told Mason about the Strigoi in Spokane. Hands down, this was my fault, and without me, none of this would have happened.

"Lissa always makes eye contact," I coached Christian as we approached the exit. "And speaks in a really, like, calm voice. I don't know what else. I mean, she concentrates a lot too, so try that. Focus on forcing your will on them."

"I know," he snapped. "I've seen her do it."

"Fine," I snapped back. "Just trying to help."

Squinting, I saw that only one guardian stood at the gate, a total stroke of luck. They were in between shifts. With the sun out, the risk of Strigoi had disappeared. The guardians would still continue in their duties, but they could relax just a bit.

The guy on duty didn't seem particularly alarmed by our appearance. "What are you kids doing out here?"

Christian swallowed. I could see the lines of tension on his face.

"You're going to let us out of the gate," he said. A note of nervousness made his voice tremble, but otherwise, he did a fair approximation of Lissa's soothing tones. Unfortunately, it had no effect on the guardian. As Christian had pointed out, using compulsion on a guardian was nearly impossible. Mia had gotten lucky. The guardian grinned at us.

"What?" he asked, clearly amused.

Christian tried again. "You're going to let us out."

The guy's smile faltered just a little, and I saw him blink in surprise. His eyes didn't glaze over in the same way Lissa's victims did, but Christian had done enough to briefly enthrall him. Unfortunately, I could tell right then and there that it wouldn't be enough to make him let us out and forget. Fortunately, I'd been trained to compel people without the use of magic.

Sitting near his post was an enormous Maglite, two feet long and easily seven pounds. I grabbed the Maglite and clocked him on the back of the head. He grunted and crumpled to the ground. He'd barely seen me coming, and despite the horribleness of what I'd just done, I kind of wished one of my instructors had been there to grade me on such an awesome performance.

"Jesus Christ," exclaimed Christian. "You just assaulted a guardian."

"Yeah." So much for getting the guys back without getting anyone in trouble. "I didn't know just how much you sucked at compulsion. I'll deal with the fallout later. Thanks for your help. You should head back before the next shift comes on."

He shook his head and grimaced. "No, I'm going with you on this."

"No," I argued. "I only needed you to get through the gate. You don't have to get in trouble over this."

"I'm already in trouble!" He pointed at the guardian. "He saw my face. I'm screwed either way, so I might as well help you save the day. Stop being a bitch for a change."

We hurried off, and I cast one last, guilty glance at the guardian. I was pretty sure I hadn't hit him hard enough to cause real damage, and with the sun coming out, he wouldn't freeze or anything.

After about five minutes of walking down the highway, I knew we had a problem. Despite being covered and wearing sunglasses, the sun was taking its toll on Christian. It was slowing us down, and it wouldn't take that long for someone to find the guardian I'd taken out and come after us.

A car—not one of the Academy's—appeared behind us, and I made a decision. I didn't approve of hitchhiking in the least. Even someone like me knew how dangerous it was. But we needed to get to town *fast*, and I prayed Christian and I could take down any creepy stalker guy who tried to mess with us.

Fortunately, when the car pulled over, it was just a middle-aged couple who looked more concerned than anything else. "You kids okay?"

I jerked my thumb behind me. "Our car slid off the road. Can you take us to town so I can call my dad?"

It worked. Fifteen minutes later, they dropped us off at a gas station. I actually had trouble getting rid of them because they wanted to help us so much. Finally, we convinced them we'd be fine, and we walked the few blocks over to the bus station. As I'd suspected, this town wasn't much of a hub for real travel. Three lines serviced the town: two that went to other ski resorts and one that went to Lowston, Idaho. From Lowston, you could go on to other places.

I'd half-hoped that we might beat Mason and the others before their bus came. Then we could have hauled them back without any trouble. Unfortunately, there was no sign of them. The cheery woman at the counter knew exactly who we were talking about, too. She confirmed that all three of them had bought tickets to Spokane by way of Lowston.

"Damn it," I said. The woman raised her eyebrows at my language. I turned to Christian. "You got money for the bus?"

Christian and I didn't talk much along the way, except for me to tell him he'd been an idiot about Lissa and Adrian. By the time we reached Lowston, I finally had him convinced, which was a minor miracle. He slept the rest of the way to Spokane, but I couldn't. I just kept thinking over and over that this was my fault.

It was late afternoon by the time we reached Spokane. It took a few people, but we finally found someone who knew the shopping center Dimitri had mentioned. It was a long ways from the bus station, but it was walkable. My legs were stiff after almost five hours of riding a bus, and I wanted the movement. The sun was a while from setting, but it was lower and less detrimental to vampires, so Christian didn't mind the walk either.

And, as often happened when I was in calm settings, I felt a tug into Lissa's head. I let myself fall into her because I wanted to know what was happening back at the resort.

"I know you want to protect them, but we need to know where they are."

Lissa sat on the bed in our room while Dimitri and my mom stared her down. It was Dimitri who had spoken. Seeing him through her eyes was interesting. She had a fond respect for him, very different from the intense roller coaster of emotions I always experienced.

"I told you," said Lissa, "I don't know. I don't know what happened."

Frustration and fear for us burned through her. It saddened me to see her so anxious, but at the same time, I was glad I hadn't gotten her involved. She couldn't report what she didn't know.

"I can't believe they wouldn't have told you where they were going," said my mother. Her words sounded flat, but there were lines of worry on her face. "Especially with your . . . bond."

"It only works one way," said Lissa sadly. "You know that."

Dimitri knelt down so he could be at Lissa's height and look her in the eye. He pretty much had to do that to look anyone in the eye. "Are you sure there's nothing? Nothing at all you can tell us? They're nowhere in town. The man at the bus station didn't see them . . . though we're pretty sure that's where they must have gone. We need something, *anything* to go on."

Man at the bus station? That was another stroke of luck. The woman who'd sold us the tickets must have gone home. Her replacement wouldn't know us.

Lissa gritted her teeth and glared. "Don't you think if I knew, I'd tell you? You don't think I'm worried about them too? I have *no* idea where they are. None. And why'd they even leave . . . it doesn't make any sense either. Especially why they'd go with Mia, of all people." A twinge of hurt flickered through the bond, hurt at being left out of whatever we were doing, no matter how wrong.

Dimitri sighed and leaned back on his heels. From the look on his face, he obviously believed her. It was also obvious that he was worried—worried in more than a professional way. And seeing that concern—that concern for *me*—ate up my heart.

"Rose?" Christian's voice brought me back to myself. "We're here, I think."

The plaza consisted of a wide, open area in front of a shopping center. A café was carved into a corner of the main building, its tables spilling out into the open area. A crowd moved in and out of the complex, busy even at this time of the day.

"So, how do we find them?" asked Christian.

I shrugged. "Maybe if we act like Strigoi, they'll try to stake us."

A small, reluctant smile played over his face. He didn't want to admit it, but he'd thought my joke was funny.

He and I went inside. Like any mall, it was filled with familiar chains, and a selfish part of me thought that maybe if we found the group soon enough, we could still get in shopping time.

Christian and I walked the length of it twice and saw no signs of our friends or anything resembling tunnels.

"Maybe we're in the wrong place," I finally said.

"Or maybe *they* are," suggested Christian. "They could have gone to some other—wait."

He pointed, and I followed the gesture. The three renegades sat at a table in the middle of the food court, looking dejected. They looked so miserable, I almost felt sorry for them.

"I'd kill for a camera right now," said Christian, smirking.

"This isn't funny," I told him, striding toward the group. Inside, I breathed a sigh of relief. The group clearly hadn't found any Strigoi, were all still alive, and could maybe be taken back before we got in even more trouble.

They didn't notice me until I was almost right next to them. Eddie's head jerked up. "Rose? What are you doing here?"

"Are you out of your mind?" I yelled. A few people nearby gave us surprised looks. "Do you know how much trouble you're in? How much trouble you've gotten *us* in?"

"How the hell did you find us?" asked Mason in a low voice, glancing anxiously around.

"You guys aren't exactly criminal masterminds," I told them. "Your informant at the bus station gave you away. That, and I figured out that you'd want to go off on your pointless Strigoi-hunting quest."

The look Mason gave me revealed he still wasn't entirely happy with me. It was Mia who replied, however.

"It isn't pointless."

"Oh?" I demanded. "Did you kill any Strigoi? Did you even find any?"

"No," admitted Eddie.

"Good," I said. "You got lucky."

"Why are you so against killing Strigoi?" asked Mia hotly. "Isn't that what you train for?"

"I train for sane missions, not childish stunts like this."

"It isn't childish," she cried. "They killed my mother. And the guardians weren't doing anything. Even their information is bad. There weren't any Strigoi in the tunnels. Probably none in the whole city."

Christian looked impressed. "You found the tunnels?"

"Yeah," said Eddie. "But like she said, they were useless."

"We should see them before we go," Christian told me. "It'd be kind of cool, and if the data was bad, there's no danger."

"No," I snapped. "We're going home. Now."

Mason looked tired. "We're going to search the city again. Even you can't make us go back, Rose."

"No, but the school's guardians can when I call and tell them you're here."

Call it blackmailing or being a tattletale; the effect was the same. The three of them looked at me like I had just simultaneously gut-punched them all.

"You'd really do that?" asked Mason. "You'd sell us out like that?"

I rubbed my eyes, wondering desperately why I was trying to be the voice of reason here. Where was the girl who'd run away from school? Mason had been right. I had changed.

"This isn't about selling anyone out. This is about keeping you guys alive."

"You think we're that defenseless?" asked Mia. "You think we'd get killed right away?"

"Yes," I said. "Unless you've found some way to use water as a weapon?"

She flushed and didn't say anything.

"We brought silver stakes," said Eddie.

Fantastic. They must have stolen them. I looked at Mason pleadingly.

"Mason. Please. Call this off. Let's go back."

He looked at me for a long time. Finally, he sighed. "Okay."

Eddie and Mia looked aghast, but Mason had assumed a leadership role with them, and they didn't have the initiative to go on without him. Mia seemed to take it the hardest, and I felt bad for her. She'd barely had any real time to grieve for her mother; she'd just jumped right on board with this revenge thing as a way to cope with the pain. She'd have a lot to deal with when we got back.

Christian was still excited about the idea of the underground tunnels. Considering he spent all his time in an attic, I shouldn't have been all that surprised.

"I saw the schedule," he told me. "We've got a while before the next bus."

"We can't go walking into some Strigoi lair," I argued, walking toward the mall's entrance.

"There are no Strigoi there," said Mason. "It's seriously all janitorial stuff. There was no sign of anything weird. I really do think the guardians had bad information."

"Rose," said Christian, "let's get something fun out of this."

They all looked at me. I felt like a mom who wouldn't buy her kids candy at the grocery store.

"Okay, fine. Just a peek, though."

The others led Christian and me to the opposite end of the mall, through a door marked STAFF ONLY. We dodged a couple of janitors, then slipped through another door that led us to a set of stairs going down. I had a brief moment of déjà vu, recalling the steps down to Adrian's spa party. Only these stairs were dirtier and smelled pretty nasty.

We reached the bottom. It wasn't so much a tunnel as a narrow corridor, lined in grime-caked cement. Ugly fluorescent lights were embedded sporadically along the walls. The passage went off to our left and right. Boxes of ordinary cleaning and electrical supplies sat around.

"See?" said Mason. "Boring."

I pointed in each direction. "What's down there?"

"Nothing," sighed Mia. "We'll show you."

We walked down to the right and found more of the same. I was starting to agree with the boring assessment when we passed some black writing on one of the walls. I stopped and looked at it. It was a list of letters.

D

B

C

O

T

D

V

L

D

Z

S

I

Some had lines and x marks next to them, but for the most part the message was incoherent. Mia noticed my scrutiny.

"It's probably a janitor thing," she said. "Or maybe some gang did it."

"Probably," I said, still studying it. The others shifted restlessly, not understanding my fascination with the jumble of letters. I didn't understand my fascination either, but something in my head tugged at me to stay.

Then I got it.

B for *Badica*, *Z* for *Zeklos*, *I* for *Ivashkov* . . .

I stared. The first letter of every royal family's name was there. There were three *D* names, but based on the order, you could actually read the list as a size ranking. It started with the smaller families—Dragomir, Badica, Conta—and went all the way up to the giant Ivashkov clan. I didn't understand the dashes and lines beside the letters, but I quickly noticed which names had an x beside them: Badica and Drozdov.

I stepped back from the wall. "We have to get out of here," I said. My own voice scared me a little. "Right now."

The others looked at me in surprise. "Why?" asked Eddie. "What's going on?"

"I'll tell you later. We just need to go."

Mason pointed in the direction we'd been heading. "This lets out a few blocks away. It's closer to the station."

I peered down into the dark unknown. "No," I said. "We're going back the way we came."

They all looked at me like I was insane as we retraced

our steps, but nobody questioned me yet. When we emerged from the mall's front, I breathed a sigh of relief to see that the sun was still out, though it was steadily sinking into the horizon and casting orange and red light onto the buildings. The remaining light would still be enough for us to get back to the bus station before we were really in any danger of seeing Strigoi.

And I knew now that there really were Strigoi in Spokane. Dimitri's information had been correct. I didn't know what the list meant, but it clearly had something to do with the attacks. I needed to report it to the other guardians immediately, and I certainly couldn't tell the others what I'd realized until we were safely at the lodge. Mason was likely to go back into the tunnels if he knew what I did.

Most of our walk back to the station proceeded in silence. I think my mood had cowed the others. Even Christian seemed to have run out of snide comments. Inside, my emotions swirled, oscillating between anger and guilt as I kept reexamining my role in everything.

Ahead of me, Eddie stopped walking, and I nearly ran into him. He looked around. "Where are we?"

Snapping out of my own thoughts, I surveyed the area too. I didn't remember these buildings. "Damn it," I exclaimed. "Are we lost? Didn't anyone keep track of which way we went?"

It was an unfair question since I clearly hadn't paid attention either, but my temper had pushed me past reason. Mason studied me for a few moments, then pointed. "This way."

We turned and walked down a narrow street between two buildings. I didn't think we were going the right way, but I didn't really have a better idea. I also didn't want to stand around debating.

We hadn't gone very far when I heard the sound of an engine and squealing tires. Mia was walking in the middle of the road, and protective conditioning kicked in before I even saw what was coming. Grabbing her, I jerked her out of the street and up against one of the building walls. The boys had done the same.

A large, gray van with tinted windows had rounded the corner and was headed in our direction. We pressed flat against the wall, waiting for it to go past.

Only it didn't.

Screeching to a halt, it stopped right in front of us, and the doors slid open. Three big guys spilled out, and again, my instincts kicked in. I had no clue who they were or what they wanted, but they clearly weren't friendly. That was all I needed to know.

One of them moved toward Christian, and I struck out and punched him. The guy barely staggered but was clearly surprised to have felt it at all, I think. He probably hadn't expected someone as small as me to be much of a threat. Ignoring Christian, he moved toward me. In my peripheral vision, I saw Mason and Eddie squaring off with the other two. Mason had actually pulled out his stolen silver stake. Mia and Christian stood there, frozen.

Our attackers were relying a lot on bulk. They didn't have the sort of background we had in offensive and defensive techniques. Plus, they were human, and we had dhampir strength. Unfortunately, we also had the disadvantage of being cornered against the wall. We had nowhere to retreat to. Most importantly, we had something to lose.

Like Mia.

The guy who'd been sparring with Mason seemed to realize this. He backed off from Mason and instead grabbed her. I barely saw the flash of his gun before its barrel was pressed against her neck. Backing off from my own adversary, I yelled at Eddie to stop. We'd all been trained to respond instantly to those kinds of orders, and he halted his attack, glancing at me questioningly. When he saw Mia, his face went pale.

I wanted nothing more than to keep pummeling these men—whoever they were—but I couldn't risk this guy hurting Mia. He knew it, too. He didn't even have to make the threat. He was human, but he knew enough about us to know that we'd go out of our way to protect the Moroi. Novices had a saying grilled into us from an early age: *Only they matter.*

Everyone stopped and looked between him and me. Apparently we were the acknowledged leaders here. "What do you want?" I asked harshly.

The guy pressed his gun closer to Mia's neck, and she

whimpered. For all her talk about fighting, she was smaller than me and not nearly as strong. And she was too terrified to move.

The man inclined his head toward the van's open door. "I want you to get inside. And don't start anything. You do, and she's gone."

I looked at Mia, the van, my other friends, and then back to the guy. Shit.

NINETEEN

I HATE BEING POWERLESS. AND I hate going down without a fight. What had taken place outside in the alley hadn't been a real fight. If it had—if I'd been beaten into submission . . . well, yeah. Maybe I could accept that. Maybe. But I hadn't been beaten. I'd barely gotten my hands dirty. Instead, I'd gone quietly.

Once they had us sitting on the floor of the van, they'd bound each of our hands behind our back with flex-cuffs—strips of plastic that cinched together and held just as well as anything made of metal.

After that, we rode in near silence. The men occasionally murmured something to each other, speaking too softly for any of us to hear. Christian or Mia might have been able to understand the words, but they were in no position to communicate anything to the rest of us. Mia looked as terrified as she had out on the street, and while Christian's fear had rapidly given way to his typical haughty anger, even he didn't dare act out with guards nearby.

I was glad for Christian's self-control. I didn't doubt any of these men would smack him if he got out of line, and neither I nor the other novices were in a position to stop them. That was what really drove me crazy. The instinct to protect Moroi was so deeply ingrained in me that I couldn't even pause to worry about myself. Christian and Mia were the focus. They were the ones I had to get out of this mess.

And how had this mess started? Who were these guys? That was a mystery. They were human, but I didn't believe for an instant that a group of dhampirs and Moroi had been random kidnapping victims. We'd been targeted for a reason.

Our captors made no attempts to blindfold us or conceal our route, which I didn't take as a good sign. Did they think we didn't know the city well enough to retrace our steps? Or did they figure it didn't matter since we wouldn't be leaving wherever they were taking us? All I sensed was that we were driving away from downtown, off toward a more suburban area. Spokane was as dull as I'd imagined. Unlike where pristine white snow lay in drifts, slushy gray puddles lined the streets and dirty patches dotted the lawns. There were also a lot fewer evergreen trees than I was used to. The scraggly, leafless deciduous trees here seemed skeletal by comparison. They only added to the mood of impending doom.

After what felt like less than an hour, the van turned down a quiet cul-de-sac, and we drove up to a very ordinary—yet large—house. Other houses—identical in the way suburban homes often are—stood nearby, which gave me hope. Maybe we could get some help from the neighbors.

We pulled inside the garage, and once the door was back down, the men ushered us into the house. It looked a lot more interesting on the inside. Antique, claw-footed sofas and chairs. A large, saltwater fish tank. Swords crossed over the fireplace. One of those stupid modern art paintings that consisted of a few lines splayed across the canvas.

The part of me that enjoyed destroying things would have liked to study the swords in detail, but the main floor wasn't our destination. Instead, we were led down a narrow flight of stairs, down to a basement as large as the floor above. Only, unlike the main floor's open space, the basement was sectioned off into a series of halls and closed doors. It was like a rat's maze. Our captors led us through it without hesitation, into a small room with a concrete floor and unpainted drywall.

The furniture inside consisted of several very uncomfortable-looking wooden chairs with slatted backs—backs that proved to be a convenient place for rebinding our hands. The men seated us in such a way that Mia and Christian sat on one side of the room, and the rest of us dhampirs sat on the other. One guy—the leader, apparently—watched carefully as one of his henchmen bound Eddie's hands with new flex-cuffs.

"These are the ones you especially have to watch," he warned, nodding toward us. "They'll fight back." His eyes traveled first to Eddie's face, then Mason's, and then mine. The guy and I held each other's gaze for several moments, and I scowled. He looked back over at his associate. "Watch *her* in particular."

When we'd been restrained to his satisfaction, he barked out a few more orders to the others and then left the room, shutting the door loudly behind him. His steps echoed through the house as he walked upstairs. Moments later, silence fell.

We sat there, staring at each other. After several minutes, Mia whimpered and started to speak. "What are you going to—"

"Shut up," growled one of the men. He took a warning step toward her. Blanching, she cringed but still looked as though she might say something else. I caught her eye and shook my head. She stayed silent, eyes wide and a slight tremble to her lip.

There's nothing worse than waiting and not knowing what'll happen to you. Your own imagination can be crueler than any captor. Since our guards wouldn't talk to us or tell us what was in store, I imagined all sorts of horrible scenarios. The guns were the obvious threat, and I found myself pondering what a bullet would feel like. Painful, presumably. And where would they shoot? Through the heart or the head? Quick death. But somewhere else? Like the stomach? That would be slow and painful. I shuddered at the thought of my life bleeding out of me. Thinking of all that blood put me in mind of the Badica house and maybe having our throats slit. These men could have knives as well as guns.

Of course, I had to wonder why we were still alive at all. Clearly they wanted something from us, but what? They weren't asking for information. And they were *human*. What would humans want with us? Usually the most we feared from humans was either running into crazy slayer types or those who wanted to experiment on us. These seemed like neither.

So what did they want? Why were we here? Over and over, I imagined more awful, gruesome fates. The looks on my friends' faces showed I wasn't the only one who could envision creative torments. The smell of sweat and fear filled the room.

I lost track of time and was suddenly jolted out of my imaginings when footsteps sounded on the stairs. The lead captor stepped into the hall. The rest of the men straightened up, tension crackling around them. Oh God. This was it, I realized. This was what we'd been waiting for.

"Yes, sir," I heard the leader say. "They're in here, just like you wanted."

Finally, I realized. The person behind our kidnapping. Panic shot through me. I had to escape.

"Let us out of here!" I yelled, straining at my bindings. "Let us out of here, you son of a—"

I stopped. Something inside of me shriveled up. My throat went dry. My heart wanted to stop. The guard had returned with a man and a woman I didn't recognize. I did, however, recognize that they were . . .

. . . Strigoi.

Real, live—well, figuratively speaking—Strigoi. It all suddenly clicked together. It wasn't just the Spokane reports that had been true. What we'd feared—Strigoi working with humans—had come true. *This changes everything.* Daylight wasn't safe anymore. None of us were safe anymore. Worse, I realized these must be the rogue Strigoi—the ones who had attacked the two Moroi families with human help. Again, those horrible memories came to me: bodies and blood everywhere. Bile rose in my throat, and I tried to shift my thoughts from the past to the present situation. Not that that was any more reassuring.

Moroi had pale skin, the kind of skin that blushed and burned easily. But these vampires . . . their skin was white, chalky in a way that made it look like the result of a bad make-up job. The pupils of their eyes had a red ring around them, driving home what monsters they were.

The woman, actually, reminded me of Natalie—my poor friend whose father had convinced her to turn Strigoi. It took me a few moments to figure out what the resemblance was because they looked nothing alike. This woman was short—probably human before becoming Strigoi—and had brown hair with a bad highlighting job.

Then it hit me. This Strigoi was a new one, much as Natalie had been. It didn't become obvious until I compared her with the Strigoi man. The Strigoi woman's face had a little life in it. But his . . . his was the face of death.

His face was completely devoid of any sort of warmth or gentler emotion. His expression was cold and calculating, laced with malicious amusement. He was tall, as tall as Dimitri, and had a slender frame that indicated he'd been Moroi before changing over. Shoulder-length black hair framed his face and stood out against the bright scarlet of his dress shirt. His eyes were so dark and brown that without the red ring, it would have been almost impossible to tell where pupil ended and iris began.

One of the guards shoved me hard, even though I'd been silent. He glanced up at the Strigoi man. "You want me to gag her?"

I suddenly realized I'd been hunching into the back of my chair, unconsciously trying to get as far away from him as possible. He realized this too, and a thin, toothless smile crossed his lips.

"No," he said. His voice was silky and low. "I'd like to hear what she has to say." He raised an eyebrow at me. "Please. Continue."

I swallowed.

"No? Nothing to add? Well. Do feel free to pipe up if something else comes to mind."

"Isaiah," exclaimed the woman. "Why are you keeping them here? Why haven't you just contacted the others?"

"Elena, Elena," Isaiah murmured to her. "Behave yourself. I'm not going to pass up the chance to enjoy myself with two Moroi and . . ." He walked behind my chair and lifted my hair, making me shudder. A moment later, he peered at Mason and Eddie's necks as well. ". . . three unblooded dhampirs." He spoke those words with an almost happy sigh, and I realized he'd been looking for guardian tattoos.

Strolling over to Mia and Christian, Isaiah rested a hand on his hip as he studied them. Mia could only meet his eyes for an instant before looking away. Christian's fear was palpable, but he managed to return the Strigoi's scrutiny. It made me proud.

"Look at these eyes, Elena." Elena walked over and stood beside Isaiah as he spoke. "That pale blue. Like ice. Like aquamarines. You almost never get that outside of the royal houses. Badicas. Ozeras. The occasional Zeklos."

"Ozera," said Christian, trying very hard to sound fearless.

Isaiah tilted his head. "Really? Surely not . . ." He leaned closer to Christian. "But the age is right . . . and that hair . . ." He smiled. "Lucas and Moira's son?"

Christian said nothing, but the confirmation on his face was obvious.

"I knew your parents. Great people. Unparalleled. Their deaths were a shame . . . but, well . . . I daresay they brought that on themselves. I *told* them they shouldn't have gone back for you. Would have been wasteful to awaken you so young. They claimed they were going to just keep you around and waken you when you were older. I warned them that that would be a disaster, but, well . . ." He gave a delicate shrug. "Awaken" was the term Strigoi used among themselves when they changed over. It sounded like a religious experience. "They wouldn't listen, and disaster met them in a different way."

Hatred, deep and dark, boiled behind Christian's eyes. Isaiah smiled again.

"It's quite touching that you should find your way to me after all this time. Perhaps I can realize their dream after all."

"Isaiah," said the woman—Elena—again. Every word out of her mouth seemed like a whine. "Call the others—"

"Stop giving me orders!" Isaiah grabbed her shoulder and shoved her away—except that the push knocked her across the room and almost through the wall. She just barely threw her hand out in time to stop the impact. Strigoi had better reflexes than dhampirs or even Moroi; her lack of grace meant he'd completely caught her off guard. And really, he'd barely touched her. The push had been light—yet it had packed the force of a small car.

This further enforced my belief that he was in another class altogether. His strength beat hers by magnitudes. She was like a fly he could swat away. Strigoi power increased with age— as well as through the consumption of Moroi blood and, to a lesser extent, dhampir blood. This guy wasn't just old, I realized. He was ancient. And he'd drunk *a lot* of blood over the years. Terror filled Elena's features, and I could understand her fear. Strigoi turned against each other all the time. He could have ripped her head off if he wanted.

She cowered, averting her eyes. "I . . . I'm sorry, Isaiah."

Isaiah smoothed his shirt—not that it had been wrinkled. His voice took on the cold pleasantness he'd affected earlier. "You clearly have opinions here, Elena, and I welcome you voicing them in a civilized manner. What do you think we should do with these cubs?"

"You should—that is, I think we should just take them now. Especially the Moroi." She was clearly working hard not to whine again and annoy him. "Unless . . . you aren't going to throw another dinner party, are you? It's a complete waste. We'll have to share, and you know the others won't be grateful. They *never* are."

"I'm not making a dinner party out of them," he declared loftily. Dinner party? "But I'm not killing them yet either. You're young, Elena. You only think about immediate gratification. When you're as old as me, you won't be so . . . impatient."

She rolled her eyes when he wasn't looking.

Turning, he swept his gaze over me, Mason, and Eddie. "You three, I'm afraid, are going to die. There's no avoiding it. I'd like to say I'm sorry, but, well, I'm not. Such is the way of the world. You do have a choice in how you die, however, and that will be dictated by your behavior." His eyes lingered on me. I didn't really get why everyone seemed to be singling me out as the troublemaker here. Well, maybe I did. "Some of you will die more painfully than others."

I didn't need to see Mason and Eddie to know their fear mirrored mine. I was pretty sure I even heard Eddie whimper.

Isaiah abruptly turned on his heels, military-style, and faced Mia and Christian. "You two, fortunately, have options. Only one of you will die. The other will live on in glorious immortality. I'll even be kind enough to take you under my wing until you're a little older. Such is my charity."

I couldn't help it. I choked on a laugh.

Isaiah spun around and stared at me. I fell silent and waited for him to throw me across the room like he had Elena, but he did nothing else but stare. It was enough. My heart raced, and I felt tears brim in my eyes. My fear shamed me. I wanted to be like Dimitri. Maybe even like my mother. After several long, agonizing moments, Isaiah turned back to the Moroi.

"Now. As I was saying, one of you will be awakened and live forever. But it will not be me who wakens you. You will choose to be awakened willingly."

"Not likely," said Christian. He packed as much snarky defiance as he could manage into those two words, but it was still obvious to everyone else in the room that he was scared out of his mind.

"Ah, how I love the Ozera spirit," mused Isaiah. He glanced at Mia, his red eyes gleaming. She shrank back in fear. "But don't let him upstage you, my dear. There's strength in common blood, too. And here's how it will be decided." He pointed at us dhampirs. His gazed chilled me all over, and I imagined I could smell the stink of decay. "If you want to live, all you have to do is kill one of these three." He turned back to the Moroi. "That's it. Not unpleasant at all. Just tell one of these gentlemen here you want to do it. They'll release you. Then you drink from them and are awakened as one of us. Whoever does this first walks free. The other will be dinner for Elena and me."

Silence hung in the room.

"No," said Christian. "No way am I killing one of my friends. I don't care what you do. I'll die first."

Isaiah waved a dismissive hand. "Easy to be brave when you aren't hungry. Go a few days without any other sustenance . . . and yes, these three will start to look *very* good. And they are. Dhampirs are delicious. Some prefer them to Moroi, and while I myself have never shared such beliefs, I can certainly appreciate the variety."

Christian scowled.

"Don't believe me?" asked Isaiah. "Then let me prove it." He walked back over to my side of the room. I realized what he was going to do and spoke without fully thinking things through.

"Use me," I blurted out. "Drink from me."

Isaiah's smug look faltered for a moment, and his eyebrows rose. "You're volunteering?"

"I've done it before. Let Moroi feed off me, I mean. I don't mind. I like it. Leave the rest of them alone."

"Rose!" exclaimed Mason.

I ignored him and looked beseechingly at Isaiah. I didn't want him to feed off me. The thought made me sick. But I *had* given blood before, and I'd rather him take pints from me before he touched Eddie or Mason.

I couldn't read his expression as he sized me up. For half a second, I thought he might go for it, but instead he shook his head.

"No. Not you. Not yet."

He walked over and stood before Eddie. I pulled against my flex-cuffs so hard that they dug painfully into my skin. They didn't give. "No! Leave him alone!"

"Quiet," snapped Isaiah, without looking at me. He rested one hand on the side of Eddie's face. Eddie trembled and had gone so pale, I thought he would faint. "I can make this easy, or I can make it hurt. Your silence will encourage the former."

I wanted to scream, wanted to call Isaiah all sorts of names and make all sorts of threats. But I couldn't. My eyes flicked around the room, searching for exits, as I had so many times before. But there were none. Just blank, bare white walls. No windows. The one precious door, always guarded. I was helpless, just as helpless as I'd been from the moment they'd pulled us into the van. I felt like crying, more from frustration than fear. What kind of guardian would I be if I couldn't protect my friends?

But I stayed quiet, and a look of satisfaction crossed Isaiah's face. The fluorescent lighting gave his skin a sickly, grayish hue, emphasizing the dark circles under his eyes. I wanted to punch him.

"Good." He smiled at Eddie and held his face so that the two made direct eye contact. "Now, you won't fight me, will you?"

As I've mentioned, Lissa was good at compulsion. But she couldn't have done this. In seconds, Eddie was smiling.

"No. I won't fight you."

"Good," repeated Isaiah. "And you'll give me your neck freely, won't you?"

"Of course," replied Eddie, tilting his head back.

Isaiah brought his mouth down, and I looked away, trying to focus on the threadbare carpet instead. I didn't want to see this. I heard Eddie emit a soft, happy moan. The feeding itself was relatively quiet—no slurping or anything like that.

"There."

I glanced back when I heard Isaiah speak again. Blood dripped from his lips, and he ran his tongue across them. I couldn't see the wound on Eddie's neck, but I suspected it was bloody and horrible too. Mia and Christian stared wide-eyed, both with fear and fascination. Eddie gazed off in a happy, drugged haze, high from both the endorphins and the compulsion.

Isaiah straightened up and smiled at the Moroi, licking the last of the blood off his lips. "You see?" he told them, moving toward the door. "It's just that easy."

TWENTY

WE NEEDED AN ESCAPE PLAN, and we needed it fast. Unfortunately, my only ideas called for things that really weren't under my control. Like us being left completely alone so we could sneak off. Or having stupid guards whom we could easily fool and slip away from. At the very least, we should have been sloppily secured so that we could break free.

None of that was happening, though. After almost twenty-four hours, our situations hadn't really changed. We were still prisoners, still securely bound. Our captors stayed vigilant, almost as efficient as any group of guardians. Almost.

The closest we got to freedom was heavily supervised—and extremely embarrassing—bathroom breaks. The men gave us no food or water. That was rough on me, but the human and vampire mix made dhampirs hardy. I could handle being uncomfortable, even though I was fast reaching a point where I would have killed for a cheeseburger and some really, really greasy french fries.

For Mia and Christian . . . well, things were a little harder. Moroi could go weeks without food and water if they were still getting blood. Without blood, they could manage a few days before getting sick and weak, so long as they still had other sustenance. That was how Lissa and I had managed while living on our own, since I hadn't been able to feed her every day.

Take away food, blood, and water, and Moroi endurance dropped through the floor. I was hungry, but Mia and Christian were ravenous. Already, their faces looked gaunt, their eyes almost feverish. Isaiah made matters worse during his subsequent visits. Each time, he would come down and ramble on in his annoying, taunting way. Then, before leaving, he'd take another drink from Eddie. By the third visit, I could practically see Mia and Christian salivating. Between the endorphins and lack of food, I was pretty sure Eddie didn't even know where we were.

I couldn't really sleep under these conditions, but during the second day, I started nodding off now and then. Starvation and exhaustion will do that to you. At one point, I actually dreamed, surprising since I didn't really think I could fall into a deep slumber under such insane conditions.

In the dream—and I knew perfectly well that it was a dream—I stood on a beach. It took me a moment to recognize just which beach it was. It was along the Oregon coast— sandy and warm, with the Pacific unfolding in the distance. Lissa and I had traveled out here once when we lived in Portland. It had been a gorgeous day, but she couldn't handle being out in that much sun. We'd kept the visit short as a result, but I'd always wished I could have stayed longer and basked in all that. Now I had all the light and warmth I could want.

"Little dhampir," said a voice behind me. "It's about time."

I turned around in surprise and found Adrian Ivashkov watching me. He had on khakis and a loose shirt and—in a surprisingly casual style for him—wore no shoes. Wind ruffled his brown hair, and he kept his hands stuffed in his pockets as he regarded me with that trademark smirk of his.

"Still got your protection," he added.

Frowning, I thought for a moment he was staring at my chest. Then I realized his eyes were on my stomach. I had on jeans and a bikini top, and once again, the little blue eye pendant dangled from my belly-button. The chotki was on my wrist.

"And you're in the sun again," I said. "So I suppose it's your dream."

"It's our dream."

I wiggled my toes in the sand. "How can two people share a dream?"

"People share dreams all the time, Rose."

I looked up at him with a frown. "I need to know what you mean. About there being darkness around me. What does it mean?"

"Honestly, I don't know. Everyone has light around them, except for you. You have shadows. You take them from Lissa."

My confusion grew. "I don't understand."

"I can't get into it right now," he told me. "That's not why I'm here."

"You're here for a reason?" I asked, my eyes wandering to the blue-gray water. It was hypnotic. "You aren't just . . . here to be here?"

He stepped forward and caught my hand, forcing me to look up at him. All amusement was gone. He was dead serious. "Where are you?"

"Here," I said, puzzled. "Just like you."

Adrian shook his head. "No, that's not what I mean. In the real world. Where are you?"

The real world? Around us, the beach suddenly blurred, like a film going out of focus. Moments later, everything steadied itself. I racked my brain. The real world. Images came to me. Chairs. Guards. Flex-cuffs.

"In a basement . . ." I said slowly. Alarm suddenly shattered the beauty of the moment as everything came back to me. "Oh God, Adrian. You've got to help Mia and Christian. I can't—"

Adrian's grip on my hand tightened. "Where?" The world shimmered again, and this time it didn't refocus. He swore. "Where are you, Rose?"

The world began to disintegrate. Adrian began to disintegrate.

"A basement. In a house. In—"

He was gone. I woke up. The sound of the room's door opening startled me back to reality.

Isaiah swept in with Elena in tow. I had to fight a sneer when I saw her. He was arrogant and mean and all-around evil. But he was that way because he was a leader. He had the strength and power to back up his cruelty—even if I didn't like it. But Elena? She was a lackey. She threatened us and made snide comments, but most of her ability to do so came from being his sidekick. She was a total suck-up.

"Hello, children," he said. "How are we doing today?"

Sullen glares answered him.

He strolled over to Mia and Christian, hands folded behind his back. "Any changes of heart since my last visit? You're taking an awfully long time, and it's upsetting Elena. She's very hungry, you see, but—I suspect—not as hungry as you two."

Christian narrowed his eyes. "Fuck off," he said through gritted teeth.

Elena snarled and lunged forward. "Don't you dare—"

Isaiah waved her off. "Leave him alone. It just means we wait a little longer, and really, it's an entertaining wait."

Elena's eyes shot daggers at Christian.

"Honestly," continued Isaiah, watching Christian, "I can't decide which I want more: to kill you or have you join us. Either option offers its own amusements."

"Don't you get tired of hearing yourself talk?" asked Christian.

Isaiah considered. "No. Not really. And I don't get tired of *this*, either."

He turned around and walked toward Eddie. Poor Eddie could barely sit upright in his chair anymore after all the feedings he'd gone through. Worse, Isaiah didn't even need to use compulsion. Eddie's face simply lit up with a stupid grin, eager for the next bite. He was as addicted as a feeder.

Anger and disgust flooded through me.

"Damn it!" I yelled. "Leave him alone!"

Isaiah glanced back at me. "Be silent, girl. I don't find you nearly as amusing as I do Mr. Ozera."

"Yeah?" I snarled. "If I piss you off so much, then use me to prove your stupid point. Bite me instead. Put me in my place, and show me what a badass you are."

"No!" exclaimed Mason. "Use me."

Isaiah rolled his eyes. "Good God. What a noble lot. You're all Spartacus, aren't you?"

He strolled away from Eddie and put a finger under Mason's chin, tilting his head up. "But you," Isaiah said, "don't really mean it. You only offer because of *her*." He released Mason and walked in front of me, staring down with those black, black eyes. "And you . . . I didn't really believe you at first either. But now?" He knelt down so that he was at my height. I refused to look away from his eyes, even though I knew that put me at risk of compulsion. "I think you really mean it. And it's not all nobility, either. You *do* want it. You really have been bitten before." His voice was magical. Hypnotic. He wasn't using compulsion, exactly, but he definitely had an unnatural charisma surrounding him. Like Lissa and

Adrian. I hung on his every word. "Lots of times, I'd guess," he added.

He leaned toward me, breath hot against my neck. Somewhere beyond him, I could hear Mason shouting something, but all of my focus was on how close Isaiah's teeth were to my skin. In the last few months, I'd only been bitten once— and that was when Lissa had had an emergency. Before then, she'd bitten me at least twice a week for two years, and I had only recently come to realize how addicted to that I'd been. There is nothing—*nothing*—in the world like a Moroi bite, like the flood of bliss it sends into you. Of course, by all accounts, Strigoi bites were even more powerful. . . .

I swallowed, suddenly aware of my own heavy breathing and racing heart. Isaiah gave a low chuckle.

"Yes. You're a blood whore in the making. Unfortunate for you—because I'm not going to give you what you want."

He backed away, and I slumped forward in my chair. Without further delay, he returned to Eddie and drank. I couldn't watch, but it was because of envy this time, not disgust. Longing burned inside of me. I ached for that bite, ached for it with every nerve in my body.

When Isaiah finished, he started to leave the room, then paused. He directed his words at Mia and Christian. "Don't delay," he warned. "Seize your opportunity to be saved." He tilted his head toward me. "You even have a willing victim."

He left. Across the room, Christian met my eyes. Somehow, his face looked even gaunter than it had a couple of hours ago.

Hunger burned in his gaze, and I knew I wore the comple-
mentary one: a desire to sate that hunger. God. We were so
screwed. I think Christian realized it at the same time. His lips
twisted into a bitter smile.

"You never looked so good, Rose," he managed, just before
the guards told him to shut up.

I dozed a little throughout the day, but Adrian didn't
return to my dreams. Instead, while hovering just at the edge
of consciousness, I found myself slipping into familiar ter-
ritory: Lissa's head. After all the weirdness of these last two
days, being in her mind felt like a homecoming.

She was in one of the lodge's banquet rooms, only it was
empty. She sat on the floor of the far side of it, trying to stay
inconspicuous. Nervousness filled her. She was waiting for
something—or rather, someone. A few minutes later, Adrian
slipped in.

"Cousin," he said by way of greeting. He sat down beside
her and drew his knees up, unconcerned about his expensive
dress pants. "Sorry I'm late."

"It's okay," she said.

"You didn't know I was here until you saw me, did you?"

She shook her head, disappointed. I felt more confused
than ever.

"And sitting with me . . . you can't really notice anything?"

"No."

He shrugged. "Well. Hopefully it'll come soon."

"How does it look for you?" she asked, burning with curiosity.

"Do you know what auras are?"

"They're like . . . bands of light around people, right? Some New Age thing?"

"Something like that. Everyone has a sort of spiritual energy that radiates out from them. Well, almost everyone." His hesitation made me wonder if he was thinking of me and the darkness I allegedly walked in. "Based on the color and appearance, you can tell a lot about a person . . . well, if anyone could actually *see* auras, that is."

"And you can," she said. "And you can tell I use spirit from my aura?"

"Yours is mostly gold. Like mine. It'll shift with other colors depending on the situation, but the gold always stays."

"How many other people out there like us do you know?"

"Not many. I just see them every once in a while. They kind of keep to themselves. You're the first I've actually ever talked to. I didn't even know it was called 'spirit.' Wish I'd known about this when I didn't specialize. I just figured I was some kind of freak."

Lissa held up her arm and stared, willing herself to see the light shining around it. Nothing. She sighed and let the arm drop.

And that's when I got it.

Adrian was a spirit user too. That was why he'd been so curious about Lissa, why he'd wanted to talk to her and ask

about the bond and her specialization. It also explained a lot
of other things—like that charisma I couldn't seem to escape
when I was near him. He'd used compulsion that day Lissa
and I had been in his room—that was how he'd forced Dimitri
to release him.

"So, they finally let you go?" Adrian asked her.

"Yeah. They finally decided I really didn't know anything."

"Good," he said. He frowned, and I realized he was sober
for a change. "And you're *sure* you don't?"

"I already told you that. I can't make the bond work
that way."

"Hmm. Well. You've got to."

She glared. "What, you think I'm holding back? If I could
find her, I would!"

"I know, but to have it at all, you must have a strong connection. Use that to talk to her in her dreams. I tried, but I
can't hang on long enough to—"

"What did you say?" exclaimed Lissa. "Talk to her in her
dreams?"

Now he looked puzzled. "Sure. Don't you know how to do
that?"

"No! Are you kidding? How is that even possible?"

My dreams . . .

I remembered Lissa talking about unexplained Moroi phenomena, how there might be spirit powers out there beyond
healing, things no one even knew about yet. It would appear

that Adrian being in my dreams was no coincidence. He'd managed to get inside my head, maybe in a way similar to how I saw Lissa's mind. The thought made me uneasy. Lissa could barely even grasp it.

He ran a hand through his hair and tipped his head back, staring at the crystal chandelier above as he pondered. "Okay. So. You don't see auras, and you don't talk to people in dreams. What *do* you do?"

"I . . . I can heal people. Animals. Plants, too. I can bring dead things back to life."

"Really?" He looked impressed. "Okay. You get credit for that. What else?"

"Um, I can use compulsion."

"We can all do that."

"No, I can *really* do it. It's not hard. I can make people do anything I want—even bad things."

"So can I." His eyes lit up. "I wonder what would happen if you tried to use it on me. . . ."

She hesitated and absentmindedly ran her fingers over the textured red carpet. "Well . . . I can't."

"You just said you could."

"I can—just not right now. I take this prescription . . . for depression and other stuff . . . and it cuts me off from the magic."

He threw his arms up in the air. "How can I teach you to walk through dreams then? How else are we going to find Rose?"

"Look," she said angrily, "I don't *want* to take the meds. But when I was off them . . . I did really crazy stuff. Danger-ous stuff. That's what spirit does to you."

"I don't take anything. I'm okay," he said.

No, he wasn't, I realized. Lissa realized it too.

"You got really weird that day when Dimitri was in your room," she pointed out. "You started rambling, and you didn't make any sense."

"Oh, that? Yeah . . . it happens now and then. But seriously, not often. Once a month, if that." He sounded sincere.

Lissa stared at him, suddenly reevaluating everything. What if Adrian could do it? What if he could use spirit with-out pills *and* without any harmful side effects? It would be everything she had been hoping for. Besides, she wasn't even sure if the pills would keep working anymore. . . .

He smiled, guessing what she was thinking.

"What do you say, cousin?" he asked. He didn't need to use compulsion. His offer was plenty tempting in its own right. "I can teach you everything I know if you're able to touch the magic. It'll take a while for the pills to get out of your system, but once they do . . ."

TWENTY-ONE

THIS WAS *SO* NOT WHAT I needed right now. I could have handled anything else Adrian did: hitting on her, getting her to smoke his ridiculous cigarettes, whatever. But not this. Lissa quitting those pills was exactly what I'd wanted to avoid.

Reluctantly, I pulled out of her head and returned to my own grim situation. I would have liked to see what further developed with Adrian and Lissa, but watching them would do no good. Okay. I *really* needed a plan now. I needed action. I needed to get us out of here. But, glancing around me, I found myself no closer to escape than I had been earlier, and I spent the next few hours brooding and speculating.

We had three guards today. They looked a little bored but not enough to slack off. Nearby, Eddie appeared unconscious, and Mason stared blankly at the floor. Across the room, Christian glared at nothing in particular, and I think Mia was sleeping. Painfully aware of how dry my throat was, I almost laughed in recalling how I'd told her water magic was useless. It might not do much in a fight, but I would have given anything for her to summon up some—

Magic.

Why hadn't I thought of this before? We weren't helpless. Not entirely.

A plan slowly coalesced in my mind—a plan that was probably insane but was also the best we had. My heart thudded with anticipation, and I immediately schooled my features to calmness before the guards noticed my sudden insight. On the opposite side of the room, Christian was watching me. He'd seen the brief flare of excitement and realized I'd thought of something. He watched me curiously, as ready for action as I was.

God. How could we pull this off? I needed his help, but I had no real way of letting him know what I had in mind. In fact, I wasn't even sure if he could help me at all—he was pretty weak.

I held his gaze, willing him to understand that something was going to happen. There was confusion on his face, but it was paired with determination. After making sure none of the guards were looking directly at me, I shifted slightly, giving a small tug at my wrists. I glanced behind me as much as I could, then met Christian's eyes again. He frowned, and I repeated the gesture.

"Hey," I said loudly. Mia and Mason both jerked in surprise. "Are you guys really going to keep starving us? Can't we at least have some water or something?"

"Shut up," said one of the guards. It was a pretty standard answer whenever any of us spoke.

"Come on." I used my best bitchy voice. "Not even like a sip of something? My throat's *burning*. Practically on fire." My gaze flicked to Christian as I said those last few words, then returned to the guard who'd spoken.

As expected, he rose from his seat and lurched toward me. "Do *not* make me repeat myself," he growled. I didn't know if he'd really do anything violent, but I had no interest in pushing it just yet. Besides, I'd accomplished my goal. If Christian couldn't take the hint, there was nothing else to be done for it. Hoping I looked afraid, I shut up.

The guard returned to his seat, and after a while, he stopped watching me. I looked at Christian again and gave the wrist tug. *Come on, come on*, I thought. *Put it together, Christian.*

His eyebrows suddenly shot up, and he stared at me in amazement. Well. He'd apparently figured out something. I just hoped it was what I'd wanted. His look turned questioning, as though asking if I was really serious. I nodded emphatically. He frowned in thought for a few moments and then took a deep, steadying breath.

"All right," he said. Everyone jumped again.

"Shut up," said one of the guards automatically. He sounded weary.

"No," said Christian. "I'm ready. Ready to drink."

Everyone in the room froze for the space of a few heartbeats, including me. This wasn't exactly what I'd had in mind.

The guards' leader stood up. "Do *not* screw around with us."

"I'm not," said Christian. He had a feverish, desperate look on his face that I didn't think was entirely faked. "I'm tired of this. I want to get out of here, and I don't want to die. I'll drink—and I want *her*." He nodded toward me. Mia squeaked in alarm. Mason called Christian something that would have earned him a detention back at school.

This *definitely* wasn't what I'd had in mind.

The other two guards looked to their leader questioningly. "Should we get Isaiah?" asked one of them.

"I don't think he's here," said the leader. He studied Christian for a few seconds and then made a decision. "And I don't want to bother him anyway if this is a joke. Let him go, and we'll see."

One of the men produced a pair of sharp pliers. He moved behind Christian and leaned down. I heard the sound of plastic popping as the flex-cuffs gave way. Grabbing a hold of Christian's arm, the guard jerked him upright and led him over to me.

"Christian," exclaimed Mason, fury filling his voice. He struggled against his constraints, shaking his chair a little. "Are you out of your mind? Don't let them do this!"

"You guys have to die, but I don't," snapped Christian, tossing his black hair out of his eyes. "There's no other way out of this."

I didn't really know what was going on now, but I was pretty sure I should be showing a lot more emotion if I was about to die. Two guards flanked Christian on either side, watching warily as he leaned toward me.

"Christian," I whispered, surprised at how easy it was to sound afraid. "Don't do this."

His lips twisted into one of the bitter smiles he produced

so well. "You and I have never liked each other, Rose. If I've got to kill someone, it might as well be you." His words were icy, precise. Believable. "Besides, I thought you wanted this."

"Not *this*. Please, don't—"

One of the guards shoved Christian. "Get it over with, or get back to your chair."

Still wearing that dark smile, Christian shrugged. "Sorry, Rose. You're going to die anyway. Why not do it for a good cause?" He brought his face down to my neck. "This is probably going to hurt," he added.

I actually doubted it would . . . if he was really going to do it. Because he wasn't . . . right? I shifted uneasily. By all accounts, if you got all your blood sucked out of you, you also got enough endorphins pumped in during the process to dull most of the pain. It was like going to sleep. Of course, that was all speculation. People who died from vampire bites didn't really come back to report on the experience.

Christian nuzzled my neck, moving his face under my hair so that it partially obscured him. His lips brushed my skin, every bit as soft as I recalled from when he and Lissa kissed. A moment later, the points of his fangs touched my skin.

And then I felt pain. Real pain.

But it wasn't coming from the bite. His teeth only pressed against my skin; they didn't break it. His tongue moved against my neck in a lapping motion, but there was no blood to suck. If anything, it was more like some kind of weird, twisted kiss.

No, the pain came from my wrists. A burning pain. Christian was using his magic to channel heat into my flex-cuffs, just as I had wanted him to. He'd understood my message. The plastic grew hotter and hotter as he continued his barely there drinking. Anyone who'd been looking closely would have been able to tell he was half-faking it, but too much of my hair was blocking the guards' view.

I knew plastic was hard to melt, but only now did I really, really understand what that meant. The temperatures required to do any damage were off the charts. It was like plunging my hands into lava. The flex-cuffs seared my skin, hot and terrible. I squirmed, hoping I could relieve the pain. I couldn't. What I did notice, however, was that the cuffs gave a little when I moved. They were getting softer. Okay. That was something. I just had to hold out a little longer. Desperately, I tried to focus on Christian's bite and distract myself. It worked for about five seconds. He wasn't giving me much in the way of endorphins, certainly not enough to combat that increasingly horrible pain. I whimpered, probably making myself more convincing.

"I can't believe it," muttered one of the guards. "He's actually doing it." Beyond them, I thought I heard the sound of Mia crying.

The cuffs' burning increased. I'd never felt anything so painful in my life, and I'd been through a lot. Passing out was rapidly becoming a very real possibility.

"Hey," the guard suddenly said. "What's that smell?"

That smell was melting plastic. Or maybe my melting flesh. Honestly, it didn't matter because the next time I moved my wrists, they broke through the gooey, scalding cuffs.

I had ten seconds of surprise, and I used them. I leapt out of my chair, pushing Christian backward in the process. He'd had a guard on either side of him, and one still held the pliers. In a single motion, I grabbed the pliers from the guy and plunged them into his cheek. He gave some kind of gurgled scream, but I didn't wait to see what happened. My window of surprise was closing, and I couldn't waste time. As soon as I let go of the pliers, I punched the second guy. My kicks were stronger than my punches as a general rule, but I still hit him hard enough to startle him and make him stagger.

By then, the guards' leader was in action. As I'd feared, he still had a gun, and he went for it. "Don't move!" he yelled, aiming at me.

I froze. The guard I'd punched came forward and grabbed my arm. Nearby, the guy I'd stabbed was moaning on the floor. Still training the gun on me, the leader started to say something and then yelped in alarm. The gun glowed faintly orange and fell from his hands. Where he'd held it, the skin burned red and angry. Christian had heated the metal, I realized. Yeah. We definitely should have been using this magic thing from the start. If we got out of this, I was going to take up Tasha's cause. The Moroi anti-magic custom was so instilled in our brains that we hadn't even thought to try this sooner. It was stupid.

I turned on the guy holding me. I don't think he expected a girl my size to put up so much of a fight, plus he was still kind of stunned over what had happened to the other guy and the gun. I managed enough room to get in a kick to his stomach, a kick that would have earned me an A in my combat class. He grunted at the impact, and the motion propelled him back into the wall. In a flash, I was on him. Grabbing a fistful of his hair, I slammed his head against the ground hard enough to knock him out but not kill him.

Immediately, I sprang up, surprised the leader hadn't come after me yet. It shouldn't have taken him that long to recover from the shock of the heated gun. But when I turned around, the room was quiet. The leader lay unconscious on the ground—with a newly freed Mason hovering over him. Nearby, Christian held the pliers in one hand and the gun in the other. It had to still be hot, but Christian's power must have made him immune. He was aiming at that man I'd stabbed. The guy wasn't unconscious, merely bleeding, but, like I had, he froze beneath that barrel.

"Holy shit," I muttered, taking in the scene. Staggering over to Christian, I held out my hand. "Give me that before you hurt somebody."

I expected a biting remark, but he simply handed the gun over with shaking hands. I shoved it into my belt. Studying him further, I saw how pale he was. He looked like he could collapse at any moment. He'd done some pretty major magic for someone who'd been starved for two days.

"Mase, get the cuffs," I said. Without turning his back on the rest of us, Mason took a few steps back toward the box where our captors had kept their stash of flex-cuffs. He pulled out three strips of plastic and then something else. With a questioning glance at me, he held up a roll of duct tape.

"Perfect," I said.

We bound our captors to the chairs. One had remained conscious, but we knocked him out too and then put duct tape over all their mouths. They'd eventually come to, and I didn't want them making any noise.

After releasing Mia and Eddie, the five of us huddled together and planned our next move. Christian and Eddie could barely stand, but at least Christian was aware of his surroundings. Mia's face was streaked with tears, but I suspected she'd be able to take orders. That left Mason and me as the most functional in the group.

"That guy's watch says it's morning," he said. "All we've got to do is get outside, and they can't touch us. As long as there are no more humans, at least."

"They said Isaiah was gone," said Mia in a small voice. "We should just be able to leave, right?"

"Those men haven't left in hours," I said. "They could be wrong. We can't do anything stupid."

Carefully, Mason opened the door to our room and peered out into the empty hallway. "Think there's a way outside down here?"

"That'd make our lives easier," I muttered. I glanced back

at the others. "Stay here. We're going to check out the rest of the basement."

"What if somebody comes?" exclaimed Mia.

"They won't," I assured her. I was actually pretty sure there was no one else in the basement; they would have come running with all that racket. And if anyone tried to come down the stairs, we would hear them first.

Still, Mason and I moved cautiously as we scouted around the basement, watching each other's backs and checking around corners. It was every bit the rat's maze I remembered from our initial capture. Twisted hallways and lots of rooms. One by one, we opened each door. Every room was empty, save for the occasional chair or two. I shuddered, thinking that all of these were probably used as prisons, just as ours had been.

"Not a goddamned window in this whole place," I muttered when we'd finished our sweep. "We've got to go upstairs."

We headed back toward our room, but before we got there, Mason caught hold of my hand. "Rose . . ."

I stopped and looked up at him. "Yeah?"

His blues eyes—more serious than I'd ever seen them—looked down at me regretfully. "I really screwed things up."

I thought about all the events that had led to this. "*We* screwed things up, Mason."

He sighed. "I hope . . . I hope when this is all done, we can sit down and talk and figure things out. I shouldn't have gotten mad at you."

I wanted to tell him that that wasn't going to happen, that when he'd disappeared, I'd actually been on my way to tell him things wouldn't be better between us. Since this didn't seem like the right time or place to bring up a breakup, I lied.

I squeezed his hand. "I hope so too."

He smiled, and we returned to the others.

"All right," I told them. "Here's how it's going to be."

We quickly hashed out a plan and then crept up the stairs. I led, followed by Mia as she tried to support a reluctant Christian. Mason brought up the rear, practically dragging Eddie.

"I should be first," Mason murmured as we stood at the top of the stairs.

"You aren't," I snapped back, resting my hand on the doorknob.

"Yeah, but if something happens—"

"Mason," I interrupted. I stared at him hard, and suddenly, I had a brief flash of my mother that day when the Drozdov attack had broken. Calm and controlled, even in the wake of something so horrible. They'd needed a leader, just like this group did now, and I tried as hard as I could to channel her. "If something happens, you get them out of here. Run fast and run far. Do not come back without a herd of guardians."

"You'll be the one who gets attacked first! What am I supposed to do?" he hissed. "Leave you?"

"Yes. You forget about me if you can get them out."

"Rose, I'm not going to—"

"Mason." I again envisioned my mother, fighting for that

strength and power to lead others. "Can you do this or not?"

We stared at each other for several heavy moments while the others held their breaths.

"I can do this," he said stiffly. I nodded and turned back around.

The basement door squeaked when I opened it, and I grimaced at the sound. Scarcely daring to breathe, I stood perfectly still at the top of the stairs, waiting and listening. The house and its eccentric decorating looked the same as when we'd been brought in. Dark blinds covered all of the windows, but along the edges, I could see bright light peeping in. Sunshine had never tasted so sweet as it did at that moment. Getting to it meant freedom.

There were no sounds, no movements. Looking around, I tried to remember where the front door was. It was on the other side of the house—really not far in the grand scheme of things but a gaping chasm at the moment.

"Scout with me," I whispered to Mason, hoping to make him feel better about bringing up the rear.

He let Eddie lean on Mia for a moment and stepped forward with me to do a quick sweep of the main living area. Nothing. The path was clear from here to the front door. I exhaled in relief. Mason took hold of Eddie again, and we moved forward, all of us tense and nervous. God. We were going to do this, I realized. We were really going to do this. I couldn't believe how lucky we'd gotten. We'd been so close to disaster—and had just barely made it through. It was one of those moments that made you appreciate your life and want to turn things around. A second chance you swear you won't let go to waste. A realization that—

I heard them move almost at the same time I saw them step in front of us. It was like a magician conjured Isaiah and Elena out of thin air. Only, I knew there was no magic involved this time. Strigoi just moved that quickly. They must have been in one of the other main floor rooms that we'd assumed were empty—we hadn't wanted to waste the extra time looking. I raged at myself internally for not having checked out every inch of the whole floor. Somewhere, in the back of my memory, I heard myself taunting my mother in Stan's class: *"It seems to me like you guys messed up. Why didn't you scope out the place and make sure it was clear of Strigoi in the first place? Seems like you could have saved yourself a lot of trouble."*

Karma's a real bitch.

"Children, children," crooned Isaiah. "This isn't how the game works. You're breaking the rules." A cruel smile played over his lips. He found us amusing, no real threat at all. Honestly? He was right.

"Fast and far, Mason," I said in low voice, never taking my eyes off the Strigoi.

"My, my . . . if looks could kill . . ." Isaiah arched his eyebrows as something occurred to him. "Are you thinking you can take us both on by yourself?" He chuckled. Elena chuckled. I gritted my teeth.

No, I didn't think I could take them both on. In fact, I was pretty sure I was going to die. But I was also pretty sure I could provide one hell of a distraction first.

I lunged toward Isaiah but pulled the gun on Elena. You could get a jump on human guards—but not on Strigoi. They saw me coming practically before I even moved. They didn't expect me to have a gun, though. And while Isaiah blocked my attacking body with almost no effort whatsoever, I still managed to get a shot off at Elena before he seized my arms and restrained me. The gun's report rang loud in my ears, and she screamed in pain and surprise. I'd aimed for her stomach but had been jostled into hitting her thigh. Not that it mattered. Neither spot would kill her, but the stomach would have hurt a lot more.

Isaiah held my wrists so hard, I thought he'd break the bones. I dropped the gun. It hit the floor, bounced, and slid toward the door. Elena shrieked in rage and clawed at me. Isaiah told her to control herself and pushed me out of reach. All the while, I flailed as much as possible, not so much to escape as to make a nuisance of myself.

And then: the sweetest of sounds.

The front door opening.

Mason had taken advantage of my distraction. He'd left Eddie with Mia and sprinted around me and the grappling Strigoi to open the door. Isaiah turned with that lightning-fast speed of his—and screamed as sunlight poured over him. But even though he was suffering, his reflexes were still fast. He jerked himself out of the patch of light into the living room, dragging Elena and me with him—her by the arm and me by my neck.

"Get them out!" I yelled.

"Isaiah—" began Elena, breaking out of his grip.

He shoved me to the floor and spun around, staring at his escaping victims. I gasped for breath now that his grip on my throat was gone and peered back at the door through the tangle of my hair. I was just in time to see Mason drag Eddie over the threshold, out into the safety of the light. Mia and Christian were already gone. I nearly wept in relief.

Isaiah turned back on me with all the fury of a storm, his eyes black and terrible as he loomed over me from his great height. His face, which had always been scary, became something almost beyond comprehension. "Monstrous" didn't even begin to cover it.

He jerked me up by my hair. I cried out at the pain, and he brought his head down so that our faces were pressed up to one another's.

"You want a bite, girl?" he demanded. "You want to be a blood whore? Well, we can arrange that. In every sense of the word. And it will *not* be sweet. And it will *not* be numbing. It will be painful—compulsion works both ways, you know, and I will make sure you believe you are suffering the worst pain of your life. And I will also make sure your death takes a very, very long time. You will scream. You will cry. You will beg me to end it all and let you die—"

"Isaiah," cried Elena in exasperation. "Just kill her already.

If you'd done it sooner like I said, none of this would have happened."

He kept his grip on me but flicked his eyes toward her. "Do not interrupt me."

"You're being melodramatic," she continued. Yeah, she really was whiny. I never would have thought a Strigoi could do that. It was almost comical. "And wasteful."

"Do not talk back to me, either," he said.

"I'm *hungry*. I'm just saying you should—"

"Let her go, or I'll kill you."

We all turned at the new voice, a voice dark and angry. Mason stood in the doorway, framed in light, holding my dropped gun. Isaiah studied him for a few moments.

"Sure," Isaiah finally said. He sounded bored. "Try it."

Mason didn't hesitate. He fired and kept firing until he'd emptied the entire clip into Isaiah's chest. Each bullet made the Strigoi flinch a little, but otherwise, he kept standing and holding on to me. This was what it meant to be an old and powerful Strigoi, I realized. A bullet in the thigh hurt a young vampire like Elena. But for Isaiah? Getting shot in the chest multiple times was simply a nuisance.

Mason realized this too, and his features hardened as he threw down the gun.

"Get out!" I screamed. He was still in the sun, still safe.

But he didn't listen to me. He ran toward us, out of his protective light. I redoubled my struggles, hoping I'd pull Isaiah's attention away from Mason. I didn't. Isaiah shoved me into Elena before Mason was halfway to us. Swiftly, Isaiah blocked and seized hold of Mason, exactly as he'd done to me earlier.

Only, unlike with me, Isaiah didn't restrain Mason's arms. He didn't jerk Mason upright by the hair or make long, rambling threats about an agonizing death. Isaiah simply stopped the attack, grabbed Mason's head with both hands, and gave a quick twist. There was a sickening crack. Mason's eyes went wide. Then they went blank.

With an impatient sigh, Isaiah released his hold and tossed Mason's limp body over toward where Elena held me. It landed before us. My vision swam as nausea and dizziness wrapped around me.

"There," Isaiah said to Elena. "See if that'll tide you over. And save some for me."

TWENTY-TWO

HORROR AND SHOCK CONSUMED ME, so much so that I thought my soul would shrivel, that the world would end right then and there—because surely, *surely* it couldn't keep going on after this. No one could keep going on after this. I wanted to shriek my pain to the universe. I wanted to cry until I melted. I wanted to sink down beside Mason and die with him.

Elena released me, apparently deciding I posed no danger positioned as I was between her and Isaiah. She turned toward Mason's body.

And I stopped feeling. I simply acted.

"Don't. Touch. Him." I didn't recognize my own voice.

She rolled her eyes. "Good grief, you're annoying. I'm started to see Isaiah's point—you *do* need to suffer before dying." Turning away, she knelt down to the floor and flipped Mason over onto his back.

"Don't touch him!" I screamed. I shoved her with little effect. She shoved back, nearly knocking me over. It was all I could do to steady my feet and stay upright.

Isaiah looked on with amused interest; then his gaze fell to the floor. Lissa's chotki had fallen out of my coat pocket. He picked it up. Strigoi could touch holy objects—the stories about them fearing crosses weren't true. They just couldn't enter holy ground. He flipped the cross over and ran his fingers over the etched dragon.

"Ah, the Dragomirs," he mused. "I'd forgotten about them. Easy to. There's what, one? Two of them left? Barely worth remembering." Those horrible red eyes focused on me. "Do you know any of them? I'll have to see to them one of these days. It won't be very hard to—"

Suddenly, I heard an explosion. The aquarium burst apart as water shot out of it, shattering the glass. Pieces of it flew toward me, but I barely noticed. The water coalesced in the air, forming a lopsided sphere. It began to float. Toward Isaiah. I felt my jaw drop as I stared at it.

He watched it too, more puzzled than scared. At least until it wrapped around his face and started suffocating him.

Much like the bullets, suffocation wouldn't kill him. But it could cause him a hell of a lot of discomfort.

His hands flew to his face, desperately trying to "pry" the water away. It was no use. His fingers simply slipped through. Elena forgot about Mason and jumped to her feet.

"What is it?" she shrieked. She shook him in an equally useless effort to free him. "What's happening?"

Again, I didn't feel. I acted. My hand closed around a large piece of glass from the broken aquarium. It was jagged and sharp, cutting into my hand.

Sprinting forward, I plunged the shard into Isaiah's chest, aiming for the heart I'd worked so hard to find in practice.

Isaiah emitted a strangled scream through the water and collapsed to the floor. His eyes rolled back in his head as he blacked out from the pain.

Elena stared, as shocked as I'd been when Isaiah had killed Mason. Isaiah wasn't dead, of course, but he was temporarily down for the count. Her face clearly showed she hadn't thought that was possible.

The smart thing at that point would have been to run toward the door and the sun's safety. Instead, I ran in the opposite direction, toward the fireplace. I grabbed one of the antique swords and turned back toward Elena. I didn't have far to go, because she'd recovered herself and was heading toward me.

Snarling with rage, she tried to grab me. I had never trained with a sword, but I had been taught to fight with any makeshift weapon I could find. I used the sword to keep distance between us, my motions clumsy but effective for the time being.

White fangs flashed in her mouth. "I am going to make you—"

"Suffer, pay, regret I was ever born?" I suggested.

I remembered fighting with my mom, how I'd been on the defensive the whole time. That wouldn't work this time. I had to attack. Jabbing forward, I tried to land a blow on Elena. No luck. She anticipated my every move.

Suddenly, from behind her, Isaiah groaned as he started to come around. She glanced back, the smallest of motions that let me swipe the sword across her chest. It cut the fabric of her shirt and grazed the skin, but nothing more. Still, she flinched and looked down in panic. I think the glass going through Isaiah's heart was still fresh in her mind.

And *that* was what I really needed.

I mustered all my strength, drew back, and swung.

The sword's blade hit the side of her neck, hard and deep. She gave a horrible, sickening cry, a shriek that made my skin crawl. She tried to move toward me. I pulled back and hit again. Her hands clutched at her throat, and her knees gave way. I struck and struck, the sword digging deeper into her neck each time. Cutting off someone's head was harder than I'd thought it would be. The old, dull sword probably wasn't helping.

But finally, I gained enough sense to realize she wasn't moving. Her head lay there, detached from her body, her dead eyes looking up at me as though she couldn't believe what had happened. That made two of us.

Someone was screaming, and for a surreal second, I thought it was still Elena. Then I lifted my eyes and looked across the room. Mia stood in the doorway, eyes bugging out and skin tinged green like she might throw up. Distantly, in the back of my mind, I realized she was the one who'd made the aquarium explode. Water magic apparently wasn't worthless after all.

Still a bit shaken, Isaiah tried to rise to his feet. But I was on him before he could fully manage it. The sword sang out, wreaking blood and pain with each blow. I felt like an old pro now. Isaiah fell back to the floor. In my mind, I kept seeing him break Mason's neck, and I hacked and hacked as hard as I could, as though striking fiercely enough might somehow banish the memory.

"Rose! *Rose!*"

Through my hate-filled haze, I just barely detected Mia's voice.

"Rose, he's dead!"

Slowly, shakily, I held back the next blow and looked down at his body—and the head no longer attached to it. She was right. He was dead. Very, very dead.

I looked at the rest of the room. There was blood everywhere, but the horror of it didn't really register with me. My world had slowed down, slowed down to two very simple tasks. Kill the Strigoi. Protect Mason. I couldn't process anything else.

"Rose," whispered Mia. She was trembling, her words filled with fear. She was afraid of me, not the Strigoi. "Rose, we have to go. Come on."

I dragged my eyes away from her and looked down at Isaiah's remains. After several moments, I crawled over to Mason's body, still clutching the sword.

"No," I croaked out. "I can't leave him. Other Strigoi might come. . . ."

My eyes burned like I desperately wanted to cry. I couldn't say for sure. The bloodlust still pounded in me, violence and rage the only emotions I was capable of anymore.

"Rose, we'll come back for him. If other Strigoi are coming, we have to get out."

"No," I repeated, not even looking at her. "I'm not leaving him. I won't leave him alone." With my free hand, I stroked Mason's hair.

"Rose—"

I jerked my head up. "Get out!" I screamed at her. "Get out, and leave us alone."

She took a few steps forward, and I lifted the sword. She froze.

"Get out," I repeated. "Go find the others."

Slowly, Mia backed up toward the door. She gave me one last, desperate look before running outside.

Silence fell, and I relaxed my hold on the sword but refused to let it go. My body sagged forward, and I rested my head on Mason's chest. I became oblivious to everything: to the world around me, to time itself. Seconds could have passed. Hours could have passed. I didn't know. I didn't know anything except that I couldn't leave Mason alone. I existed in an altered state, a state that just barely kept the terror and grief at bay. I couldn't believe Mason was dead. I couldn't believe I'd just summoned death. So long as I refused to acknowledge either, I could pretend they hadn't happened.

Footsteps and voices eventually sounded, and I lifted my head up. People poured in through the door, lots of them. I couldn't really make out any of them. I didn't need to. They were threats, threats I had to keep Mason safe from. A couple of them approached me, and I leapt up, lifting the sword and holding it protectively over his body.

"Stay back," I warned. "Stay away from him."

They kept coming.

"Stay back!" I yelled. They stopped. Except for one.

"Rose," came a soft voice. "Drop the sword."

My hands shook. I swallowed. "Get away from us."

"Rose."

The voice spoke again, a voice that my soul would have known anywhere. Hesitantly, I let myself finally become aware of my surroundings, let the details sink in. I let my eyes focus on the features of the man standing there. Dimitri's brown eyes, gentle and firm, looked down on me.

"It's okay," he said. "Everything's going to be okay. You can let go of the sword."

My hands shook even harder as I fought to hold on to the hilt. "I can't." The words hurt coming out. "I can't leave him alone. I have to protect him."

"You have," said Dimitri.

The sword fell out of my hands, landing with a loud clatter on the wooden floor. I followed, collapsing on all fours, wanting to cry but still unable to.

Dimitri's arms wrapped around me as he helped me up. Voices swarmed around us, and one by one, I recognized people I knew and trusted. He started to tug me toward the door, but I refused to move just yet. I couldn't. My hands clutched his shirt, crumpling the fabric. Still keeping one arm around me, he smoothed my hair back away from my face. I leaned my head against him, and he continued stroking my hair, murmuring something in Russian. I didn't understand a word of it, but the gentle tone soothed me.

Guardians were spreading throughout the house, examining it inch by inch. A couple of them approached us and knelt by the bodies I refused to look at.

"She did that? Both of them?"

"That sword hasn't been sharpened in years!"

A funny sound caught in my throat. Dimitri squeezed my shoulder comfortingly.

"Get her out of here, Belikov," I heard a woman say behind him, her voice familiar.

Dimitri squeezed my shoulder again. "Come on, Roza. It's time to go."

This time, I went. He guided me out of the house, holding onto me as I managed each agonizing step. My mind still refused to really process what had happened. I couldn't do much more than follow simple directions from those around me.

I eventually ended up on one of the Academy's jets. Engines roared around us as the plane lifted off. Dimitri murmured something about coming back shortly and left me alone in my seat. I stared straight ahead, studying the details of the seat in front of me.

Someone sat beside me and draped a blanket over my

shoulders. I noticed then just how badly I was shivering. I tugged at the edges of the blanket.

"I'm cold," I said. "How am I so cold?"

"You're in shock," Mia answered.

I turned and looked at her, studying her blond curls and big blue eyes. Something about seeing her unleashed my memories. It all tumbled back. I squeezed my eyes shut.

"Oh God," I breathed. I opened my eyes and focused on her again. "You saved me—saved me when you blew up the fish tank. You shouldn't have done it. You shouldn't have come back."

She shrugged. "You shouldn't have gone for the sword."

Fair point. "Thank you," I told her. "What you did . . . I never would have thought of that. It was brilliant."

"I don't know about that," she mused, smiling ruefully. "Water isn't much of a weapon, remember?"

I choked on a laugh, even though I really didn't find my old words that funny. Not anymore.

"Water's a great weapon," I said finally. "When we get back, we'll have to practice ways to use it."

Her face lit up. Fierceness shone out from her eyes. "I'd like that. More than anything."

"I'm sorry . . . sorry about your mom."

Mia simply nodded. "You're lucky to still have yours. You don't know how lucky."

I turned and stared at the seat again. The next words out of my mouth startled me: "I wish she was here."

"She is," said Mia, sounding surprised. "She was with the group that raided the house. Didn't you see her?"

I shook my head.

We lapsed into silence. Mia stood up and left. A minute later, someone else sat down beside me. I didn't have to see her to know who she was. I just *knew*.

"Rose," said my mother. For once in my life, she sounded unsure of herself. Scared, maybe. "Mia said you wanted to see me." I didn't answer. I didn't look at her. "What . . . what do you need?"

I didn't know what I needed. I didn't know what to do. The stinging in my eyes grew unbearable, and before I knew it, I was crying. Big, painful sobs seized my body. The tears I'd held back so long poured down my face. The fear and grief I'd refused to let myself feel finally burst free, burning in my chest. I could scarcely breathe.

My mother put her arms around me, and I buried my face in her chest, sobbing even harder.

"I know," she said softly, tightening her grip on me. "I understand."

TWENTY-THREE

THE WEATHER WARMED UP ON the day of my *molnija* ceremony. In fact, it was so warm that a lot of the snow on campus began melting, running down the sides of the Academy's stone buildings in slim, silvery streams. Winter was far from being over, so I knew everything would just freeze up again in a few days. For now, though, it felt as though the entire world was weeping.

I had walked away from the Spokane incident with minor bruises and cuts. The burns from the melting flex-cuffs were the worst of my injuries. But I was still having a hard time dealing with the death I'd caused and the death I'd seen. I'd wanted little more than to go curl up in a ball somewhere and not talk to anyone, except maybe Lissa. But on my fourth day back at the Academy, my mother had found me and told me it was time to receive my marks.

It had taken me several moments to grasp what she was talking about. Then it occurred to me that in decapitating two Strigoi, I'd earned two *molnija* tattoos. My first ones. The realization had stunned me. All my life, in considering my future career as a guardian, I'd looked forward to the marks. I'd seen them as badges of honor. But now? Mainly they were going to be reminders of something I wanted to forget.

The ceremony took place in the guardians' building, in a large room they used for meetings and banquets. It was nothing at all like the great dining room at the resort. It was efficient and practical, like the guardians were. The carpet was a bluish gray shade, low and tightly woven. The bare white walls held framed black-and-white photos of St. Vladimir's through the years. There were no other decorations or fanfare, yet the solemnity and power of the moment were palpable. All the guardians on campus—but no novices—attended. They milled around in the building's main meeting room, hanging out in clusters but not talking. When the ceremony started, they fell into orderly ranks without being told and watched me.

I sat on a stool in the corner of the room, leaning forward with my hair hanging over the front of my face. Behind me, a guardian named Lionel held a tattooist's needle to the back of my neck. I'd known him the whole time I'd been at the Academy, but I'd never realized he was trained to draw *molnija* marks.

Before he started, he had a murmured conversation with my mother and Alberta.

"She won't have a promise mark," he said. "She hasn't graduated."

"It happens," said Alberta. "She made the kills. Do the *molnijas*, and she'll get the promise mark later."

Considering the pain I regularly put myself through, I didn't expect the tattoos to hurt as much as they did. But I bit my lip and stayed silent as Lionel made the marks. The process seemed to go on forever. When he finished, he produced a couple of mirrors, and with some maneuvering, I was able to see the back of my neck. Two tiny black marks sat there, side by side, against my reddened and sensitive skin. *Molnija* meant "lightning" in Russian, and that's what the jagged shape was meant to symbolize. Two marks. One for Isaiah, one for Elena.

Once I'd seen them, he bandaged them up and gave me some instructions about caring for them while they healed. Most of it I missed, but I figured I could ask again later. I was still kind of shocked by it all.

After that, all the gathered guardians came up to me one by one. They each gave me some sort of sign of affection—a hug, a kiss on the cheek—and kind words.

"Welcome to the ranks," said Alberta, her weathered face gentle as she pulled me into a tight embrace.

Dimitri didn't say anything when his turn came, but as always, his eyes spoke legions. Pride and tenderness filled his expression, and I swallowed back tears. He rested one hand gently on my cheek, nodded, and walked away.

When Stan—the instructor I'd fought with the most since my first day—hugged me and said, "Now you're one of us. I always knew you'd be one of the best," I thought I'd pass out.

And then when my mother came up to me, I couldn't help the tear that ran down my cheek. She wiped it away and then brushed her fingers against the back of my neck. "Don't ever forget," she told me.

Nobody said, "Congratulations," and I was glad. Death wasn't anything to get excited about.

When that was done, drinks and food were served. I walked to the buffet table and made a plate for myself of miniature feta quiches and a slice of mango cheesecake. I ate without really tasting the food and answered questions from others without even knowing what I said half the time. It was like I was a Rose robot, going through the motions of what was expected. On the back of my neck, my skin stung from the tattoos, and in my mind, I kept seeing Mason's blue eyes and Isaiah's red ones.

I felt guilty for not enjoying my big day more, but I was relieved when the group finally started dispersing. My mother walked up to me as others murmured their good-byes. Aside from her words here at the ceremony, we hadn't talked much since my breakdown on the plane. I still felt a little funny about that—and a little embarrassed as well. She'd never mentioned it, but something very small had shifted in the nature of our relationship. We weren't anywhere near being friends . . . but we weren't exactly enemies anymore either.

"Lord Szelsky is leaving soon," she told me as we stood near the building's doorway, not far from where I'd yelled for her on that first day we'd talked. "I'll be going with him."

"I know," I said. There was no question she'd leave. That was how it was. Guardians followed Moroi. They came first.

She regarded me for a few moments, her brown eyes

thoughtful. For the first time in a long time, I felt like we were actually looking eye to eye, as opposed to her looking down on me. It was about time, too, seeing as I had half a foot of height on her.

"You did well," she said at last. "Considering the circumstances."

It was only half a compliment, but I deserved no more. I understood now the mistakes and lapses of judgment that had led to the events at Isaiah's house. Some had been my fault; some hadn't. I wished I could have changed some of my actions, but I knew she was right. I'd done the best I could in the end with the mess before me.

"Killing Strigoi wasn't as glamorous as I thought it'd be," I told her.

She gave me a sad smile. "No. It never is."

I thought then about all the marks on her neck, all the kills. I shuddered.

"Oh, hey." Eager to change the subject, I reached into my pocket and pulled out the little blue eye pendant she'd given me. "This thing you gave me. It's a *n-nazar*?" I stumbled over the word. She looked surprised.

"Yes. How'd you know?"

I didn't want to explain my dreams with Adrian. "Someone told me. It's a protection thing, right?"

A pensive look crossed her face, and then she exhaled and nodded. "Yes. It comes from an old superstition in the Middle East. . . . Some people believe that those who want to hurt you can curse you or give you 'the evil eye.' The nazar is meant to counteract the evil eye . . . and just bring protection in general to those who wear it."

I ran my fingers over the piece of glass. "Middle East . . . so, places sort of like, um, Turkey?"

My mother's lips quirked. "Places exactly like Turkey." She hesitated. "It was . . . a gift. A gift I received a long time ago . . ." Her gaze turned inward, lost in memory. "I got a lot of . . . attention from men when I was your age. Attention that seemed flattering at first but wasn't in the end. It's hard to tell the difference sometimes, between what's real affection and what's someone wanting to take advantage of you. But when you feel the real thing . . . well, you'll know."

I understood then why she was so overprotective about my reputation—she'd endangered her own when she was younger. Maybe more than that had been damaged.

I also knew why she'd given the nazar to me. My father had given it to her. I didn't think she wanted to talk anymore about it, so I didn't ask. It was enough to know that maybe, just maybe, their relationship hadn't been all about business and genes after all.

We said goodbye, and I returned to my classes. Everyone knew where I'd been that morning, and my fellow novices wanted to see my *molnija* marks. I didn't blame them. If our roles had been reversed, I would have been harassing me too.

"Come on, Rose," begged Shane Reyes. We were walking out of our morning practice, and he kept swatting my ponytail.

I made a mental note to wear my hair down tomorrow. Several others followed us and echoed his requests.

"Yeah, come on. Let's see what you got for your swordsmanship!"

Their eyes shone with eagerness and excitement. I was a hero, their classmate who'd dispatched the leaders of the roving band of Strigoi that had so terrorized us over the holidays. But I met the eyes of someone standing at the back of the group, someone who looked neither eager nor excited. Eddie. Meeting my gaze, he gave me a small, sad smile. He understood.

"Sorry, guys," I said, turning back to the others. "They have to stay bandaged. Doctor's orders."

This was met with grumbles that soon turned into questions about how I'd actually killed the Strigoi. Decapitation was one of the hardest and rarest ways to kill a vampire; it wasn't like carrying a sword was convenient. So I did my best to tell my friends what had happened, making sure to stick to the facts and not glorify the killings.

The school day couldn't end a moment too soon, and Lissa walked with me back to my dorm. She and I hadn't had the chance to talk much since everything had gone down in Spokane. I'd undergone a lot of questioning, and then there'd been Mason's funeral. Lissa had also been caught up in her own distractions with the royals leaving campus, so she'd had no more free time than me.

Being near her made me feel better. Even though I could

be in her head at any time, it just wasn't the same as actually being physically around another living person who cared
about you.

When we got to the door of my room, I saw a bouquet of
freesias sitting on the floor near it. Sighing, I picked up the
fragrant flowers without even looking at the attached card.

"What are those?" asked Lissa while I unlocked the door.

"They're from Adrian," I told her. We walked inside, and I
pointed to my desk, where a few other bouquets sat. I put the
freesias down beside them. "I'll be glad when he leaves campus. I don't think I can take much more of this."

She turned to me in surprise. "Oh. Um, you don't know."

I got that warning twinge through the bond that told me I
wouldn't like what was about to come.

"Know what?"

"Uh, he isn't leaving. He's going to stay here for a while."

"He has to leave," I argued. To my knowledge, the only
reason he'd come back at all was because of Mason's funeral,
and I still wasn't sure why he'd done that, since he barely knew
Mason. Maybe Adrian had just done it for show. Or maybe to
keep stalking Lissa and me. "He's in college. Or maybe reform
school. I don't know, but he does something."

"He's taking the semester off."

I stared.

Smiling at my shock, she nodded. "He's going to stay and
work with me . . . and Ms. Carmack. All this time, he never even
knew what spirit was. He just knew he hadn't specialized but

that he had these weird abilities. He just kept them to himself, except for when he occasionally found another spirit user. But they didn't know any more than he did."

"I should have figured it out sooner," I mused. "There was something about being around him. . . . I always wanted to talk to him, you know? He just has this . . . charisma. Like you do. I guess it's all tied into spirit and compulsion or whatever. It makes me like him . . . even though I don't like him."

"Don't you?" she teased.

"No," I replied adamantly. "And I don't like that dream thing, either."

Her jade eyes went wide with wonder. "*That* is cool," she said. "You've always been able to tell what's going on with me, but I've never been able to communicate with you the other way. I'm glad you guys got away when you did . . . but I wish I could have figured out the dream thing and helped find you."

"Not me," I said. "I'm glad Adrian didn't get you to go off your meds."

I hadn't found that out until a few days after being in Spokane. Lissa had apparently rejected Adrian's initial suggestion that stopping the pills would let her learn more about spirit. She had admitted to me later, however, that if Christian and I had stayed missing much longer, she might have cracked.

"How are you feeling lately?" I asked, recalling her concerns about the medication. "You still feel like the pills aren't working?"

"Mmm . . . well, it's hard to explain. I still feel closer to the magic, like maybe they aren't blocking me so much anymore. But I'm not feeling any of the other mental side effects . . . not upset or anything."

"Wow, that's great."

A beautiful smile lit her face. "I know. It makes me think there might be hope for me to learn to work the magic after all someday."

Seeing her so happy made me smile back. I hadn't liked seeing those dark feelings starting to return and was glad they'd vanished. I didn't understand the how or the why, but as long as she felt okay—

Everyone has light around them, except for you. You have shadows. You take them from Lissa.

Adrian's words slammed into my mind. Uneasily, I thought about my behavior these last couple of weeks. Some of the angry outbursts. My rebelliousness—unusual even for me. My own black coil of emotion, stirring in my chest . . .

No, I decided. There were no similarities. Lissa's dark feelings were magic-based. Mine were stress-based. Besides, I felt fine right now.

Seeing her watching me, I tried to remember where we'd left off in the conversation. "Maybe you'll eventually find a way to make it work. I mean, if Adrian could find a way to use spirit and doesn't need meds . . ."

She suddenly laughed. "You don't know, do you?"

"What?"

"That Adrian does medicate himself."

"He does? But he said—" I groaned. "Of course he does. The cigarettes. The drinking. God only knows what else."

She nodded. "Yup. He's almost always got something in his system."

"But probably not at night . . . which is why he can poke his head into my dreams."

"Man, I wish I could do that," she sighed.

"Maybe you'll learn someday. Just don't become an alcoholic in the process."

"I won't," she assured me. "But I *will* learn. None of the other spirit users could do it, Rose—well, aside from St. Vladimir. I'll learn like he did. I'm going to learn to use it—and I won't let it hurt me."

I smiled and touched her hand. I had absolute faith in her. "I know."

We talked for most of the evening. When the time came for my usual practice with Dimitri, I parted ways with her. As I walked away, I pondered something that had been bothering me. Although the attacking groups of Strigoi had had many more members, the guardians felt confident Isaiah had been their leader. That didn't mean there wouldn't be *other* threats in the future, but they felt it'd be a while before his followers regrouped.

But I couldn't help thinking about the list I'd seen in the tunnel in Spokane, the one that had listed royal families by size. And Isaiah had mentioned the Dragomirs by name. He knew they were almost gone, and he'd sounded keen on being the one to finish them. Sure, he was dead now . . . but were there other Strigoi out there with the same idea?

I shook my head. I couldn't worry about that. Not today. I still needed to recover from everything else. Soon, though. Soon I'd have to deal with this.

I didn't even know if our practice was still on but went to the locker room anyway. After changing into practice clothes, I headed down into the gym and found Dimitri in a supply room, reading one of the Western novels he loved. He looked up at my entrance. I'd seen little of him in these last few days and had figured he was busy with Tasha.

"I thought you might come by," he said, putting a bookmark between the pages.

"It's time for practice."

He shook his head. "No. No practice today. You still need to recover."

"I've got a clean bill of health. I'm good to go." I pushed as much patented Rose Hathaway bravado into my words as I could.

Dimitri wasn't falling for any of it. He gestured to the chair beside him. "Sit down, Rose."

I hesitated only a moment before complying. He moved his own chair close to mine so that we sat directly across from each other. My heart fluttered as I looked into those gorgeous dark eyes.

"No one gets over their first kill . . . kills . . . easily. Even with Strigoi . . . well, it's still technically taking a life. That's hard to come to terms with. And after everything else you went through . . ." He sighed, then reached out and caught my hand in his. His fingers were exactly like I remembered, long and powerful, calloused with years of training. "When I saw your face . . . when we found you in that house . . . you can't imagine how I felt."

I swallowed. "How . . . how did you feel?"

"Devastated . . . grief-stricken. You were alive, but the way you looked . . . I didn't think you'd ever recover. And it tore me apart to think of that happening to you so young." He squeezed my hand. "You will recover—I know that now, and I'm glad. But you aren't there. Not yet. Losing someone you care about is never easy."

My eyes dropped from his and studied the floor. "It's my fault," I said in a small voice.

"Hmm?"

"Mason. Getting killed."

I didn't have to see Dimitri's face to know compassion was filling it. "Oh, Roza. No. You made some bad decisions . . . you should have told others when you knew he was gone . . . but you can't blame yourself. You didn't kill him."

Tears brimmed in my eyes as I looked back up. "I might as well have. The whole reason he went there—it was my fault. We had a fight . . . and I told him about the Spokane thing, even though you asked me not to. . . ."

One tear leaked out of the corner of my eye. Really, I

needed to learn to stop that. Just as my mother had, Dimitri delicately wiped the tear off my cheek.

"You can't blame yourself for that," he told me. "You can regret your decisions and wish you'd done things differently, but in the end, Mason made his decisions too. That was what he chose to do. It was his decision in the end, no matter your original role." When Mason had come back for me, I realized, he'd let his feelings for me get in the way. It was what Dimitri had always feared, that if he and I had any sort of relationship, it would put us—and any Moroi we protected—in danger.

"I just wish I'd been able to . . . I don't know, do any-thing. . . ."

Swallowing back further tears, I pulled my hands from Dimitri's and stood up before I could say something stupid.

"I should go," I said thickly. "Let me know when you want to start practice again. And thanks for . . . talking."

I started to turn; then I heard him say abruptly, "No."

I glanced back. "What?"

He held my gaze, and something warm and wonderful and powerful shot between us.

"No," he repeated. "I told her no. Tasha."

"I . . ." I shut my mouth before my jaw hit the floor. "But . . . why? That was a once-in-a-lifetime thing. You could have had a baby. And she . . . she was, you know, into you. . . ."

The ghost of a smile flickered on his face. "Yes, she was. Is. And that's why I had to say no. I couldn't return that . . . couldn't give her what she wanted. Not when . . ." He took a few steps toward me. "Not when my heart is somewhere else."

I almost started crying again. "But you seemed so into her. And you kept going on about how young I acted."

"You act young," he said, "because you *are* young. But you know things, Roza. Things people older than you don't even know. That day . . ." I knew instantly which day he referred to. The one up against the wall. "You were right, about how I fight to stay in control. No one else has ever figured that out—and it scared me. *You* scare me."

"Why? Don't you want anyone to know?"

He shrugged. "Whether they know that fact or not doesn't matter. What matters is that someone—that you—know me that well. When a person can see into your soul, it's hard. It forces you to be open. Vulnerable. It's much easier being with someone who's just more of a casual friend."

"Like Tasha."

"Tasha Ozera is an amazing woman. She's beautiful and she's brave. But she doesn't—"

"She doesn't *get* you," I finished.

He nodded. "I knew that. But I still wanted the relationship. I knew it would be easy and that she could take me away from you. I thought she could make me forget you."

I'd thought the same thing about Mason. "But she couldn't."

"Yes. And, so . . . that's a problem."

"Because it's wrong for us to be together."

"Yes."

"Because of the age difference."

"Yes."

"But more importantly because we're going to be Lissa's guardians and need to focus on her—not each other."

"Yes."

I thought about this for a moment and then looked straight into his eyes. "Well," I said at last, "the way I see it, we aren't Lissa's guardians *yet*."

I steeled myself for the next response. I knew it was going to be one of the Zen life lessons. Something about inner strength and perseverance, about how the choices we made today were templates for the future or some other nonsense.

Instead he kissed me.

Time stopped as he reached out and cupped my face between his hands. He brought his mouth down and brushed it against my lips. It was barely a kiss at first but soon increased, becoming heady and deep. When he finally pulled away, it was to kiss my forehead. He left his lips there for several seconds as his arms held me close.

I wished the kiss could have gone on forever. Breaking the embrace, he ran a few fingers through my hair and down my cheek. He stepped back toward the door.

"I'll see you later, Roza."

"At our next practice?" I asked. "We *are* starting those up again, right? I mean, you still have things to teach me."

Standing in the doorway, he looked over at me and smiled. "Yes. Lots of things."

Like always, this book couldn't have been written without the help and support of my friends and family. In particular, I need to thank my IM Counseling Team: Caitlin, David, Jay, Jackie, and Kat. You guys logged more late-night online hours than I can even begin to count. I couldn't have gotten through this book and the rest of this year's craziness without you.

Thanks also to my agent, Jim McCarthy, who has moved heaven, earth, and deadlines to help me finish what I need to. I'm glad you've got my back. And finally, many thanks to Jessica Rothenberg and Ben Schrank at Razorbill for their continued support and hard work.

CAN'T GET ENOUGH OF ROSE HATHAWAY?
JUST WAIT UNTIL YOU MEET DRU.

IN BOOKSTORES NOW

TURN THE PAGE FOR A SNEAK PEEK. . . .

didn't tell Dad about Granmama's white owl. I know I should have.

There's that space between sleep and dreaming where things—not quite dreams, not fully fledged precognition, but weird little blends of both—sometimes get in. Your eyes open, slow and dreamy, when the sense of *someone looking* rises through the cotton-wool fog of being warm and tired.

That's when I saw it.

The owl ruffled itself up on my windowsill drenched in moonglow, each pale feather sharp and clear under icy light. I hadn't bothered to pull the cheap blinds down or hang up the curtains. Why bother, when we—Dad and me—only spend a few months in any town?

I blinked at the yellow-eyed bird. Instead of the comfort that means Gran is thinking about me—and don't ask how I know the dead think of the living; I've seen too much *not* to know—I felt a sharp annoyance, like a glass splinter under the surface of my brain.

The owl's beak was black, and its feathers had ghostly spots like cobwebs, shadows against snowy down. It stared into my sleepy eyes for what seemed like eternity, ruffling just a bit, puffing up the way Gran always used to when she thought anyone was messing with me.

Not again. Go away.

It usually only showed up when something interesting or really foul was about to happen. Dad had never seen it, or at least I didn't think so. But he could tell when I had, and it would make him reach for a weapon until I managed to open my mouth and say whether we were going to meet an old friend—or find ourselves in deep shit.

The night Gran died the owl had sat inside the window while she took her last few shallow, sipping breaths, but I don't think the nurses or the doctor saw it. They would have said something. By that point I knew enough to keep my mouth shut, at least. I just sat there and held Gran's hand until she drained away; then I sat in the hall while they did things to her empty body and wheeled it off. I curled up inside myself when the doctor or the social worker tried to talk to me, and just kept repeating that my dad would know, that he was on his way—even though I had no clue *where* he was, really. He'd been gone a good three months, off ridding the world of nasty things while I watched Gran slide downhill.

Of course, that morning Dad showed up, haggard and unshaven, his shoulder bandaged and his face bruised. He had all the ID, signed all the papers, and answered all the questions. Everything turned out okay, but sometimes I dream about that night, wondering if I'm going to get left behind again in some fluorescent-lit corridor smelling of Lysol and cold pain.

I don't like thinking about that. I settled further into the pillow, watching the owl's fluffing, each feather edged with cold moonlight.

My eyes drifted closed. Warm darkness swallowed me, and when the alarm clock went off it was morning, weak winter sunshine spilling through the window and making a square on the brown carpet. I'd thrashed out of the covers and was about to freeze my ass off. Dad hadn't turned the heater up.

It took a good twenty minutes in the shower before I felt anything *close* to awake. *Or* human. By the time I stamped down the stairs, I was already pissed off and getting worse. My favorite jeans weren't clean and I had a zit the size of Mount Pinatubo on my temple under a hank of dishwater brown hair. I opted for a gray T-shirt and a red hoodie, a pair of combat boots and no makeup.

Why bother, right? I wasn't going to be here long enough for anyone to care.

My bag smacked the floor. Last night's dishes still crouched in the sink. Dad was at the kitchen table, his shoulders hunched over the tray as he loaded clips, each bullet making a little clicking sound. "Hi, sweetheart."

I snorted, snagging the orange juice and opening the carton, taking a long cold draft. I wiped my mouth and belched musically.

"Ladylike." His bloodshot blue eyes didn't rise from the clip, and I knew what that meant.

"Going out tonight?" That's what I said. What I meant was, *without me?*

Click. Click. He set the full clip aside and started on the next. The bullets glinted, silver-coated. He must have been up all night with that, making them and loading them. "I won't be in for dinner. Order a pizza or something."

Which meant he was going somewhere more-dangerous, not just kinda-dangerous. And that he didn't need me to zero the target. So he must've gotten some kind of intel. He'd been gone every night this week, always reappearing in time for dinner smelling of cigarette smoke and danger. In other towns he'd mostly take me with him; people either didn't care about a teenage girl drinking a Coke in a bar, or we went places where Dad was reasonably sure he could stop any trouble with an ice-cold military stare or a drawled word.

But in this town he hadn't taken me anywhere. So if he'd gotten intel, it was on his own.

How? Probably the old-fashioned way. He likes that better, I guess. "I could come along."

"Dru." Just the one word, a warning in his tone. Mom's silver locket glittered at his throat, winking in the morning light.

"You might need me. I can carry the ammo." *And tell you when something invisible's in the corner, looking at you.* I heard the stubborn whine in my voice and belched again to cover it, a nice sonorous one that all but rattled the window looking out onto the scrubby backyard with its dilapidated swing set. There was a box of dishes sitting in front of the cabinets next to the stove; I suppressed the urge to kick at it. Mom's cookie jar—the one shaped like a fat grinning black-and-white cow—was next to the sink, the first thing unpacked in every new house. I always put it in the bathroom box with the toilet paper and shampoo; that's always the last in and first one out.

I've gotten kind of used to packing and unpacking, you could say. And trying to find toilet paper after a thirty-six-hour drive is no fun.

"Not this time, Dru." He looked up at me, though, the bristles of his cropped hair glittering blond under fluorescent light. "I'll be home late. Don't wait up."

I was about to protest, but his mouth had turned into a thin, hard line and the bottle sitting on the table warned me. Jim Beam. It had been almost full last night when I went to bed, and the dregs of amber liquid in it glowed warmer than his hair. Dad was pale blond, almost a towhead, even if his stubble was brown and gold.

I've got a washed-out version of Mom's curls and a better copy of Dad's blue eyes. The rest of me, I guess, is up for grabs. Except maybe Gran's nose, but she could have just been trying to make me feel better. I'm no prize. Most girls go through a gawky stage, but I'm beginning to think mine will be a lifelong thing.

It doesn't bother me too much. Better to be strong than pretty and useless. I'll take a plain girl with her head screwed on right over a cheerleader any day.

So I just leaned down and scooped up my messenger bag, the strap scraping against my fingerless wool gloves. They're scratchy but they're warm, and if you slip small stuff under the cuff, it's damn near invisible. "Okay."

"You should have some breakfast." *Click.* Another bullet slid into the clip. His eyes dropped back down to it, like it was the most important thing in the world.

Eat something? When he was about to go out and deal with bad news alone? Was he *kidding*?

My stomach turned over hard. "I'll miss the bus. Do you want some eggs?"

I don't know why I offered. He liked them sunny-side up, but neither Mom or me could ever get them done right. I've been breaking yolks all my life, even when he tried to teach me the right way to gently jiggle with a spatula to get them out of the pan. Mom would just laugh on Sunday mornings and tell him scrambled or over-hard was what he was going to get, and he'd come up behind her and put his arms around her waist and nuzzle her long, curling chestnut hair. I would always yell, *Ewwww! No kissing!*

And they would both laugh.

That was Before. A thousand years ago. When I was little.

Dad shook his head a little. "No thanks, kiddo. You have money?"

I spotted his billfold on the counter and scooped it up. "I'm taking twenty."

"Take another twenty, just in case." *Click. Click.* "How's school going?"

Just fine, Dad. Just freaking dandy. Two weeks in a new town is enough to make me all sorts of friends. "Okay."

I took two twenties out of his billfold, rubbing the plastic sleeve over Mom's picture with my thumb like I always did. There was a shiny space on the sleeve right over her wide, bright smile. Her chestnut hair was as wildly curly as mine, but pulled back into a loose ponytail, blonde-streaked ringlets falling into her heart-shaped face. She was beautiful. You could see why Dad fell for her in that picture. You could almost smell her perfume.

"Just okay?" *Click.*

"It's fine. It's stupid. Same old stuff." I toed the linoleum and set his billfold down. "I'm going."

Click. He didn't look up. "Okay. I love you." He was wearing his Marines sweatshirt and the pair of blue sweats he always worked out in, with the hole in the knee. I stared at the top of his head while he finished the clip, set it aside, and picked up a fresh one. I could almost feel the noise of each bullet being slid home in my own fingers.

My throat had turned to stone. "'Kay. Whatever. Bye." *Don't get killed.* I stamped out of the kitchen and down the hall, one of the stacked boxes barking me in the shin. I still hadn't unpacked the living room yet. Why bother? I'd just have to box it all up in another couple months.

I slammed the front door, too, and pulled my hood up, shoving my hair back. I hadn't bothered with much beyond dragging a comb through it. Mom's curls had been loose pretty ringlets, but mine were pure frizz. The Midwest podunk humidity made it worse; it was a wet blanket of cold that immediately turned my breath into a white cloud and nipped at my elbows and knees.

The rental was on a long, ruler-straight block of similar houses, all dozing under watery sunlight managing to fight its way through overcast. The air tasted like iron and I shivered. We'd been in Florida before this, always sticky, sweaty, sultry heat against the skin like oil. We'd cleared out four poltergeists in Pensacola and a haunting apparition of a woman even Dad could see in some dead-end town north of Miami, and there was a creepy woman with cottonmouths and copperheads in glass cages who sold Dad the silver he needed to take care of something else. I hadn't had to go to school there—we were so busy staying mobile, moving from one hotel to the next, so whatever Dad needed the silver for couldn't get a lock on us.

Now it was the Dakotas, and snow up to our knees. Great.

Our yard was the only one with weeds and tall grass. We had a picket fence, too, but the paint was flaking and peeling off and parts of it were missing, like a gap-toothed smile. Still, the porch was sturdy and the house was even sturdier. Dad didn't believe in renting crappy bungalows. He said it was a bad way to raise a kid.

I walked away with my head down and my hands stuffed in my pockets.

I never saw Dad alive again.

WILL DRU DISCOVER JUST HOW SPECIAL SHE REALLY IS?

FIND OUT IN BETRAYALS COMING NOVEMBER 2009